The
Guardian

The Guardian

JANE HAMILTON

A JAN DENNIS BOOK

THOMAS NELSON PUBLISHERS
Nashville

Published in Nashville, Tennessee, by Jan Dennis Books, an imprint
of Thomas Nelson, Inc., and distributed in Canada by Word Commu-
nications, Ltd., Richmond, British Columbia.

Library of Congress Cataloging-in-Publication Data

Hamilton, Jane
    The Guardian: A Novel/ by Jane Hamilton
        p.   cm.
    "A Jan Dennis Book"
    ISBN 0-7852-8209-2 (pbk.)
    1. Guardian angels—Fiction. I. Title
PS3558.A4427G8 1994
813'.54—dc20   93-30197
                                                 CIP

Printed in the United States of America

1 2 3 4 5 6 7 — 99 98 97 96 95 94 93

DEDICATION

For Jameson Brewer:
Thank you for answering a little girl's fan mail.

ACKNOWLEDGEMENTS

Thanks to all who have helped me in writing this: my parents, everyone at 133 Linden, Toni, who spelled his name wrong, Dan and Val (for cheddar and "pop" at midnight), MFR, E.A. Miller (poet and teacher), "Murph," James, P.M. Griffin (who helped more than she knew), and Evan.

"I thank my God upon every remembrance of you, always in every prayer of mine making request for you all with joy, for your fellowship in the gospel from the first day until now."

Philippians 1:3–5

1

RAGUEL WATCHED FROM THE BACK OF THE JUDG-
ment hall as the verdict was passed on the small boy
standing at the front. Election. He nodded tersely as he
registered the word, but his strained smile showed he was
not as happy as he ought to have been, and judging from
the expressions, neither was any one else in the chamber.
Almost half the angels in the room were watching the boy
as he smiled broadly and was hugged by the angel at his
side, but the larger number were studying Tabris, who
was standing a distance away.

Tabris had not reacted to the echoing sound of the
verdict. Staring tightly at the chains binding his wrists
together and securing him to the smooth stone floor as
though he were a horse at a hitching post, he seemed the
soul of restraint. Raguel's mouth twitched as he watched
Tabris look up once, trying to see the boy, but the other
angels had crowded into his line of sight, and the boy was
taken away from him without exchanging a word.

There were two Archangel guards flanking Tabris,
and they were smiling icily. Everything about their posture read *duty* to Raguel, broadcast nonverbally in their
feet which were planted solidly on the floor, their hands
which held their sword hilts, and their chins which remained firm and raised. Tabris seemed smaller as he
stood between the two, slumped, his head down, his
hands almost trembling. His two-toned wings dropped
down and touched the floor. With a shudder, Raguel realized the two guards had probably been his friends.

Now that the boy had been taken away, movement
suddenly animated the tremendous space. Some celestials left but more arrived to sit on the benches in front of
and to the right of the judgment throne, angels as well as

demons. The light of the Father heightened in intensity to a brilliance that danced in Raguel's eyes, but Tabris turned his face aside, staring at the heavy iron ring that fastened him to the floor.

The two Archangels glanced at each other, still wearing their chilled smiles.

Raguel's eyes burned, and he flashed to the trio. He had the highest status of all present—one of the Seven Elite as well as the supervisor over all guardian angels—and he had every intention of pulling rank now. The Archangels saluted him. Tabris did not raise his head.

Raguel snapped his fingers and the chains binding Tabris vanished. The guards protested, but Raguel not only outranked them, he was also much taller, much stronger, and he glistened with God's glory.

"You will not degrade him," Raguel said. "He's not running anywhere. And unless God damns him he's still one of us. Don't forget that."

The first guard glared angrily.

Tabris was trembling as though he were terribly cold. He had not looked up at Raguel, and even with the chains gone he did not move.

The muscular angel tried to convey reassurance to Tabris through both body language and the nonverbal communication process angels use more efficiently than words, but Tabris stared at his hands.

Somewhat confused, Raguel walked toward one of the long tables at the front of the room and settled his large but not unwieldy form on the edge. His wings raised as he inspected the broken angel from a distance. Then with a sigh, Raguel looked toward the throne of God.

What followed was a trial. God, who knew the entire situation without the presentation of evidence, revealed to all exactly what Tabris had done and what he clearly deserved for the crime.

Ordinarily, the two guards flanking Tabris should have leaped forward to catch him if he had collapsed, but now their revulsion would keep them distant. Tabris, however, remained steady, and his eyes did not move from his hands.

"Do you have a statement in your own defense?" asked Raguel, who had turned slightly pale.

"No."

"Then I do," said Raguel. He turned to the great throne of the Lord, his face bathed in the white radiance of the light that had dispelled the darkness since time unremembered. He smiled suddenly, glimpsing infinity with his soul visibly thrilling at the ancient touch of the Lord his Creator, but then he focused himself and said, "I ask for leniency." A palpable annoyance—and hope—arose from the other angels in the room, but Raguel ignored these and continued. "Tabris panicked—I don't think his crime was premeditated. If he had thought about it at all, I think he would have stopped."

"The boy's dead!" shouted another angel, rising from the bench and moving across the room.

"He didn't intend—"

"Regardless," the angel continued, "completely regardless of that, the effect was the same—Sebastian died. Tabris thwarted God's plan, the plan everyone has to fulfill! One third of the host was thrown into Hell for not fulfilling that plan, and now you want—"

"One more angel in Hell isn't going to resurrect the boy," said Raguel.

"But it would exact justice," said the accuser.

"I don't think so," Raguel said. "He's sorry he did it."

"But the boy," the accuser said, "is dead."

"It was a rash action."

At that point all the angels in the room abruptly turned to face the Lord, who had become visible in the person of Jesus Christ. Most bowed, but Tabris completely prostrated himself. Jesus advanced to the accuser, regarding him steadily. The accuser responded with eyes as insensitive as ice.

"Your point," said Jesus, "is understandable."

"If I'm damned," said the demon, "then I fail to see why *he* should receive the leniency you denied to the rest of our species."

"Because Tabris still loves me," Jesus said.

"His demonstration of that love, you must admit, falls short of the ideal."

Jesus turned to Raguel, His eyes suddenly gentler. "Why are you pleading for him? He hasn't even pleaded for himself."

Raguel bowed his head, but Jesus touched his shoulder and made him look up. "My Lord," said Raguel, "he's still in shock. I'm convinced that he really had no intention beforehand of violating your plan, and that given the chance he would change his own actions. He's practically condemned himself!"

"How much do you believe in him?" asked Jesus.

"I wouldn't challenge your judgment on this."

"But do you think the judgment should be favorable?"

"Yes." Raguel looked aside. "Please, can you be merciful to him?"

Tabris, still distant, still prostrated, had not yet reacted, and it seemed he had prevented himself from listening to his own Creator debating whether or not he should be discarded.

"He does still love you," said Raguel. "For that alone you might be able to show him mercy."

Jesus walked forward and looked more closely at Tabris, whose wings pressed tightly over his head when the footsteps turned in his direction. Christ's eyes scintillated as He watched the angel. Tabris had stopped breathing, his fear had filled the room, and it seemed that with Him near he began again to plumb the depth of his action.

Looking at this angel, Jesus said, "Raguel, how much do you believe in him?"

"Completely."

"Then I'll release him into your custody."

The room reacted with simultaneous surprise and relief. After a moment, some anger arose.

"My Lord," said Raguel with a short bow.

"Tabris," Jesus said, but Tabris did not raise his head even then, "you're on probation. One more act of disobedience means instant damnation. Is that clear?"

Still facedown and shaking, Tabris nonverbalized that he understood.

"Raguel, accompany him to his next assignment." Then He vanished from the tribunal. All the angels looked at Tabris, who first raised his head and then stood, his face still devoid of expression.

Raguel walked forward and said, "Shall we go?"

Tabris looked across the room at the demon who had accused him, and the hollow expression in the guardian's eyes resounded with distant loss, far-removed pain. He nodded to Raguel, his voice almost breaking as he said, "Yes, let's."

Tabris, the two-toned angel, still shaking with fear, with hopelessness, and with desperate love, followed Raguel by doing automatically what would confuse any creature with a body. Tabris remembered the one time he had tried to explain the process: the human had tried for hours to comprehend how one could simply *go* oblivious of a destination. Angels hardly need that, of course—they think about where they want to go, and without passing through the intermediate space they are there, whether the thought is specifically "corner of 83rd and Park," or more generally "wherever he's taking me," or "wherever Gabriel is right now." This time Tabris' intention had been the second, so he felt mildly surprised when he found himself surrounded by the paperish smell of Raguel's study, in the East wing of one of the Many Mansions.

Raguel led Tabris to one of the sofas and said, "I'm going to leave you here for a while—"

"Please," said Tabris, "I'd rather you didn't."

Raguel sat beside him. The two-toned angel regarded him, inclining his body away yet meeting his eyes hungrily so that Raguel was left with the impression that Tabris needed comfort but would refuse sympathy.

"I was going to go ahead of you."

"To explain to all my future comrades that I'm a 'good guy,' even though I—" Tabris stopped short of completing the sentence.

There are unwritten laws, laws no angel would break for any reason—actions that are not necessarily sinful but that they avoid anyway. For instance, angels don't sneak onto the end of the communion line since communion is reserved for humanity alone. Some laws are written, primarily laws for humans, such as *Thou shalt not steal.* For guardian angels, there is only one written rule, and that rule forbids them killing their charges.

Ever since Adam fell, that law has been in force, written and shown to all guardian angels before beginning their assignments. *Do not kill your charge.* This might seem unnecessary, given the nature of angels, but guardians are different, more reckless—after rubbing shoulders with sin for years they begin to take risks for their charges, pushing themselves to the limits of their power to keep the people under their care from falling deeper into sin, desperate to exact a conversion. Their contact with humans changes them in an interesting fashion, so that the guardians begin to form a class of angels distinctly their own. They see God's mercy at work every hour, and their understanding of God deepens even as their love of their charges intensifies.

They usually *offer* themselves in exchange for their charges if it appears the judgment will be damnation. They have modeled themselves after Christ, whose sacrifice on the cross gave the world's guardians all the instruction they ever would need in how to perform their jobs.

Unfortunately, an angel who would damn himself to save his charge would very quickly realize that if he killed the charge while he was in a state of grace, the charge would of course be saved. This makes the one written law necessary. And this is the law Tabris had broken.

The child—Sebastian—had been saved. It was not, after all, his fault that the guardian had altered the Divine Will. Tabris, however, was guilty of murder and therefore had merited nothing less than full damnation—sharp and swift. In fact, if only to keep the other guardians faithful, his damnation seemed the only answer.

Christ's mercy on Tabris had upset a great number of angels, and Tabris himself was unsure of how he felt. Even now, however, sitting on the couch beside Raguel, he knew he was by no means out of danger.

"I—" he said, quelling the instinctual nonverbal sentence and translating it into clumsy words, "I wanted to thank you for pleading on my behalf. I—" The emotions roiling in his heart burst upward into his throat and stopped his speech.

"Please, Tabris, it's all right. I'd have done it for anyone."

"But you did it for me," he said. "That—" Tabris lost his voice again for a time, while Raguel watched the strangled emotions play for control of his features.

They stayed in silence until Raguel said, "I'll go ahead of you."

"I know what's going to happen," said Tabris. "If you make me the guardian of a small country, a corporation, a province—Raguel, even if I'm assigned guardian over a souvenir stand you'll have complaints from every guardian in the area."

Raguel said, "I'm going ahead of you to intercept those," and nonverbally added that Tabris had not guessed correctly.

Tabris paused. "A star?"

"Let me go ahead," Raguel said. "I won't do it against your will, but it might be easier if you don't hear the reaction."

"The reality couldn't possibly exceed imagination. What am I guarding?"

"Not what, who."

Tabris leaped from the couch, backing away from Raguel with eyes as round as a full moon. "I hope," he stammered, "you mean an animal or something."

Raguel shook his head.

"No!" Tabris shouted. "Absolutely *not*! I—you can't! What about the one-person rule?"

Raguel had stood. "It's been suspended in your case to permit you to guard a second person, and besides, you won't be the primary caregiver. It's just a co-guardianship."

Tabris managed to seat his trembling form again before he collapsed.

Raguel could feel the emotions locked inside the two-toned angel, each ricocheting ever faster until somewhere it could find an outlet, in the process giving Tabris untold frantic energy as though he were an emotional reactor and every attempt to regain control would only add more energy to the system he had closed. Tabris' eyes sparkled with nascent fire that made their mahogany color seem hazel. He had gripped the sides of his chair almost as tightly as he had clenched his teeth.

Eventually he said, "The other guardian . . ."

"He has no choice. He's under the same orders you are."

The word *Sebastian* came to Raguel's mind, a presence strong enough to say itself even though Tabris had bitten back the name. Smiling tentatively, Raguel crouched before Tabris' chair. "Maybe the connection to this charge won't be quite so strong since you're not the primary guardian."

This close, Raguel could feel his stomach tightening with the nausea that seemed to radiate from Tabris, who had almost deflated between the arms of his chair. With a concerned look Raguel reached up to touch him, but Tabris moved away first.

"If you're going to do it," Tabris said, "let's do it quickly."

Raguel regarded him uncertainly.

"I've got to do it eventually," Tabris said, "and it isn't going to get easier."

Raguel helped Tabris to stand, the concern not leaving his eyes as he watched Tabris darken once more, his wings' colors enriching to deep jade and darker mahogany that glittered like old amber. Tabris regarded himself momentarily, and then looked back at Raguel.

"Let the games begin," he said, and that moment they were gone.

2

"NO!" THE GUARDIAN ANGEL SHOUTED. "YOU can't!"

"Rock," Raguel was saying, "Rachmiel, please calm yourself. Tabris—"

"—murdered the last one, and I'm certainly not letting him even *near* mine!"

Tabris, backing against the corner of the cluttered bedroom and silently enduring every verbal lash, observed the guardian with utter quiet. Rachmiel had drawn his sword in the grainy midnight obscurity. His angry eyes and the icy sharpness of his weapon shed a blue light on the tiny form who slept beneath the tousled covers on the bed across the room. So far the noise of the argument and the glow which only angels could sense had left the child undisturbed.

Raguel nonverbally pressured Rachmiel to be reasonable, and Rachmiel's eyes narrowed while his grip tightened on the sword. He drew it so rarely that Tabris might have crumbled if he had realized what kind of upheaval his appearance had caused. "If you think," Rachmiel said, "even once, that I'd let him touch—"

Raguel darted forward and used his tremendous strength of will to disarm the angry guardian, who was so driven that he was almost able to withstand him. Rachmiel's wings were spread in a battle stance. Just as one cat will back away from another who is hissing and has his fur raised, Tabris found himself pressing even harder against the cold security of the bedroom wall, which if he concentrated did not have to exist for him at all.

Raguel finally released Rachmiel, moving intangibly through the small heaps of clothing on the floor. Tabris hardly listened to the argument now, or at least he seemed not to feel the whiplash of words spoken in protective rage. Instead he surveyed the walls, the posters and the pictures which in daylight would be landscapes, fluffy animals, ballet slippers, and piano keyboards. A soft teddy bear lay on the floor where it had been pushed out of bed by a sleeping arm. Tabris leaned forward toward the bear and then jerked back against the wall, reminding himself that this child was not really his to guard.

"And don't forget that!" Rachmiel said, his pallor now given way to a deep flush. He stood silently, breathing heavily.

"These are Divine orders," Raguel said.

Rachmiel looked ready to either defy the orders or spit contemptuously, but he locked his teeth and exhaled raggedly. There glittered something in his eyes, almost a denial of his nature, a great battle within the guardian himself, and a question of exactly how specifically those orders were worded.

Then Rachmiel's eyes closed, feeling God answer the questions before Raguel had the chance, trembling with resistance as God stroked his heart and lay like a shawl over his shoulders. He relented quickly—infinite love melts any heart that can love in return—and Tabris leaned forward from the room's corner with round, bright eyes as he watched the Creator's hand easing away the stubbornness. He stepped forward, closer to Rachmiel, closer to the child. Rachmiel was not ready for that. "You," he said with a half turn and a near hiss, "get out!"

Tabris blazed from the room like a comet, hardly realizing that what he feared, he could not evade, could never escape; it was impossible for him to leave behind. He streaked across the clear sky like a laser, arcing parallel to the earth's surface for almost two full miles before realizing in panic that he had been bound to the child by a spiritual tether. At exactly two miles it snapped taut, and he dropped to the ground in agony.

To move forward any further would hurt beyond endurance, and even here his eyes stung and his fingers tingled with the numbness of the distance from his spiritual home base.

Guardian.

Tabris backed up a little on his hands and knees through the brown grass until full sensation returned to his fingers and his lips no longer trembled with cold. The whistling left his ear. Lurching to his feet and rubbing his temples to clear his mind, he looked up at the stars.

When semi-corporeal, as they are most of the time, angels have limits and must observe them. In their purest form they exist as unalloyed intelligences, knowing and loving God in His most profound and incomprehensible aspects. In order to act, however, angels become more solid, taking on the shapes humans recognize as winged men and women—although the image of fat babies with tiny wings nauseates most angels. Tabris knew that if he had persisted in widening the distance between him and the child he would not have died, because angels are immortal; but he would have begun to suffer and might have lost consciousness if he had flown very much further.

Dusting himself off, Tabris scanned the area briefly and realized that Raguel had brought him to the countryside, far enough from any city that the sky looked deep, the stars eerily distant, and the universe heartless. His soul could have filled with abandonment if he had let it, but he returned his gaze to the hills. Squinting upward again after a moment, he remarked to himself that a sky unpolluted by city lights looks like a dome that gets more distant toward its apex.

He walked. The hum of crickets gave him some pleasure—not all in the world had changed. His last assignment had been in one of the city walls people call *suburbs,* long rows of cookie-cutter houses, each with an identical lawn and tree and driveway, each with its own picture window, each with a potted plant on the kitchen sill.

Guardian.

The child, two miles away, he reflected—and then paused. He wanted to think the child unlucky, but he knew already the purity of its heart. Of her heart, he corrected himself. He knew the purity of her heart and the innocence of her youth. A part of him feared corrupting her, feared dropping the fragile porcelain of her spirit. But there was another part of him, the part a human would have called instinct because God had installed it without any angel's permission, and this part wanted fiercely to protect her and fight anyone with harm in his soul.

Rachmiel and I, he thought, *are a lot alike.*

Except of course that Rachmiel had never raised his hands against the girl—Tabris never could forget that cardinal difference. When danger had appeared, Rachmiel had driven off the attacker, and Tabris had turned on the victim.

He spread his wings and flew the perimeter of his tether, knowing that once he had settled into the job and accepted all its responsibilities and all its pains, when what bound him to the girl was love and not force, then the spiritual chain would loosen. Then he could travel anywhere in creation and still feel her heart beating within his own. Now he hardly detected her and would not have realized she existed at all except for the manacles pinning him to one spot and making him a living radius that strained ever outward.

No, that's wrong, he thought. *Do that and she'll grow up feeling abandoned.*

He reflected on his first human guardianship, a textbook case until the disaster. Nine months curled in the womb beside a developing embryo, snuggling the child and shielding it from all the traps that might be set for one, semiconscious days of dreaming protection, loving what as yet had only four cells and an immortal soul and was rooted in the body of another living thing. Then birth, the laughter and admiration when he first saw clearly the tiny body, the quiet pride as he stood in

silence over the bassinet where the little boy lay—
Sebastian. His vows still rang in his ears. He turned
his head aside.

He glided over a sagging white fence and cupped
his wings, angled upright, and dropped to a stand. The
long grass licked against his calves and knees, tickling
him where it could; but he had no energy to play with the
plant life, to talk to it of God, to encourage it to grow and
to stretch its slender blades toward the sun. The grass
settled back disappointed after he passed by, then forgot
him and returned to dodging moonbeams at the behest
of the wind.

Chilled by the night, Tabris walked. He breathed,
loving the cold and embracing it, draining all the warmth
from his body for an instant to crystalize the evanescence
that was him. He loved God's world. He felt glad to be
here.

A distant trickle caught his attention, and he walked
the perimeter toward it. He reflected that his favorite
season was fall—autumn, he corrected hastily. Within a
few weeks the delightful chill of winter snow and blister-
ingly wild wind would settle on the land, and he could lie
down on the snow-covered rooftops and share all his experiences with his Father.

He paused sharply.

He knew he had to answer the question which had
pierced his conscience, and his eyes snapped shut in sudden fear. Instantly he decided to delay, knowing that a
positive answer would leave him uncomfortable and a
negative one would destroy him. Even so, the worry
gnawed at his heart and forced him to stop walking and
to think.

A small stream lapped over his feet, but for now he
ignored it.

The dark trees and very distant roads provided the
silence Tabris both needed and feared. He had not
prayed since the accident. He had been too stunned at
the time, too numb afterward, too afraid now. Just as
Sebastian's parents had not spoken to each other when

they had learned of the accident, gripping each other's hands in silence that joined them more closely than words; so too had Tabris gripped God's hand wordlessly, constantly, until the verdict had been passed on him. He had only let go when Raguel took him away.

Or rather, a few moments before that, Tabris realized. His Vision of God had been strangled so that what he saw now was only a glimpse in comparison to what he had seen in the past. That small view kept him strong, but the shock of partial separation from God had made him release his last grip on the love he had feared would desert him forever, and rightly so.

Tabris shuddered with a movement that shook his whole body, and he gripped himself tightly with his arms.

Can I pray? he wondered.

He had to answer the question, so he supposed he could pray as a human does, with words, but not in the higher way. He forbore trying because he was still shaking.

Finally the stream caught his attention. He stepped into the middle and walked against the flow of the white water to the farthest reach of the tether binding him to the tiny bedroom and the unsuspecting human soul. Then, numb and afraid and weary, he lay down full length, feeling the sharp wet cold penetrate his clothes, untangle his hair, and saturate the two-toned feathers of his wings. The trickles of water pooled over his eyes and streamed over his cheekbones, glided alongside his nose and dripped down off his chin. He gasped because of the needles of the extreme cold, but then lay still and let the water cover him like a blanket.

It was good.

He dug his hands into the small stones on the bottom, wriggling until his fingertips contacted the softer sediment, and then closed his eyes.

Guardian.

"I'll do it, God," he said.

The moon shone all its round glory on the sleeping hill country rolling along beneath it, casting its white haze on the inhabitants of the night. Tabris, his eyes closed and ears deafened by the water, realized that the glow was vanishing when he felt a hand on his shoulder.

Rachmiel.

"Come back," said the other guardian. "It's not right for you to stay out here all night."

Tabris followed, dry the instant he left the water, and was brought directly to the girl's bedroom. Full sensation returned to him as the tether's grip on his soul slackened, and he looked at Rachmiel.

"Sit on the bed," said the other guardian. Tabris followed instructions mutely, realizing abruptly that Rachmiel too remained wordless, speaking with only his gestures, and that his heart, not his voice, conveyed tension and distant worry.

Rachmiel settled himself in the reading chair by the window in the corner of the room so that the moon bathed him in its waning shine like a spotlight. The white haze revealed Rachmiel's hard features which were normally sensitive, his blond hair with a gentle curl to its soft strands, and the orange wings he kept folded at his back. The moonlight accentuated the color of his eyes, sunset-toned so that they would range the full spectrum which a night sky might achieve, probably orange when he was happy and calm but deepening to purple when he was upset. Now they were purple. As if the eyes were not indication enough of his emotions, he had drawn his knees up against his chest in the semidarkness and now rested his chin on his cupped hands. He regarded Tabris.

For a while they stayed in this still-life pose, Tabris all the time more uncomfortable with his soul exposed to the scrutiny of this other angel in a way no clothing, nor any curled fetal position could hide. A part of him longed to cover himself, to obfuscate his soul in a cloudy density of chaotic folds and twists, but because he was co-guardian with Rachmiel, he resisted these feelings, tensed himself, and allowed his co-worker to inspect all of him.

Rachmiel had watched with interest while Tabris fought to control himself, and now he looked at the girl who still slept beneath the white blankets behind Tabris.

"We'll be working together for a while," Rachmiel nonverbalized, saying it primarily by thinking in images and adding to them the appropriate gestures: thinking of time, of compelled acceptance, and of the child as he unclenched his fists. He smiled, studying the child, and now spoke using no words at all.

"Elizabeth?" Tabris asked.

Rachmiel's nonverbal confirmation filled Tabris with inexplicable sadness. Rachmiel sat dreamily in the chair seven feet away. Tabris felt his mind expanding, filled with facts about this girl, Elizabeth Hayes: she was ten years old; she had three brothers; she liked to pound on the piano; she was smart but shy. Her whole personality unfolded for Tabris to read, and underlying all Rachmiel's nonverbal description was strong love that nearly shattered Tabris' heart.

The love changed then to fierceness—if Tabris hurt her, Rachmiel would defend the child with his own existence.

"I wouldn't," Tabris said, almost stammering.

Rachmiel's eyes flared.

Tabris turned away, ostensibly to look at the girl more closely, to examine the thin and wavy red hair that covered her shoulders and the edge of her arm before it disappeared beneath the pillow. He reached out and then stopped himself, turning to Rachmiel. "May I touch her?"

Sullen for only a moment, Rachmiel nodded.

Tabris extended a hand to her cheek, freckled and smooth, winter-whitened by the loss of a tan she had deepened every day of the summer by running about in the sun. He traced the curve of her cheek with two fingers, the information now coming to him directly from the child as readily as if he were a doctor reading a patient's wall chart. She had good health except for a scab on one knee that would heal soon. Her eyes, he learned, were horizon blue beneath the closed lids. Her face had not yet lost its baby-roundness. His mind filled quickly with trivial information: her shoe size, the length of her hair, her blood pressure, her lung capacity, what she had eaten for dinner. But also he learned her pulse and her temperature, and he could feel her dreams.

"She'll wake in an hour?" Tabris asked.

Rachmiel shrugged, meaning a little longer.

Tabris winced, looking again at Elizabeth to control the hollow depth of his eyes. Sensing this, Rachmiel uncurled from his place in the reading chair and looked at Tabris deliberately. He nonverbalized a question—would Tabris like to meet the other household angels?

"I would."

Rachmiel flashed them both downstairs into the living room. Two angels sat on the thick carpet talking and a third sat on the carved mantelpiece. Rachmiel nonverbalized to the others, who turned to face Tabris and extended a greeting, either by bowing or smiling or opening their hands.

When Rachmiel finally spoke aloud, his voice conveyed a gentility that surprised Tabris. "This is Hadriel, who guards Connie, Elizabeth's mother."

Hadriel stood and smiled, but Tabris could feel the tension in his greeting. Rachmiel continued, "This is Josai'el, who guards Elizabeth's grandmother Bridget." Josai'el bowed, her straight and shiny brown hair tripping down over her shoulders and hitting the low wooden coffee table as she did so. "And lastly—"

"I've met Mithra," Tabris said. "Hello."

"I guard John, her father," said the smaller angel.

"I remember," Tabris said, his eyes dark.

Josai'el sent a nonverbal command, and the guardians of the three sons arrived in the living room. Tabris' eyes absorbed the sight, and he nodded at the sound of each angel's name as though he knew that was all he could take in now, that he would have to wait a while for them to become personalities he could recognize and enjoy.

"Katra'il," said the first, a female angel with blond hair in tight curls. "I guard Martin."

"Voriah," said the second, his eyes gleaming faintly white and blue. "I'm with Alan."

"Miriael," said the last. "Kyle is my charge."

All the introductions made, Tabris felt the others waiting as though he were supposed to say something, but maybe their awkwardness stemmed only from their own confusion. Tabris looked away, eyes glittering as though he were trapped, realizing that they all knew what he had done. Conscious that he only barely remained before them, that he rode the fringes of God's mercy, he smiled hesitantly.

"You'll get into the routine of the day pretty quickly," Rachmiel said, his eyes quick but now a bit softer, as if he had suddenly begun feeling protective of Tabris in addition to Elizabeth. "It's usually so hectic during the day that we need the night times to recover."

"I know," Tabris said, his heart clinging to the past—yesterday, but a yesterday behind him by eternity—when he and the guardians of Sebastian's parents had sat on the rooftop and prayed together or sometimes curled beside their charges in their warm beds and idly fingered their hair, an angelic wing thrown protectively over human shoulders.

"The demons around here—" and Miriael's words brought Tabris out of his reverie, "like to attack in groups. This household is large enough to ward off most strikes, and usually we'll assist the others nearby."

"There's a woman who lives alone up the hill," said Mithra. "We help her guardian a lot."

Tabris nodded, taking in the group with one glance, noticing how the six of them, Rachmiel included, knew each others' motions and habits so well that they felt completely familiar in each others' presence. Right now, in this living room that long since had given up elegance for practicality, this team resonated with unity and flexibility. They trusted each other. Tabris wondered, *Will I ever feel that comfortable again, with anyone?*

They knew what he had done. Even a human would have been able to decipher the tension in their hands, the darkness at the corners of their eyes that said, *Why are you here?* Raguel, he realized, must have prepared them, sat them together on the worn sofas and explained that damnation had been as close as the dotting of an *i.* He had probably teased out their concerns, persuaded them to confide their worries, and then reassured them. Like a session for friends of a teen suicide, Tabris realized, *God has to be sure no one will do what I did, that no one else will end the life he's sworn to protect.*

The guardian's supervisor must have explained his need, given them instructions, and gone. Then the meeting had dispersed, Rachmiel had been sent to get him, and the three elders had remained in the living room talking about him.

Tabris shivered.

"Thanks for taking me in," he said, because he thought it was expected and because he promised himself he would never let himself forget that these angels, this household community, were doing him a favor.

"Enjoy your stay," said Josai'el. "We're glad to have you."

3

JOSAI'EL, AT LEAST, WAS GLAD TO HAVE TABRIS. One more angel meant that much more strength against demon attacks, but most importantly, she knew that Tabris needed them. They were a solid household, exactly what would be best to help him regain his confidence and resolve his pain.

She had seen how much his heart hurt the instant he had arrived beside Rachmiel, and she had sensed immediately that despite Rachmiel's best efforts to the contrary, he had been harsh. Tabris wore the most ashamed and hollow look in his eyes that Josai'el ever had seen, and her first impulse had been to run forward and tell him that he would be all right. The wounds of the past twenty-four hours were etched into his face, in his eyes especially, and Josai'el wondered how many more signs of pain she had not recognized.

The family would be waking within the hour, so she invited Mithra and Tabris to accompany her on a quick tour. "You have to know the place if you'll be working here," she said.

Both Mithra and Tabris remained silent for the most part while she lead them from room to room, introducing each human in his turn, letting Mithra introduce John. Tabris took in all the names and faces without comment. Josai'el then showed him the grounds, both the places she loved and the spots where demons were most likely to hide.

"It's a far cry from suburbia," Tabris said, once again outdoors and relieved to be able to stare into the cold expanse of the sky. "I'll enjoy the locale."

"The Hayes family has been here for over a century," Josai'el said. "Bridget was born in this house."

"John was born in the hospital in the city," Mithra said, giving half a smile as he poked fun at Josai'el's sentimentality.

"How far is the city?" Tabris asked.

"About twenty minutes' drive south," said Mithra. "Elizabeth's school is in the town, though, so you won't have to visit there often."

Tabris nodded as though he were going to speak, but he stopped before there were words. They continued walking, Josai'el wondering what would be better—questioning him or leaving him alone. Mithra was quiet. As they passed the woodshed, a hiss stopped them.

"Tab-riss!"

He and Mithra whirled instantly, their swords drawn and blazing. Josai'el rose into the air and lit the countryside with a shine from her heart.

"No need," said an angelic form sitting on a wood pile, his sharp shadow waving up and down as it passed over chopped logs and brown grass. "None at all—Tabris and I go way back. He's my pal. Tell them, Tabris."

Tabris' mouth had tightened into a line, and Mithra advanced.

"Tell them," said the demon again.

"Zeffar," he said.

"I go by another name now," said the demon. "Call me Accuser."

Tabris trembled and Josai'el moved closer to him. "Thank you, Accuser. You may go."

"Tabris missed his destiny," said Accuser. "I tried to help him along, but you know your Jesus—sinks in His claws and never lets go, even though Tabris chose freedom. I told him to fight for it, to demand his release, but he was too weak."

"That's quite enough," said Josai'el. "Go!"

The demon vanished, and even though Mithra and Josai'el relaxed, Tabris kept his sword raised.

"He asked for your damnation?" asked Mithra.

"Yes."

Mithra nonverbalized that Satan always sent someone to the trials. Tabris nodded, extinguishing his sword and looking aside.

"Maybe we should return," said Mithra, and Josai'el smiled suddenly, realizing that Mithra had swung to Tabris' side. "Do you feel like continuing?"

"I'd rather stay outside," said Tabris.

"Then I'll show you the pond," said Josai'el. "The pond is my favorite place."

The pond turned out to be the source of the stream Tabris had seen earlier, and he admitted that this was the most peaceful area he had seen in a long time. Josai'el's prayers decorated the multicolored branches of the various trees like limp streamers, ringing the whole area and making it feel already familiar. Pines and oaks mingled with willows around the water, sharing their neighborhood readily with shrubbery and wild strawberry plants that had lost their fruit to birds and insects and small children. The mobile inhabitants, mostly winged with chitin or feathers, came in search of the three angels and passed right through them. Then, confused, they returned to their morning hunt. A muskrat swam on the surface of the lake and then dove down under the water.

Tabris' soul vibrated as though he were very close to nonverbalizing, but he chose to speak instead. "This is lovely."

"It's far removed and silent," said Josai'el. "Bridget likes to come here on sunny days to read or just sit. I come whenever I can."

Mithra walked a few paces away, talking to a small finch on the branch of a tree, and Josai'el moved closer to Tabris. "You can come here, too," she said. "Please, feel free to make use of everything we do."

"I'm still tethered."

"That will extend within the year. You know that. You're not at your limit now, are you?"

"No, but close. My hands are numb."

Tabris stopped, his eyes widening as he saw his fingers, his opened palms, the smooth flesh of his hands. He realized, not even a full day before, these very hands had made one quick gesture and robbed the world of a life.

Josai'el put her hands on his, and Tabris looked up with round mahogany eyes, meeting hers and shuddering at the contact. Her eyes, like faceted garnets, spoke without words, with an opened heart, and told him that all was forgiven.

"When will Elizabeth wake up?" Tabris asked.

Josai'el paused, then her mouth twitched and she said, "Soon."

"Maybe I should return," Tabris said. "I—I want to see her, to get to know her better. You understand." And he vanished.

Mithra looked up from the bird. Josai'el stood with her hands opened and her eyes wide—because she did understand.

Tabris noted that Rachmiel at least pretended to be happy upon his return, offering a smile from where he sat beside Elizabeth on the bed. Tabris sat on the floor by her discarded teddy bear.

"Sleepyhead," said Rachmiel, bending over her still body, "little one, it's time to get up."

Elizabeth rolled over beneath the covers, making a muffled cooing sound that coaxed a smile from Tabris.

"Come on, Sleepy," Rachmiel said. "It's morning."

Elizabeth sat up in bed and rubbed her eyes. Tabris sprang forward and beamed.

Rachmiel continued watching her, and quite aware of Tabris' reaction, sat straighter as though to ask if he hadn't a right to be proud of her.

"She's very sweet," Tabris said, but clearly he wanted to say more.

Rachmiel accompanied Elizabeth while she pulled her clothes from the closet and started getting dressed.

"She's small for her age," Tabris said.

He rose from the floor and drifted to the girl's side while she brushed her hair, running the soft bristles through the snarled red length of it.

"She's the only one of the children with red hair," said Rachmiel. "The rest are blond."

Tabris perched on the headboard, not having heard Rachmiel's last sentence. He stared as though bewitched. God had linked him to this girl as a co-guardian, so he could see her soul as it was—youthfully innocent. His comments about stature had been inane, silliness composed to try to explain why this one little girl in a world filled with thousands of little girls would be so special to him. God, in binding him to this girl, had shown him some of His own brightness manifested in her heart—bright despite Tabris' reduced Beatific Vision. The amazing craftsmanship of the Most High was visible in its full glory within her young and yet undeveloped soul, intricate interlocking pieces that existed in their full form in every part of her body. Naturally Tabris loved her.

About to speak, he stopped.

Rachmiel looked up with sudden concern.

Tabris stood and paced as heavily as a spirit can. Rachmiel stood too, his eyes wider.

Tabris gestured as though fighting what he wanted to communicate. "I can't," he said, and then he looked away.

Rachmiel could almost see the emotions trying to win their way free of his heart, but Tabris had battened down his soul, had reefed the sails that normally would be filled with the changing winds that at any moment would take him wherever God wanted. For a moment Rachmiel felt angry, as though Tabris were being coy and wanted him to coax the story from him, but he regretted that when Tabris turned abruptly toward the window.

"How old was Sebastian?" asked Rachmiel.

"Twelve."

Rachmiel had no idea what questions to ask or how to get Tabris to open himself without actually prying. *Did you love him?* would be painful and redundant; *What did he look like?* would be useless. He wished Tabris would say something more, but the two-toned angel stayed taciturn by the window.

Tabris said nothing for the rest of the morning. The others behaved normally, but at times a worried glance would shoot from one to another, and each would wonder what he could do.

When Connie drove the four children to school, the group enlivened somewhat, taking their places on the roof of the car, laughing and playing as only angels can play, able to be perfectly reckless with their hands holding tightly to God, secure that His eyes are watching them. The five angels who had been a part of this routine for years engaged in their usual activity, calling to angels they passed by the sides of the road, talking and relaxing. They watched for demonic attacks, of course, and during the short ride they had to fend off a few, but for the most part they were free to act as they pleased—all but Tabris, who still trembled at the thought of so recently having brushed shoulders with damnation.

He sat in the back seat behind the driver, his arms locked around the seat in front of him, his eyes mesmerized by the road that stretched ahead of him. He pulled forward his two-toned wings and thought.

He thought about Hell. Not the way humans do, but with a deeply personalized knowledge that comes from watching one's best friend abandon God and in turn be abandoned by Him. His thoughts of Hell did not linger over the flames and the pain—those, he found, were far less real in his mind than the fact that he would have lost his whole personality if God had condemned him. He had seen his friends praise God one moment and curse Him the next, hating Him, hating everything that resembled their Creator, wanting not to possess things but to destroy them, and most of all striking at the image of God embedded in their hearts. Tabris feared that change in himself. He loved God. His accuser had said that his demonstration of that love "fell short of the ideal," and the words rang back at Tabris constantly, every minute louder and more certain in his mind. He should have been condemned. A just God could hardly do otherwise.

A merciful God had.

Tabris had not been facetious when he had reflected on his being only the dot of an *i* away from damnation—the *t* had already been crossed, and by his own hand, his own actions. A part of him believed he should have been thrown into Hell.

Tabris suddenly leaped onto the hood of the car and stared into the wind, letting it sting the tears in his eyes and whip back his hair. He cupped his two-toned wings and caught the wind.

"Glad you could come on board, Tab," said Voriah.

Tabris smiled into the wind, and one might have wondered if he had heard Voriah at all. His ears rang with the sound of the air, the motor that rattled under his knees, the laughter of the children in the car, and the angels atop it.

"I like the wind," he said.

"Then this is the place to be," said Voriah.

Having satisfied their curiosity, Tabris tried to return to his thoughts but found it too difficult to think about Hell with five angels behind him laughing and praying.

"Join us, Tabris," said Rachmiel, so Tabris moved from the hood to the roof. He stayed with them and listened but felt too scared to try any prayer of his own. His eyes stayed down, and his fingers had woven around one another tightly. He felt all too glad when they arrived at the school and he could stop what had become, for him, almost a charade.

4

TABRIS HAD TROUBLE DECIDING WHICH WAS worse: the day at the school, surrounded by hundreds of angels whom he did not know but who knew about him, or the afternoons and evenings at home, with six angels whom he was expected to get to know well and who in turn would try to become close to him.

He had no reason for not wanting to become friends with them—on principle he thought it would be a good idea. These angels had adopted him as a service, however, and so he had to maintain distance. He preserved the utmost formality at all times and said nothing unless directly asked. He suspected that if he did so for a week or two, the others would stop condescending and would treat him as he deserved.

That was how he explained it to himself that night, alone by Josai'el's lake, tossing pebbles into the quiet water one after the next, avoiding the gaze of the waning moon. A musical world greeted his ears, a song no human has ever heard. The tones had been formed long ago by the stars, sent on notes of light aimlessly through the empty distances until somehow they all collided on earth around Tabris and serenaded him. He could hear the rhythmic foundation provided by the water that lapped at the pond's edge, harmony contributed by the deep breaths of sleeping birds and the sniffing of rodents that searched for food in the fallen leaves. A descant of promised and awaited snow hovered in the air, and all for Tabris, since he was the only one out that night.

"Raguel," he said, as though dictating a letter, "I think I'm doing all right. Nothing spectacular. I'm surviving. So is Elizabeth Hayes. She's very sweet, by the way. I think I could—she's ten. I . . . The other angels have been very friendly. Please let me know if I'm in danger of violating probation in any way. Please. Tabris."

He sat by the dying cattails and threw another pebble into the pond.

"Tabris," drawled a voice.

"Accuser," he said, his features unchanged although his voice had deepened.

"No, I've tired of that name. Call me Unbridled."

"Unbridled—are you the wind?"

"Yes," said the demon, inching forward from the shade of a pine tree and sitting very close to the two-toned angel. "I'm just like the wind, free to go wherever I please rather than chained within a circle that has a two-mile radius."

"And in all creation, Unbridled, you can't find the beauty I have in my circle."

Tabris smiled, a tight and symmetrical expression which strained his face but grew easier to maintain the longer he did it. He pulled his wings close to his body, fingering the green outer feathers.

"Are you going to kill Elizabeth?" asked Unbridled.

"Are you going to repent?"

"Tabris, Tabris—how can *you* ask me such a question? You're not qualified."

Tabris maintained his non-smile.

"The other angels don't want you around."

"Should that surprise me?"

"I want you." Unbridled moved closer. "Please, Tabris, come with me."

"Sorry," said Tabris. He tilted his head as though gesturing. "Tether."

"Shed it. Let go of the girl and come with me. Let's dance together in the Alps, or slip over Niagara Falls, or dive under the Arctic ice. Please—it's been so long."

The smile seemed to have frozen on Tabris' face. "No, but thank you for the kindness."

The demon sighed. "Then may I rest my head upon your shoulder and sit beside you in silence?"

"Don't involve me," said Tabris. "Other than that, do as you wish, *Unbridled.*"

"Ah, irony," said Unbridled, curling up with his head against a stone. "I could use someone with your sense of humor."

"Have you tried an employment agency?"

"You see!" said Unbridled, sitting upright. "You can do it every time! That's the Tabris I like to see."

Tabris lay back and closed his eyes.

"Let's go North and ride a good cold front."

"No."

"Tabris, if I could get you to say yes to any one question, what would that question be?"

"'Tabris, would you like me to go away and leave you in peace?'"

Silence ensued for a moment, and when Tabris dared to check, exploring with his heart, the demon had gone.

Tabris did not move from his spot beside the lake for a while. The nearby trees each were losing leaves one by one to the childlike hands of either gravity or the wind and had begun to add to the midnight music. He lay back to linger among the notes when Raguel arrived.

Tabris leaped to his feet and bowed deeply, his two-toned wings scissoring open as he bent.

"Please relax," Raguel said. "I'm sorry I couldn't arrive sooner."

"You didn't have to arrive at all," Tabris said, his eyes squinting until he managed to look up without any spark in them. "I wanted to give you an update. Am I doing something wrong?"

"Not at all, please relax," Raguel said, sitting on a rock. "Come sit with me."

Tabris perched on a fallen tree that would have either crumbled or slid down the banks of the lake had he weighed any more than moonlight. He smiled, the same non-smile he had worn for Unbridled.

"Then they're treating you well here?"

"Oh, yes."

"And Elizabeth is what you expected?"

"Yes."

Raguel paused, studying Tabris in the shine of the moon. "Remember," said Raguel, "you're in my custody. I'm directly involved in everything that happens here. If for any reason you want me around, call for me. Please, Tabris, I can help you if you need anything."

"But everything is fine," said Tabris, still smiling. "I'm having no difficulties at all."

"Call on me for any reason," Raguel said, his soul vibrating with tension which told Tabris that the chief of all guardian angels knew something was wrong. His eyes were wide.

"Of course," Tabris said. "Don't you trust me?"

They said nothing for a moment, and then Raguel said, "I took your side at the trial, didn't I?"

"Then trust me once more," Tabris said. "I'll call you if I need to."

Raguel watched him hesitantly and then took his leave. Tabris turned around on the rotting log and stared out over the lake.

5

THE NEXT DAY, AFTER LUNCH, ELIZABETH AND HER friends played with a handball against the brick wall of the school. Some of their guardians played alongside the girls, having just as good a time.

Rachmiel said to Tabris, "I'm going to sit on the roof—you'll watch her?"

"I will." Tabris settled himself against an unused space on the wall and regarded Elizabeth with dark eyes.

Rachmiel had gone to the rooftop where he joined Voriah and a few other angels.

"How's it going, Rock?" asked Voriah. The short wall that trimmed the edge of the roof to keep the maintenance workers from falling, but trapped any balls thrown injudiciously high, also served as a perch for guardians. Rachmiel stood behind the wall and leaned over the edge, too intently watching Elizabeth to answer right away. When he did speak, he did so distractedly.

"You're not giving yourself any time off, are you?" one of the other angels asked with a flash of his green eyes.

Rachmiel huffed, nonverbalizing "Are you kidding?" Then his mouth twitched and he spoke. "I'm not leaving him alone with her. At least with a demon I'd know where I stood, but him . . . No, I can't leave her alone with him."

Voriah rested on the roof beside Rachmiel, looking over the edge at Tabris, who leaned stoically against the wall three stories beneath them. "Has he spoken to you at all?"

"You mean more than to all of you?" Rachmiel chuckled. "Not really."

"The strong, silent type?" asked the green-eyed angel.

"Oh, no," Rachmiel said. "No, that came out wrong. Look, Sebastian died on Wednesday, four P.M. mountain time. It's now Friday, twelve Eastern standard time. That's not long at all for him. I'm surprised he can talk."

"That's sweet, Rock."

"Voriah! You saw him, the shock was still on his face when Raguel brought him to us. He wanted to be quiet, I think, to have some time to recover, but for some reason God sent him directly to us."

Despite his more understanding words, Rachmiel still watched Elizabeth and Tabris constantly.

Voriah squinted tightly, nonverbalizing to the third angel.

"I'd like to know his thoughts, too," said the green-eyed angel. "He really doesn't speak?"

"Oh, he'll answer you if you ask a question, he's just not verbose on his own. That's probably still shock. Mithra used to know him, and he says that the changes are obvious, whatever that means, and that Tabris used to speak on his own and laugh just like the rest of us. Now he hardly opens his mouth."

"Nonverbalizes everything?" asked the other angel.

"Well—no."

Voriah stopped. Rachmiel reached forward when Elizabeth abruptly lost her balance, but Tabris steadied the girl. Voriah continued, "Now that you mention it, I don't think he's ever nonverbalized anything."

"He hasn't to me," said Rachmiel. "We should ask Mithra."

Beneath them, Tabris had moved to stay closer to Elizabeth, and the other angels around him had stopped their bantering while playing.

Voriah waited a moment before saying, "He has this effect of silencing all."

"Well naturally," said the green-eyed angel. "He's a murderer."

Rachmiel's mouth twitched, and he half closed his eyes—but not enough that he let Tabris out of his sight.

"It's the truth," said the other angel.

"Rachmiel doesn't want to condemn him," Voriah said. "They'll be working together for the next eighty years."

"I don't know the whole story," said Rachmiel. "I can't judge him."

"God judged. He put Tabris on probation. Not damnation."

The other angel shrugged. "Your name means Compassion. You have to say that."

"Not at all. Ask Voriah what Raguel had to do to get me to accept him."

Voriah whistled.

The complicated nonverbalization settled on the green-eyed angel for a few seconds before he absorbed the whole thing. Then he looked aside. "You would see his good side anyway. You're the one who tried to explain what Lucifer was feeling before he fell."

"I never said he was justified, just that he might have thought he had a case." Rachmiel frowned. "I don't think Tabris is justified either. He's in serious trouble—but that's why he needs our help."

"Because you certainly don't need his."

Rachmiel frowned, his sunset eyes darkening to purple. The other angel detected the near anger and left.

Voriah moved closer. His heartbeat gave Rachmiel some reassurance until the color of his eyes calmed back to orange and red, and he sighed. "Am I Tabris' guardian too?"

Voriah smiled wryly, as though to say *You're certainly his defender.*

"I'm sure he has a case, if only he'd present it." Rachmiel looked closely at Elizabeth and then shuddered as if a chill had settled on his skin and dropped down into his blood.

"Don't think about it," said Voriah.

"It's too pervasive."

"Then tell me, and let it out of your system."

Rachmiel leaned further over the edge of the building and smiled at Elizabeth, then drew back. "I can't imagine—but I guess I *can* imagine it—him sitting on the edge of the child's bed one night and planning on killing him. I can't see him premeditating the act, saying 'This is how I'll do it.' God would have removed him long before it actually happened."

"What about free will?" asked an angel who had been gliding overhead but now cupped his wings and landed beside them. "Wouldn't that compromise—"

"No, God would only have been removing him from the situation until he had a better grip over himself."

The other angel came closer. "Raguel came to my household also, Rock."

Rachmiel's eyes expressed surprise, question.

"He's having meetings with all the guardians during the next few days, he and the rest of the Seven. They're talking about what happened and how we can take steps to prevent a repeat of Tabris. From what they said, my guess is that Tabris had no plan, that thought and action were simultaneous."

Voriah nonverbalized what a human would express with a gasp. "No time at all for second thoughts."

"Pretty much so, is my guess. That's why Raguel intervened. Tabris made a mistake but he never stopped loving God, or at least that's what Raguel claims. No one contests that he was wrong. He looks to me like he was ready to throw himself into Hell."

Rachmiel had stopped watching Elizabeth and had tilted his head to watch Tabris instead, who turned his own head and returned the look. Rachmiel squinted and pointed at Elizabeth. Tabris turned back.

Voriah laughed out loud. "That'll show him, Rock."

"I didn't mean to be funny. He should be watching her."

The third angel was frowning with thought. "He doesn't nonverbalize, does he? I would have expected he'd radiate laughter or hurt when you did that, but I couldn't read anything off him."

"He just doesn't," said Voriah.

"I've never seen him laugh," said Rachmiel.

The other angel sat on the edge of the roof, his feet hanging free against the wall. "Have you tried talking to him?"

"Not yet. He spent last night alone outside, by the pond. I would have gone to him, but I wasn't sure if that was what he wanted." Rachmiel suddenly straightened. His eyes narrowed and he paused.

The other angel answered the thought in Rachmiel's mind. "Raguel's advice was that we not let pressure build up in us, that we share our difficulties."

"So maybe I should try to talk to him first, rather than wait for him." Rachmiel looked down into the schoolyard at the only angel whose wings were two colors. "I could talk about something else first, to get him warmed up to speaking."

"Rock, no offense, but small talk would upset him." Voriah nodded slowly. "Do you remember the look in his eyes the night he arrived, when he realized we had been talking about him?"

Rachmiel winced as though cut with a knife.

The third angel shook his head. "He must really resent being the object of so much attention. How would you feel?"

Rachmiel closed his eyes and, keeping his heart trained on Elizabeth constantly, tried to imagine the shame of having crossed God's will, the uneasiness of knowing that everyone else knew exactly what he had done. He realized then why Adam had needed to clothe himself in the garden.

"I want to talk to him," Rachmiel said.

"Maybe you should just let him know you're available," said the third angel.

Voriah half snickered.

Although the meaning of the nonverbalization was obvious to Rachmiel, it was not so to the other angel and Rachmiel translated it. "We'll wait a long time if we want him to open up on his own."

In the yard beneath, Tabris stood leaning against a tree, his eyes downcast, his whole attention centered on Elizabeth, his ears and heart closed to the discussion of him that occupied the angels of the school children that played after lunch.

6

ONE NIGHT JOSAI'EL APPEARED IN ELIZABETH'S bedroom. "Tabris, Rachmiel, we're going to have a night off. Come downstairs."

They were not the last to arrive, and they waited in silence among the fragile knickknacks on high shelves until all eight of the household angels were present.

"Has Rachmiel explained this to you?" Josai'el asked Tabris.

"No."

"Once in a while we leave the house and relax. All but one of us go someplace outside and do whatever we wish for the night—like a picnic. The last one stays here and guards the house."

Tabris asked, "Is that safe?" but his facial features did not change.

"The one who stays behind places a Guard around the structure of the house that will repel demons or at least inform him if any try to enter. We can be recalled instantly."

Tabris finally frowned. "But a Guard that size would be weak—the last one could be overwhelmed."

"It hasn't happened yet," said Katra'il from where she sat on an end table, her gold eyes sharp. "Didn't your other household do this?"

"No."

"I thought it was strange, too, when I arrived," said Hadriel. "Connie's family never left their charges, but it's very helpful in relieving the pressure of constant vigilance."

Tabris nodded, his face once again a mask.

"Whose turn is it to stay behind?" asked Katra'il.

Rachmiel sat straighter. "I think's it's—"

"I'll stay," said Miriael.

Rachmiel turned to face the angel on the window sill.

"Oh, I'm sure," said Miriael, standing to pull his shorter stature to its full height and his eyes glinting like steel or silver. "Go, have a good time."

Rachmiel hesitated, clearly uncertain.

"Your turn on the rotation will come soon enough," said Miriael. "Please go. Enjoy yourself. I'll set the Guard."

"Wait," Tabris said, watching the others with his eyes wide and glazed, as though he were forcing himself to remain strong. Then he spoke quickly. "I can't exceed two miles yet."

"We'll stay close this time," said Josai'el, her eyes glimmering and reflecting against her lashes. "Whenever Connie or Bridget was pregnant we had this difficulty, but it's easy enough to circumvent."

Tabris nodded, not openly reluctant, and the next instant seven of the household angels stood outside on the grass of a gently sloping hill.

Very quickly they spread themselves across the grass. Katra'il called her guitar to her hands and strummed something that sounded vaguely like hard rock, but then she laughed and softly played Spanish guitar music. Hadriel leaned against a tree so that he could read a book. The other five looked at each other.

"We have enough for pinochle," said Voriah. "What do you say, Rock?"

"Not now, thank you." Rachmiel settled on the grass, looked up at the stars and lay backward. He flung his arms back behind his head and sighed. "Guess how long it's been since my last nap?"

"At least eleven years," said Josai'el.

"You can't use your night off to sleep!" Voriah said. "That's crazy!"

"Playing pinochle on a night like this—now *that's* crazy, Voriah."

Tabris sat watching the others, but slowly his attention drifted until he found himself staring into the deep darkness of the trees on the next hill. Something in the isolation and distance of that small copse fascinated him, and he felt its darkness separate from the darkness of the star-bright night which the household had chosen for its leisure time.

He startled when Rachmiel spoke. "Tabris, what do you think of Elizabeth?"

As soon as he spoke the words, Rachmiel wished almost violently that he could recall them.

In an even voice, Tabris said, "She's an adorable child. You've done a good job."

Rachmiel nonverbalized thanks, but the nonverbalization was tinged with self-consciousness.

That conversation died there. Voriah asked Josai'el a question, and Rachmiel listened past his rapidly beating heart.

"You tried," said God to Rachmiel.

"What a dumb question, though," he prayed. "Please help me with him. Is he offended?"

"No."

A very disquieted Tabris lay down on his stomach and closed his eyes. He thought about sleeping, the dark emptiness of unconsciousness, the slight disorientation of eventually waking, the friendly cold of the numbness that would steal over his mind.

When he noticed Josai'el's hands slowly massaging his shoulders, he sat up and looked around.

"I'm sorry," Josai'el said. "Weren't you going to sleep?"

"I hadn't planned on it," Tabris said. He shook his head, closed his eyes, and forced the soft and dreamy look to change into the extremely aware, sharply deep mahogany focus he normally wore. Sitting up, he glanced at the others. Mithra and Hadriel were speaking to each other about an event of the day, and Josai'el and Rachmiel were in a group that included him.

Mithra looked towards Tabris. "Has that demon bothered you again?"

"Once. I sent him away."

Josai'el smiled gently, coaxingly. "You used to be friends?"

"Before the Fall," said Tabris, and he looked back to the dark cluster of trees.

Rachmiel's eyes rounded.

Smiling tentatively still, Josai'el said, "It's always difficult meeting someone who used to be a friend. I always feel a great sense of loss when it happens to me."

"Senseless loss," said Mithra.

"None of my close friends fell," said Voriah, "but I can imagine it."

"Their whole personality changes," said Mithra. "There isn't much left of the original soul, because once they hate God they try to destroy every facet of Him they can find—destroying each other, eventually turning on themselves, slicing off the parts of their names that mention Him, some changing their names altogether. Whenever one of them meets with a former friend he's almost unrecognizable, except for remnants of the old personality which float into view from time to time, and those are painful to see."

Tabris was completely still, as though he had looked into a mirror and seen only a skull, and Rachmiel watched his expressionless face intently, leaning forward a little as though to catch any trace of emotion that would escape him. Josai'el caught the hungry look in Rachmiel's eyes and paused, looking at Tabris and seeing the same mask he did, realizing the complete control. Briefly she wondered what was best—to ask him a question in terms that demanded an answer or to change the subject completely and give Tabris time to open himself at his own pace.

Even so, she realized, for most angels their own pace would be to open their whole souls immediately.

Rachmiel said, "Tell us about your friend."

"He fell," said Tabris.

"What did he say to you?" Rachmiel asked, and then his eyes flashed with eagerly brilliant orange light. "Why is he visiting you now? What's his name? What does he want?"

Tabris recoiled, his eyes larger and darker than anyone had supposed they might become. His hands were not shaking only because he had pressed them into the ground. "I—I don't know. I don't speak to him, he doesn't—he doesn't say."

"Rachmiel," Josai'el said, her voice as stern as a rap with a ruler, "ease up on him. This isn't an interrogation. Please," and Rachmiel looked at her now, trembling somewhat and radiating awkwardness and a need to find some identifiable feature on Tabris' soul—some feature with which he could commiserate, "please don't press him."

"No," Tabris said coldly. "Let him ask."

While everyone had watched the Rachmiel-Josai'el exchange, no one had seen Tabris breathe deeply, his eyes flash and then narrow, his whole face come once again under iron control, his hands forcibly stop their shaking. The effects were visible now, as though what had addressed them was a suit of armor and the knight that had worn it gone home. Rachmiel shivered when his eyes snapped back to regard the two-toned angel.

"He's changed his name," said Tabris, "but for now he calls himself Unbridled. He obviously wants to witness my damnation. He pleaded for just that at my trial."

Tabris glittered in the darkness, his shape absorbing the starlight and letting escape only faint points now and again. His eyes seemed like infinitely deep pits, and his smile, when it came, might have been pressed from a stamp. "Have I answered all your questions, Rachmiel?"

Rachmiel gaped, then shook his head. In the distance, Katra'il's fingers had slowed on her guitar, and Hadriel had looked up from his book.

The shell of a spirit where Tabris sat gave off a resonance almost demonic in its emptiness.

Rachmiel stammered when he tried to speak, but he did not trust his heart to give a clear nonverbalization. "I—I'm sorry. No more questions. Really."

"Any time," Tabris said slowly, precisely, "please feel free to ask."

The smile that Tabris had worn for Raguel had appeared again, and he turned to the rest with that same smile. Then he fixed his eyes closely on Rachmiel.

The others might have stayed in silence for a while if Mithra had not mentioned meeting a demon he used to know, successfully changing the focus of the conversation. Like that same empty suit of armor, Tabris sat in perfect silence through the next two turns of subject, with Rachmiel beside him feeling both sorry and mortified. Eventually the orange-winged guardian stood and walked to where Katra'il played her guitar.

"Nice move, Rock," she said.

His purpled eyes wandered, his hands fingering the dying leaves of a tree, and he watched Tabris from a distance. The stars blazed, obvious to an angel as they shed their burning light onto the planet—old light—light shed hundreds of years ago that had traveled unrefracted until this moment; and now that it had struck, the earth would never again be the same. Quietly, Rachmiel climbed the tree, following his hands as they grasped higher, hauling on the branches, filling his fingers with thick fistfuls of dying leaves, pulling himself upward until he had reached the crown.

The angels had spread themselves over the hilltop, still talking, now more lively, with the exception of Tabris, who seemed as though he hardly belonged to this frivolous gathering. The group looked like a double exposure of a stern war memorial statue and a family picnic.

Rachmiel let the breeze that caressed the dry and withered branches of the tree rock him as well, feeling like a kitten being stroked by the fingers of an old, old woman. He closed his eyes, drew up his wings, hummed appreciatively as the hands of God relaxed his tense but tired spirit, laid to rest every one of his worries, and reassured him of infinite love.

The battle cry startled him most when it came since he had been drowsily curled in the leaves. The call awoke him immediately—Miriael's soul was summoning help, and Rachmiel had hardly moved before he realized that Tabris had already gone to the house, Mithra close behind. The others were waiting in silence.

Tabris and Mithra landed in the living room with their swords drawn and shining. Tabris' wings were spread their full length, displaying perfectly the jade green outer feathers that yielded to inner mahogany ones.

Immediately Tabris and Mithra had checked the bedrooms (Tabris checked Elizabeth's first), to make certain that no demons had actually entered the house, and then both returned to Miriael.

"We're uncompromised," said Tabris.

"They're pressing it," Miriael said, his voice and his blue eyes both trembling with strain. "I can't keep the Guard together."

"Let's fight them outside," Mithra said.

The pair of angels flashed outside the Guard, slicing ferociously into the evil throng that had been pressing the spiritual shell lacing the structure of the house. Tabris lifted his two-handed sword and began slashing, the black fire of his eyes and the mad energy of his arms driving away the demons. Mithra, beside him, added his strength and the force of his will to Tabris. Mithra used a sword and shield, more traditional than Tabris' heavy two-handed engine, but together they carved apart the hungry demonic hoard that clung to the outside of the house like barnacles on the bottom of an old sea barge.

When finally the last demons had retreated, Mithra looked at Tabris. "We're done," said his eyes. "Let's go."

Mithra returned to the group on the hilltop, but Tabris flashed to the inside of the house.

"The Guard held," said Miriael when Tabris arrived. "You can return to the others."

"I'd rather not just now," said Tabris.

"Is something wrong?"

Tabris smiled, a successful venture, and then shrugged.

Miriael flung himself backward onto the couch. "I'm all right. I know I was shaken before, but there's no problem now."

Tabris nodded, standing in place and regarding Miriael blankly.

Miriael cocked an eyebrow.

"Tonight was Rachmiel's turn to stand guard," said Tabris.

"He needed the time off more than I did."

"But it was his turn?"

"Yes." Miriael shrugged. "I thought he might want to get to know you better."

Miriael had half-expected Tabris to roll his eyes and say "You'd better believe it!" Rachmiel's curiosity at times became palpable, a distinct flavor that angels could drink out of the air and then long for more. Tabris had to have felt the tingle of incorporeal fingers that trembled, stroking the questions that surrounded his existence. Miriael had expected acknowledgment, but Tabris made no response at all to the offhanded statement, and suddenly Miriael understood why Rachmiel had grown so inquisitive.

"I watched you fighting outside," Miriael said tentatively, "and you were very powerful."

"Thank you."

The verbalization visibly startled Miriael, whose eyes opened a little wider. "I was wondering if I might spar with you a little."

Tabris nodded.

"There's no one here who really enjoys a good fight," Miriael said. "The closest one is Mithra, and he keeps himself constantly in check. I want to go all out, to fight as though I'm defending God's throne or my charge's life. It's been years," he added quickly, "since I've been able to exert myself to the full extent. The demons here tend to flash in and out. Temptation is seldom violent. If the demons see two angels with drawn swords they fly back to Hell."

"They fought me."

"You're new here," said Miriael, his eyes scintillating with new laughter. "They probably wanted to test you."

Tabris smiled in return, but then his eyes tightened. "Have I passed?"

"They fled at the end, didn't they? You gave a number of them blows that they'll remember for a while."

Tabris looked at his hands.

"Could you spar with me?" Miriael asked again, missing the gesture.

"Now?"

The eagerness in Miriael's eyes brightened his whole face.

Tabris produced a sword, this one lighter and shorter than the one he had used outside.

"No," Miriael said. "All out, as though you were battling Satan himself."

"We'll knock each other unconscious!"

"Good—Josai'el would come back the instant she sensed the Guard dropping, and after a display like that the local demons would give a wide berth to both of us."

Miriael smiled as Tabris made his sword heavier, longer, two-handed, and then his own sword appeared in his hands. They spread their wings. Miriael crouched.

He raised one eyebrow.

"Yes," said Tabris.

Miriael launched forward and they fought for a few minutes before Tabris pulled away breathlessly.

"You weren't kidding, were you?"

"To the *death*," gasped Miriael.

They clashed again, Tabris this time better prepared for the savagery of Miriael's attack. The pair moved faster than one might have guessed they could, but within moments it became obvious that Tabris had the greater strength. Miriael, though extremely powerful, would have to rely on quickness and agility in addition to strength to overcome Tabris; immediately Miriael shortened his sword, lightening it, changing his clothes to more supple armor, making the leather of his boots and gloves more flexible even though that afforded less protection.

They seemed grim, fully intent on slicing each other apart, but for quite a long time neither one scored a hit. Despite Miriael's fractionally faster movements, Tabris was able to avoid contacting the blade, and though hard pressed, Miriael danced around the bite of Tabris' sword. In short, the pair were almost perfectly matched, and they might never have decided the battle except for one hesitation on Tabris' part, when he could have brought his sword down toward Miriael's neck. Miriael twisted and plunged his short sword up into Tabris' stomach.

For the next minutes, which Tabris spent in quiet recovery, they stayed silent. Sweating, glowing happily, Miriael cleaned the blood from his sword and whistled.

Tabris felt the wound close, then stood and stretched. "That was a good workout. You're a worthwhile opponent."

"You're no slouch either. A couple of times I thought you'd win."

"We'll do this again sometime."

The spiritual blood evaporated from Tabris' clothes, and the tear in the fabric mended under his fingers. Angels heal from the inside out. Rubbing his hands together to flake off the blood, Tabris said, "You really were serious."

"Of course." But Miriael's voice had not spoken as much as had his full smile, his raised eyebrows. He winked, as though to add, "But I warned you."

"Oh, you did, no mistake," said Tabris.

The wound had been painless—Miriael had wanted only to cause temporary damage, not to inflict suffering, and when angels strike their intention is the greatest part of their weaponry. This is why angels seldom miss their targets, and why a blow intended to cause serious harm usually causes just that if the recipient cannot defend himself; it means death if he is human. Angelic bodies recover almost instantly from any strike, which is one reason damnation is so terrible. Hell is eternal because angelic nature is such that it cannot die. Human soul-material, almost the same substance, also cannot be slaughtered no matter how much the body is decayed or the conscience corrupted.

His wound gone, Tabris stretched out on the floor, spreading his two-toned wings and sighing deeply. "It was a long time for me too, since the last really good workout. I'd forgotten the fun."

Miriael chuckled, his battle armor now changed to sweatpants and a T-shirt. "You're by no means rusty, though. You'll be a great co-guardian for Elizabeth."

Tabris said, "I'm glad you think so."

"Don't be sarcastic," said Miriael, failing to realize that he had picked up a stray emotional emanation from Tabris, who immediately capped his spirit again. "You're good. You've got strong reflexes, vigilance, energy, all the things that make a good guardian. You're the perfect compliment to Rachmiel. He does an amazing job keeping her soul in order but doesn't always fight. Don't get me wrong, he can run intellectual rings around any demon—so can Josai'el—but he's reluctant to grab his sword and drive demons away from her. My guess is, you wouldn't even let them near."

Tabris had his eyes squinted closed, and nodded. Miriael paused, wondering why there had been no nonverbalization accompanying the gesture, as though the emotional well that fed the streams of consciousness had emptied a while ago, and nothing remained to say.

Miriael made a startling realization as the Spirit flooded his heart: Tabris faced such an important crossroad that no small talk could interest him. Certainly it could not before the matter had been resolved, and Miriael knew he was not the one to settle it. In the instant before saying something else about Elizabeth, the instant this knowledge filled him, Miriael bit back the words and closed his eyes to mentally test the Guard around the house, instinctively reaching for the soul of his charge Kyle, and found that all was well. The boy slept quietly (dreaming of swordplay, which made Miriael laugh), and the Guard remained unbreached.

Tabris left the living room to look at Elizabeth and then returned. He sat against the wall now, beneath the mantle piece, and regarded Miriael.

"Do you like to fly?"

Miriael smiled. "I suppose I do—it's not just transportation, although I guess I don't have much chance to fly for fun."

"I enjoy flying. I love cold nights when the stars are visible and the wind is brutally frigid."

"Why don't you fly now? You have the time."

Tabris nodded and left the house.

His range had been limited—he would have flown impressively high if only he were not bound to Elizabeth. So in that two-mile sphere in which he was allowed to roam he did his best to soar freely, closing his eyes as if to transform the world around him to whatever skies he imagined. Skies feel as different to angels as varied landscapes feel to humans. Some skies are more turbulent, some placid, some smooth and others grainy, and angelic spirits are so fine that they can detect changes which to a human might seem ridiculously minute. Here the sky felt to Tabris as smooth as Jell-O, silken against his face, gently cold like still water to a slow swimmer. This type of air might be great for gliding and reflecting, but it served only poorly for the type of flight that Tabris had spoken of—rugged, fast, almost painful. The richness of the air could only slow a speeding angel. During his time in the suburbs, on the rare occasions when he could leave his charge to stretch his wings, Tabris had flown through the polluted air of Los Angeles, so cluttered and foreign that he might have choked if he had required oxygen to breathe. That brown haze, with its sharp pollutants and curving tendrils of poison waiting to dissipate into the global system, had been amazingly good for diving since an angel can slide along the thin streams of carbon monoxide that rise ever upward into higher levels of the atmosphere.

Three time zones distant from Los Angeles, much farther than two miles from any polluted city, Tabris found himself trapped in thick oxygen-rich air in the way that a world-champion skier might detest having to ski on granular wet snow.

Tabris cupped his wings and landed by the pond, knowing that until Elizabeth's bond with him had aged and the tether lengthened, he would be trapped here.

Here—where was here, anyway? He spread his hands in the dying grass and pressed his palms against the ground, asking the earth where he was. The fallen planet gave only a reluctant answer, and Tabris was filled with sudden information that knew neither name nor border, but rather what neighbored it and relative distances that functioned much better than a push-pin on a map. Nodding, Tabris recognized that he was in Chittenden County, Vermont, north of Burlington and south of St. Albans. The land continued talking to him as though it could read his soul in return and had found a peer. He learned of the animals preparing to hibernate underground, the dead things decomposing in the brush around him, the multicolored leaves that had already begun to rot.

Tabris leaped into the air suddenly, his eyes round and a little surprised, like a grandmother who asked what her granddaughter learned that day in school and was treated to a dirty joke. His mind reeled slightly from the broken contact, but he knew that nature had turned perverse and would next have informed him of all the bacteria decomposing the animals recently alive, and if it could have, would have told him the direction and condition of the newly buried.

Looking about with trembling eyes at the lake, Tabris bit his lower lip, then took a deep breath and touched ground where Rachmiel and the others were finishing their evening.

"We were wondering where you had gone," said Josai'el.

"I stayed with Miriael after we defeated the demons," said Tabris.

Rachmiel's eyes followed Tabris as he sat among them, fixed on the angel as though they were binoculars with an almost-focused view of a rare bird.

"We hope we didn't make you feel uncomfortable before," said Mithra.

"Don't worry about it," said Tabris as he smiled with force. "I'm sure you didn't intend any harm."

Rachmiel caught the edge of Tabris' words, an edge that might have sliced an apple in half or split a hair. He was distant enough that his reaction went unnoticed, and the others must not have perceived the tension that might one day develop into anger.

"How's Elizabeth?" asked Rachmiel.

"Sleeping."

Rachmiel wondered briefly if his own fears could cast Tabris' words in a light different from what Tabris intended, and even if that was true, if it was wrong to take note of which things Tabris tried to hide.

But what, he wondered, *does he want hidden?*

Katra'il stood, took his hand, and forcibly flashed Rachmiel to the shade of some trees that only now had begun picking up the beginning of dawn on their crowns. He looked at her with a startled expression, and she glared into his eyes as if to say, "You're radiating curiosity."

Rachmiel swallowed hard. He shook his head with a worried expression in his eyes.

"Keep it under control," said Katra'il, her golden ringlets disheveled and framing her round face.

She returned to the group without Rachmiel, who stood alone on the hill for the time being, his heart rate and breathing slowing to normal levels, his eyes becoming less round, his hands no longer curled into fists. He pulled his wings closer and knelt on the ground. Closing his eyes, he extended his heart to the Lord.

The returning hold met him instantly, surrounding Rachmiel, engulfing his heart and making him gasp, flooding him so that he fell forward in an angelic prostration: his body curled and resting on the calves of his tucked legs, his hands flat on the ground beneath his shoulders, his wings spread forward over his head, and his forehead touching the ground. The gasping of his breathing quieted immediately, and then the awe that he felt at God's presence in him began to abate under the Divine reassurance of immortal love. He sat upright, eyes still closed, and smiled. God smiled in return, Rachmiel glorying in a hug from a God great enough to have created every star but also personal enough to have formed him and breathed life into him.

God wordlessly asked Rachmiel to speak. Rachmiel opened his heart so that all his love poured out, an oblation of spiritual wine on an altar that was the whole of creation. He revealed all of his soul to God like a child showing his mother a shoebox full of his favorite priceless objects: butterfly wings and small red trucks and baseball cards and plastic jewelry that glitters in the light. Rachmiel opened all the boxes in his soul, gave God every thought, rededicated his every deed.

God thanked him and Rachmiel laughed, almost crying. Gradually the presence withdrew and Rachmiel sat breathlessly, seeing the world through eyes like diamonds and nearly bursting with the grandeur of creation—this earth sustained countless lives and housed beautiful lifeless structures, and even these mutely gave glory to and pointed toward their Creator. He longed in that moment to show Elizabeth, to take the diamonds from his sight and put them into her eyes, then to hold her hand while she wondered at marvels he only could imagine.

Rachmiel flashed to Elizabeth's bedside and beamed as radiantly as the sun that just now began to shine into her room.

"Wake up, Sleepyhead," he whispered as the other angels began returning. "Wake up—see what God's done for you today!"

7

THAT DAY SAW A CHANGE IN TABRIS, WHO HAD found inspiration in camaraderie—although not the type Josai'el had hoped. He had learned a lot from Rachmiel's large eyes that constantly scrutinized his every action, from Rachmiel's soul that operated like a gigantic radar dish scanning to detect any emotion he allowed to stray.

After Rachmiel had left the group, ostensibly because Katra'il had wanted to show him something but more likely because she had wanted to reprimand him in private, Tabris had taken note of the angels surrounding him. The relaxing guardians had continued their aimless conversation, and he forced himself to contribute to the small talk: he etched the smile onto his face, nodded at the end of every phrase, and kept his eyes on the one who spoke. The others had responded well to this, and Tabris had not had to avert his eyes again.

He learned that the more he acted what they considered "normal," the more they acted normally themselves. In time, they might even neglect to remember they were associating with a near-demon.

Pleased with the results, Tabris continued the effort, concentrating primarily on Rachmiel because he was the one most suffused with curiosity. Tabris' first venture, carefully calculated to appease Rachmiel, was a verbal decision to get to know the family members better.

In Tabris' mind the family was a nebulous unit: two parents, a grandmother, and three brothers floating about Elizabeth, the clear center in his understanding. To any angel other than Rachmiel, of course, some other member would have been the focus, but to Tabris the family members were little more than names, and he told Rachmiel of his intent to learn more about them. This delighted the guardian, who immediately commenced the introductions.

Tabris asked about Kyle first, Miriael's charge. Rachmiel and Miriael gave long descriptions: he was the oldest of the children, a responsible boy who liked to read and had an intense interest in the sciences and computers. Miriael's eyes flashed as he spoke about the boy, and he had one hand on the boy's shoulder the entire time, as though to mark Kyle as his heart's property. Tabris tried to avoid seeing that hand or the glow of pride in Miriael's eyes, and he continually looked toward whatever Miriael mentioned, be it the boy's eyes, his small hands, the strength in his arms, the internal pensiveness that imbued his spirit. At sixteen, Kyle was already thinking about colleges, and Miriael could have spoken for a whole day on just the possibilities of location and majors and never have touched upon the gentleness of Kyle's spirit or the openness of his heart.

Kyle's roommate was Martin, guarded by Katra'il. She spoke softly, with deliberate control, about Martin's interests, mostly sports but also any type of competitive gaming. He especially enjoyed any sort of logical challenge, questions that could engage the engines within his mind and occupy all of his attention until he had solved the puzzle. He could be very intent on whatever task claimed him at any given moment—so much so that at times, Katra'il confessed, she would become absorbed and work with him to piece together the answer. Martin had celebrated his fourteenth birthday just a month before Tabris' arrival.

Only a year younger than Martin was his brother Alan. Voriah had been assigned to him, and Tabris seemed particularly intent on Voriah's description, perhaps because Sebastian had been close to Alan's age. Full of his usual energy, Voriah bounded madly from topic to topic, barely mentioning facets of Alan's character before launching into a detailed analysis of his physique, and hardly brushing the surface of that before going on to list his achievements. Alan, it became apparent, had become a type of household mediator, not terribly prominent in any one area but rather quietly efficient everywhere. His mother trusted him implicitly, and all the adults he met liked him. Of the three boys Alan was the most quiet, a strange complement to such an angel as Voriah.

After meeting the boys, Tabris decided to postpone the adults, saying that the delay would help him to differentiate.

He had made polite remarks about each of the boys, of course, and during the day they had been transformed from three brothers with identical bowl-shaped haircuts to three human beings, with their differences and faults, whose angels loved them dearly—fiercely. Tabris often recalled the look in Miriael's eyes when he had equated protecting Kyle to defending God's throne. If angels could die, then these angels were willing to give their lives in the service. The three brothers' angels emanated love and pride that might have snatched away Tabris' breath. Rachmiel, he knew, felt the same. No doubt Josai'el, Hadriel, and Mithra would also.

Tabris wondered about himself.

Certainly he would defend Elizabeth—but Sebastian . . . if he could have met himself then, in Sebastian's earlier life, would he have seen that same spark in his eyes, felt the same love radiating from the heart of Sebastian's guardian?

Whenever Tabris felt himself growing pensive, he would talk about inanities, and the more he did this the less Rachmiel felt curious. The fits of needing to know still overtook him occasionally but not to the same degree and certainly not as often. Tabris never voluntarily supplied the answers to the questions Rachmiel might have asked on his own, the deep sort of questions whose answers would require a look through the pages of the soul. Rather, he spoke about inconsequences, the angelic equivalent of discussing the weather, and managed to skirt any issue that might have involved a deeper probe. Tabris had discovered his own version of supply and demand—if he spoke at all, Rachmiel felt satisfied with the little information he received. If Tabris said nothing, then he wanted to know every deep turn of his mind.

Tabris felt uncomfortable with the schoolyard scene—oddly enough, only a few weeks ago he and Sebastian had been very much a part of the frivolity and freedom that knew it had no need yet for responsibility. Now Tabris felt above that need to forget cares and troubles in play—or perhaps below the ability. Certainly he felt apart. The other angels treated him as a loner far too often for him even to pretend to camaraderie.

Hundreds of small children of assorted ages ran about, shrieking and laughing, shouting at each other, arguing sometimes, and pushing the limits of the schoolyard rules. Some of the older girls clustered in small groups by the fences; younger girls played tag with the boys or jumped rope close to the building. Every section of the wall was being used for handball, neatly divided by classroom since each room was the same size and between each room was a narrow strip of windowless brick. Park benches cut the yard into two sections, the larger side for running games, the smaller for hopscotch and jump rope or just talking.

Tabris paced through the mélee, his consciousness trained on Elizabeth all the time so that it might have been only he and she in the playground. He walked past other angels wearing a deep silence. He had nothing to say to them. Like small angry suns the other angels radiated—most of them. Righteous indignation boiled in their hearts, and he knew a lot of them wanted him condemned. Or else, he corrected himself, anger is the loudest emotion and it drowns the others.

Elizabeth stumbled as she played hopscotch, and Rachmiel steadied her. Tabris had reached forward but then hesitated, and he now stood in a forced relaxed pose as though he had not just made a motion toward her. A few angels turned at his sudden movement.

This is eerie, he thought, knowing even as he did so that *eerie* was the wrong word and that the right one would pierce his heart if he admitted what he really felt.

Rachmiel smiled, deliberately refracting the sunlight through his orange eyes, a form of nonverbal communication that did not involve his emotions at all. "This will be one of the last warm days before winter sets in for good."

Tabris smiled as though winter had set into his veins already. "I like the snow," he said quietly.

Rachmiel inhaled. "There's a very invigorating quality to cold weather, but I prefer it like this. Actually, so does she." He smiled at the girl who right now was waiting her turn at the hopscotch grid. "The earth is alive now, but gets much colder and all the living things die or hibernate. Hibernation is amazing too—*God* is amazing—but the creatures that are up and about interest me more."

Rachmiel beamed in one of the final autumn rays of sunlight, and Tabris watched without changing expression, fighting the parts of his heart that wanted to argue, to say that he had always loved the lifeless cold. He had especially relished the cold of deep space that could kill a corporeal creature and even could sting semi-corporeal angels. He had flown through that eternal night between stars, empty and isolated except for his soul's constant touch with the Lord, and in those quiet times he had been happy. He had often delayed in temperatures near absolute zero until the numbness made his wings ache and then had flashed back to his home in Heaven—a small log cabin in the mountains—and sat wrapped in a blanket before a hot fire until the love of God and the warmth of his native country could return to his feathers and his fingers.

Tabris pried himself from the world of his thoughts and looked at Elizabeth. There was no cold aspect to her, nothing isolated or stagnant, nothing in need of the distances of space. She needed people—as did Rachmiel, Tabris realized. Rachmiel instinctively reflected and expressed the feelings of any creature nearby—he comforted by sharing the problem, by commiserating.

Tabris stood a little taller and looked around the schoolyard until he found what he knew had to be nearby. Every school had one. After a moment he nodded and said, "Elizabeth," and kept looking.

Elizabeth, awaiting her turn at hopscotch, looked around the yard until her eyes fell on the same thing Tabris had found: a girl alone on a park bench, reading. To Tabris, this girl also radiated loneliness and awkwardness.

Rachmiel saw her too—Tabris knew because he felt him suddenly nonverbalizing how it felt to be a misfit. Rachmiel was about speak to Elizabeth, but Tabris stopped him.

Rachmiel's eyes flashed with questions.

"Wait," said Tabris.

Elizabeth looked back down at the hopscotch grid chalked on the ground, and Tabris continued bringing up that girl in her mind.

Breathing deeply, Rachmiel suddenly understood what Tabris was doing. By letting Elizabeth think of the action herself, he was making sure she got the maximum credit possible and the guardians a minimum. It also made her slightly more prone to doing it again in the future with less prompting. In time, it might become automatic for her to reach out to people in trouble. Of course, not all people would respond without a good push, but Elizabeth was innocent enough and the reaction innate enough to her that maybe the knowledge of the need would be all the motivation she required.

Elizabeth took her turn hopping, and then Tabris said, "Elizabeth," dragging the thought of that lone figure on the park bench back to her mind.

Fidgeting, she looked up. Rachmiel had flown behind Tabris and was holding his shoulders, but neither angel realized. Tabris looked at the distant girl once more. He noticed suddenly that her guardian was staring back at him—deeply protective, powerfully mistrustful.

An arrow of hurt self-defense shot through Tabris, slicing deep into his heart, and it continued into Elizabeth, who just then in an untutored imitation of her true guardian was imagining how it must feel to be all alone and outcast in a schoolyard full of people who should have been friends. She winced as the pain struck her, and then she told her friends that she would be back shortly. She crossed the schoolyard to the benches and sat beside the other girl. She introduced herself.

Rachmiel shone brightly, proudly. Tabris flashed to an empty corner of the rooftop and watched as Elizabeth made at least one lonely soul a little happier.

"I was surprised," Rachmiel said later.

"Why?" Voriah asked, sitting balanced on the ridge-pole of the Hayes house. "He's still an angel."

"But it was so *nice*, that's all." Rachmiel sent a small stone skittering down the slanted roof and then called it back to him before it dropped off the edge. "He just looked for her and sent Elizabeth to her spontaneously. I was shocked. I still am."

Voriah smiled like stardust in the night. "You must be—you're verbalizing everything, just like him. Where is he now, by the way?"

"By the lake. He's always there at night. It must give him peace of mind. Maybe he prays."

Voriah huffed as though to say Tabris certainly did not pray with them.

"That's not funny," Rachmiel said. "He's been hurt by all that happened."

"Oh get off it, Rock. Keep your priorities straight. He killed a boy—his own charge! If he's hurt, then it's richly deserved."

Rachmiel's mouth twitched, and his eyes darkened to purple.

"You can't say it's right," Voriah said, glaring out over the rooftop. His teeth had locked together, and the tense anger emerged from his heart like a pulse. "I would never kill Alan—only if ordered directly by God and maybe not even then. Maybe not even then. Rock, what kind of disordered mind would kill his own charge?"

Rachmiel slumped forward and put his hands over his eyes. "I can't get over the feeling, though, that there were extenuating circumstances."

"So extenuating that he didn't speak a word in his own defense—or did you forget what Raguel told us? We're dealing with the makings of a mortal sin here!"

Rachmiel paled.

"What are the three requirements?" Voriah asked, his face flushed. "A serious matter—check! Willful consent—check! Sufficient reflection—" Rachmiel brightened. "No," Voriah said, "he must have known. It couldn't have been accidental. I don't care what Raguel said. For God's own love, I don't know why he wasn't damned."

"Voriah!"

"You're not angry?" Voriah asked, his eyes flaring.

At the moment, actually, Rachmiel was absorbing and amplifying Voriah's anger against his will, but a part of him remembered standing beside Tabris and feeling the emotional vacuum of an angel in denial, and that haunted hollow feeling had never quite left his soul since then.

"I can't wish him damned," Rachmiel finally said.

"I don't wish it," Voriah said, "but for the life of me I don't understand why God refrained."

"Tabris still loves Him."

"Love is as love does. If Tabris could strike down his charge in 'love,' then why wouldn't God do the same to him?"

Rachmiel shuddered. "And you're on his side?"

"Not *once* did I say he was right, Rock."

"Neither has he."

"He'd be in Hell for certain if he had." Voriah paused. "But I guess I'm on his side, I mean, I'll give him a chance to try again. I'll go with God's judgment on this one, that Tabris sinned but not enough to condemn him."

Rachmiel looked up with a hesitant smile, as though intoning, "That's all he asked."

"No, that's all *you're* asking. He never asked anything for himself." Voriah looked aside. "What worries me is that he might try again."

"I've thought of that too, and I doubt he would. He's very hesitant around Elizabeth, almost as though he's afraid to escape his own control."

Voriah looked Rachmiel in the eyes. "You've got to find out how it happened—no matter how much pain it causes you or Tabris, you can't let him stew. For Elizabeth's sake alone you've got to talk to him. Find out all the circumstances surrounding Sebastian's death. As her guardian it's your right to know any possible source of harm. Rock!" he exclaimed when he saw how Rachmiel had looked away shakily, "do you want him to kill her?"

"No—it's just that I can't make him open himself if he doesn't want it."

"Force him."

"You know I wouldn't." Rachmiel's eyes dimmed. "I—almost don't want to know. I'm afraid it could happen to me."

They stayed silent for a moment, and then Voriah nonverbalized, "I'm afraid too."

The stars overhead drifted in their precision formation, careful and certain, quiet because of their distance.

"But Rock," he continued, "hearing how it happened can't cause it. It's not something that happens to you, it's something you have to *do*. It's not spontaneous."

"No, but if I learn why he did it, I might find myself in the same situation and do the same thing reflexively."

Voriah extended his wing to touch Rachmiel's, and they quieted for a while. The breeze troubled the dead and drying leaves that still clung to a few trees, and in their rustling Rachmiel heard Tabris—cut off from the Life-giver, in the last stages of spiritual starvation before falling forever.

Voriah squeezed his hand. "Don't do that to yourself."

"It's my nature." Rachmiel looked aside. "I'm scared."

The pair opened their hearts to God, interacting with the Holy with their total beings, giving Him their fears and concerns, learning once again how surprisingly near He stayed. God illuminated every corner of the translucent material that made their souls—material which conducted His light like fiber optics so that one touch irradiated all of them.

Voriah returned inside while Rachmiel continued to shine in the light of the Lord.

8

TABRIS ASKED TO MEET THE THREE ADULTS OF the house, and Rachmiel was more than delighted to continue the introductions. John Hayes, Mithra's charge, had a job in St. Albans that kept him busy even when he was at home. Some of the work he did during the evenings in his basement office, however, was an escape from his family. He stayed quiet, a powerful presence in the family that sometimes quelled conversation but at times could be surprisingly friendly. He had developed for himself the idea that the model father was emotionally distant but a good provider and had successfully achieved both, which he sometimes regretted. Mithra had the same gleam in his eyes that Tabris had seen in Miriael, Katra'il, and Voriah, but it was painfully dimmed as though Mithra had seen the heights of which his charge was capable but also the depths. Tabris avoided Mithra's eyes while he talked, and later Hadriel's and Josai'el's.

Hadriel guarded Connie, Elizabeth's mother, who had recently started working again so that the family could store some money to defray college expenses. She had a part-time secretarial position at the public school which allowed her time off to drive the children home and to be with them on weekends and holidays. She seemed tired, and Hadriel confessed that most of his energy he consigned to her to help maintain her strength, especially on days when the children needed her. The job was boring, and her husband retreated into the basement. If she had needed to do the housework as well she might have died from the strain, but luckily her mother-in-law took care of that. Hadriel chuckled wryly that Con-

nie was too tired to sin, but Tabris detected the worry in
his voice.

Bridget, John's mother and the grandmother of the
brood of children, was sixty-four and guarded by Josai'el,
who consequently had seniority among the household
angels. The house and property had been in Bridget's
family ever since their arrival in the United States, and
she had inherited it from her father. Josai'el confessed
that at times Bridget resented having to share the house
with her son's family, but it was too big for her alone, too
expensive to maintain, and far too important to sell, so
she shared it with John and Connie. She enjoyed taking
long walks through the grass and breathing the cold air
that migrated across the U.S.-Canadian border. Tabris
brightened as Josai'el discussed Bridget. Josai'el had first
matched and then exceeded his enthusiasm, talking excitedly about her charge's nearly finished soul, visible to
her in the unique way that an individual soul is visible to
the single guardian angel it will have in all its existence,
although that view is not so specific or piercing as the
understanding God has. Rachmiel had listened, enraptured, as Josai'el had talked, and he had noted with delight that Tabris felt secure enough to share her intensity.
It made him wonder what was Tabris like long ago, before God had given him a child to guard and Tabris had
given it back?

Josai'el said that Bridget sometimes talked to her,
and Rachmiel bolted up from where he was sitting at her
feet. "She *talks* to you?"

"Not often."

"But—she *talks* to you?"

Tabris' eyes burned softly. "How does she know?"

"She doesn't know my name—I'd rather keep it that
way for the time being, actually," Josai'el said with a
laugh. "We don't want to slip into idolatry. But she tells
me about her pains and sometimes she asks me for help.
I immediately relay all her prayers to God, of course, but
it helps me to help her if I know more specifically what
she wants and needs."

Rachmiel whistled. "You couldn't—maybe—get her to tell Elizabeth about me?—and Tabris," he added. "How well can she hear you?"

"Probably no better than Elizabeth hears you two."

"But she *talks* to you," Rachmiel gasped. "How can— I'd be so . . . overwhelmed!"

"I was too, the first time it happened," said Josai'el. She laughed, her pretty pale eyes bright in the light of God, her long hair catching and reflecting His radiance. "But that's all beside the point. Tabris wanted me to talk about her."

Tabris shrugged. "This is fine. She sounds a lot like—well, I know her better now. Thank you.

"Do you have any questions?" asked Josai'el.

"Well," Tabris said, and his eyes drifted toward Rachmiel who still seemed enraptured by the concept of an angelphile under Elizabeth's roof, "in a way. Did Bridget—does she ever—" He paused and his eyes grew much more sharply brown. "Did she ever steal anything?"

"As a child, once," said Josai'el. "But I worked with her until God's grace penetrated her heart and she felt guilty, and then she returned it. It was a small doll. She was nine."

Tabris studied his hands. He nodded.

Rachmiel excused himself from the room abruptly to check on Elizabeth, he said, and his eyes were wide.

Josai'el's mouth opened a little as she watched Rachmiel leave, and she smiled softly with pride. Tabris still looked down, and it was doubtful that he ever realized how great a sacrifice Rachmiel had just made for him: Rachmiel's curiosity for Tabris' peace of mind.

"It's difficult," Tabris said, "that first serious sin."

"I know it is," said Josai'el. "They usually recover from that, though. The worse ones are the sins they love, when you try to open the channels for grace and they refuse to let God inside. Those are the excruciating sins, the damning ones."

"I could almost imagine it if I tried," said Tabris. "I guess I have that to look forward to in Elizabeth. They say it happens to even the best guardians."

"Who are 'they'?" asked Josai'el.

"Everyone I've asked," said Tabris, naming a few.

Then his eyes flickered about and he stood. "Thank you for talking to me."

"Any time," said Josai'el. "I look for excuses to talk about Bridget."

Tabris attempted a smile and then left the room.

Reputation. Tabris had such a commanding presence that on his entrance to any room every angel would turn toward him and automatically lay one hand on his charge's shoulder. At church on Sundays, Tabris must have sensed the confusion, the anger, the questions about his mere presence. No one ever confronted him, but he might have felt easier if someone had challenged him. Rachmiel usually waited until Tabris was involved somewhere else and then intercepted whoever radiated the most anger or distrust, speaking quietly and quickly and recommending that the fires be brought under control. Tabris might either have appreciated that or resented it, but he never mentioned the incidents.

Everyone knew Tabris. He had once been a very high ranking angel of his choir. Mithra had known him since before the Fall and said that Tabris had to be in the highest percentile of his choir, that if he were not in the top twenty then he almost certainly had hit the top thirty. His two-toned wings and dark, dark eyes gave him a peculiar presence, an appearance that disconcerted most angels—almost every angel has wings of one solid color, and an angel with two-toned wings is like a human with one green eye and one brown.

Tabris' outer feathers had a hue of jade green, far deeper than emerald and approaching the color of a forest during a wet summer. The inner feathers imitated the brown of redwood bark. When Tabris lay outside during the first snowfall of the year, he spread his wings to their full span on the snow, relishing the cold and watching the sharp but naive sunlight which had been snared inside tiny ice crystals like an intricate butterfly imprisoned in amber. While he did this, however, Rachmiel and Voriah were on the roof staring with fascination at his wings. They remarked nonverbally to each other about the sudden change of brown feathers to green, and Rachmiel finally approached Tabris, hesitant and knee-deep in snow.

Tabris sat up quickly.

"No, I don't want to disturb you," Rachmiel said. "I wanted to see your wings."

Tabris' eyes popped. "Why?"

"I never saw wings like yours before," said Rachmiel. "I wanted to look at them closely, if you don't mind."

"All of me?" Tabris asked, his voice tense as a high wire.

"No, just the wings," Rachmiel said, a little flustered. "You didn't lay out all of yourself on the snow, just your wings. That's all I'm asking."

The two angels locked gazes for a very long moment, and then Rachmiel turned his head aside.

"You can inspect me," said Tabris, resting back again on the surface of the snow, a surface his weight did not even dent. "You too, Voriah!" he called.

Voriah flashed down, a little shaken, and nonverbally thanked Tabris. He tried to meet Rachmiel's eyes, nervous because angels will not lie and Tabris obviously knew he had been scrutinized.

Rachmiel touched the feathers, running the small structures between his fingers, realizing that the green ones felt stiffer than the brown, that the change was not gradual, that the green feathers continued beneath the brown, but the brown were packed tight enough to hide them completely at their bases.

"Rock," Voriah said, "let me see your wings . . . Your outer feathers are tougher than the inner ones also."

"I hadn't realized that," Rachmiel said. "Tabris, you're color coded!"

A fourth angel's laughter stole over the trio in the sun, and that sound brought all three to their feet in a hurry.

"Tabris, you're a carnival freak to them!" said the demon who recently had called himself Unbridled. "They inspect you and gratify their lust for curiosities on you. They're indulging their intellect against your peculiarities, Tabris! Tabris—they're exploiting your soul!"

"Get out," Tabris growled. "In the name of the Holy—"

"But you can't say His name, can you?" asked Unbridled, almost sneering. "Try it!"

Tabris said it slowly, softly.

Unbridled turned paler when his gamble failed—he had been almost positive Tabris would be forbidden the use of God's name—then looked at the other two. "They don't love you, Tabris. They just want—"

"Shut up," he said. "I told you to leave."

"But you're mine, Tabris. By virtue of one flick of the wrist, you're mine."

Tabris backed away, into Voriah's wings, and suddenly Rachmiel found himself holding a sword.

"You can't fight all his battles," said the demon, his amber eyes blazing with the sunlight that reflected off the snow.

"You're not all his battles," Rachmiel said, "and I can fight you. Leave us!"

Unbridled sneered for almost half a second before Miriael's sword came down off the roof and halved him lengthwise. Voriah had flashed Tabris into the house as Miriael had jumped, but Rachmiel had watched the whole scene. He stood in shock for an instant before he reacted, letting the horror and disgust burst out of his heart without being channeled in any direction.

Mithra had his arms and wings around Rachmiel like a strong cocoon, and Miriael plunged his sword into the snow by the body before rushing to join Mithra. Rachmiel was stammering.

"You just—"

"I wanted to get him away without a long fight. I didn't want him to battle Tabris," Miriael said, his eyes round and concerned. "Josai'el is with Tabris now, and he's pretty shaken as it is."

"Are you all right?" asked Mithra, his voice a little higher in pitch and his arms supporting almost all of Rachmiel. He looked at the guardian's eyes, but they were fixed on the cloven corpse which had begun to reconstitute itself slowly. Soon it would knit completely and go away of its own accord, maybe returning to Hell, maybe finding someone else to harass.

"Could you—remove him?" Rachmiel asked.

"I will," Mithra said, helping Rachmiel to stand on his own, noting with concern that the ordinarily vibrant orange wings had turned butter yellow, and Rachmiel's sunset eyes shone black. "Let's get you inside first."

Elizabeth was watching television, and Rachmiel leaned on her slackly for a moment. Tabris sat on the couch, his head bowed and his body mostly limp. Seeing him, Rachmiel forced himself to recover some strength and flashed beside him.

"Could I hug you?" he almost said, but before speaking he gave Tabris the hug he had to offer, keeping his own eyes closed and breathing deeply, letting Tabris know nonverbally that he had strong friends.

Miriael and Mithra returned from dropping Unbridled into the middle of the Atlantic ocean, their hands and clothes still stained with the residue of Unbridled's pain and Rachmiel's emotional outburst. "Are you all right, Tabris?" asked Mithra.

"Yes—thank you."

Miriael had to leave the room before the surprise pulsed off him tangibly, but Mithra managed to contain himself well, and Rachmiel stayed with one arm and wing protectively over Tabris.

"Do you think he'll attack again?" asked Rachmiel.

"Probably. Pain never daunts those things. They return only to annoy you enough to attack them again. Like horseflies."

Rachmiel's fingers idly moved on Tabris' shoulder. "But you and Miriael did well. He didn't hurt you, did he?"

"No, but *you* nearly did." Mithra laughed. "You practically exploded—are you all right?"

Rachmiel smiled and nonverbalized that he was fine. Being able to be strong for Tabris had injected more strength into him than he had anticipated.

Tabris did not know that and sat away from him suddenly. "Are you okay? I didn't realize he'd hurt you."

Rachmiel shook his head. "It was shock." He paused. "You can . . . lean against me . . . if you want."

Tabris paused for a long time, as though he intended to move forward again, but then stiffened and shook his head. "No, thank you though. I'm fine now."

Rachmiel hardly realized he was forming a nonverbalization before it emerged, a mixture of need and care and asking and hurt self-consciousness. He said quickly, "Just tell me if you want to."

Tabris had frozen as if in the sight of a hunter's rifle. He tightened his mouth and eyes into perfect lines and then said, "I'm fine, Rachmiel. You look shaken, though. Why don't you take off the rest of the day?"

Rachmiel had just overflowed with emotion twice, and his control was shaken. Water courses most easily along the paths water has taken before, and right now Rachmiel's emotions had begun flowing as if on tap. Tabris smiled frigidly. "You can leave her with me."

Rachmiel visibly shrank away from the mahogany eyes as fierce as ice picks, the tight smile. Mithra said to Tabris, "He'll be all right."

It would be the first time Rachmiel left Tabris alone with Elizabeth. The guardian looked at the red-headed girl and his eyes clouded.

"You'll distress her," Tabris said, "if you stay. She'll pick up your shock. You know that."

He might have been a devil, and Rachmiel had no idea what to do because everything he said was exactly true, but perhaps his conclusions were faulty. Leaving might be good, but staying might be a greater good. The confusion in Rachmiel's heart radiated from him like a small cloud, and he grabbed for God's hand with his heart and clung tightly, afraid.

"I can handle her," Tabris said.

God sent wordless assurance and Rachmiel fled the room to His arms.

Mithra turned to Tabris. "You weren't playing fairly."

"Rules change," he said. His dark eyes narrowed. "But that isn't fair of me either. Rachmiel's a rule-book player. He tries to do what's best, what he thinks is best, and even when it's inadequate he's still trying."

Mithra watched silently, and Tabris turned to Elizabeth. "He'd give his life for her. She's his one gem, his pearl of great price, and he would give up everything for her."

Mithra and Tabris looked at the TV, a mindless series of colors accompanied by a noise that served only to dispel spiritual peace. Tabris pulled his two-toned wings up close to his body. "Mithra, do you hate me?"

"No."

Tabris shrugged and flashed down to the floor beside Elizabeth.

"Do you hate Rachmiel?" asked Mithra.

"How could I?" asked Tabris. "He's a child of God in all the senses you can imagine." He caught the nonverbal challenge in Mithra's eyes. "I can ask if you hate me for the reason that I'm not a child of God in every sense of the word. I'm capable of being hated."

"God loves you, too."

"Not like Rachmiel or you."

"Would you want Him to? He loves us all differently."

"You know what I mean."

"Explain it."

"No." Tabris rolled onto his stomach.

Mithra watched him silently. Tabris thought, his eyes narrow, his mouth tight. He sat up, looked intently at

Mithra, and squinted with a combined dare and question wrapped in one nonverbalized concept: Trust?

Abruptly Mithra vanished.

Tabris looked around the room, empty now except for Elizabeth and himself. He stood and surveyed the area. Mithra was with John (again in the basement), and the other angels were with their respective charges; Katra'il with Martin and the other boys out playing in the snow, Hadriel away with Connie at the supermarket, and Josai'el in the kitchen with Bridget.

With gleaming eyes, Tabris walked toward the ten-year-old watching the TV, and he towered over her, spreading his ominously bi-colored wings in a wide arc.

He crouched behind the girl, who was giggling at a funny commercial, and he put his hands around her neck. Then he closed his eyes.

"God," he whispered, "they do trust me!"

He flashed backward to the couch and frowned. He had half expected that they were watching him from a distance, ready to flash down and stop him the moment he acted even slightly untoward.

His hands tightened on the arm of the sofa, and his teeth locked together while he thought.

For no apparent reason, Tabris' sword appeared by his side.

Elizabeth laughed, the bright giggle of a little girl, the innocent half-shock of an unself-conscious soul, a soul untouched by serious sins. She clapped her hands together as she laughed, and Tabris watched her intently.

A good guardian, he thought, would be ever-vigilant, would always stand on his watch, would stare into the girl's soul resolutely for the first signs of demonic penetration. A good guardian, he realized, a perfect guardian who took his care seriously, would not lie out in the crystal cold of the first snowfall. A good guardian would not test the tether locking him to his charge, every day glad for the extra inches, because he would dread to leave the pupil, the young soul under his care. And also, most importantly he knew, a really good guardian would not sulk or hesitate to perform his job because of his personal difficulties.

"Don't you deserve the best, Elizabeth?" he asked, but the child stared at the TV, spiritually linked to a god of electrodes and simulated wood grain. "Don't you really? And if God put me here, shouldn't I do for you what I never did for Sebastian? You deserve the perfect guardian, and I can't promise anything, but I can do my best."

Tabris stood from the couch and girded on his sword, then concentrated and changed his relaxed clothing to something more uniform, tighter and more sedate, complete with boots and gloves. He smoothed the feathers of his wings, the short brown and long green ones that glistened in the afternoon sunlight of Chittenden County, Vermont.

9

RACHMIEL RETURNED AFTER AN HOUR AND paused sharply.

"Welcome back," said Tabris, completely uniformed as if he were a soldier and standing as straight as a ramrod behind Elizabeth, who still sat in the living room. "I think Elizabeth's watching too much television. May I have permission to encourage her to play outside in the snow?"

"Ah—sure," Rachmiel said, his eyes flickering to the girl and back to Tabris. "You don't need my okay."

Tabris nodded, and Rachmiel could feel him surrounding the girl's mind with images of playing in the snow, ideas of her brothers pulling her on the sled, and thoughts of snowmen. What captivated her most, however, was Rachmiel's contribution of icicles hanging from the eaves of the house. Despite his late addition to the imagined scene, Rachmiel realized how powerful Tabris could be, and he sat on the couch to watch as the girl began staring out the window.

"You can sit down," Rachmiel said.

"I'm fine," Tabris said, his deep eyes shining even more when offset by his black shirt. "I trust you're recovered?"

"Yes," Rachmiel said, almost drawling into a "yeah . . ." because he was uncertain of Tabris, of this changed and new formality. His eyes flickered again to Elizabeth, who had begun regarding the windows more than the television.

"Elizabeth's been well," Tabris said. "Where did you go?"

"I prayed. Yourself?"

"I guarded Elizabeth," he said, gesturing to the girl with a gloved hand.

"She was attacked?" Rachmiel asked, groping in his mind for a possible reason.

"Does she show signs of attack that your deeper insight can detect?" Tabris asked, his eyes suddenly troubled.

"No, but you're wearing your sword, and you're all but wearing battle armor."

"I've decided," said Tabris very deliberately, "that I have to take this guardianship seriously. That's all."

Elizabeth walked to the window and looked out at her three brothers who were building snow forts. Rachmiel took a deep breath and said, "Were you given a warning about the status of your probation?"

"No," Tabris said, the panic as far from his voice as he could thrust it. "I made a decision. You don't need to worry about me. There's nothing wrong."

For a long instant Rachmiel teetered on the brink of saying that such an amazing level of formality had to be wrong, but then Elizabeth shut off the television and ran to get her coat. The pair of guardians followed her. Tabris was always what Rachmiel would have called 'at attention,' and even out in the snow, he did not play with the children and other angels so much as watch Elizabeth intently and deflect any snowballs that the brothers hurled at her.

"Tab's getting serious?" Voriah asked Rachmiel quietly.

"Seems like it. He's guarding her physically, and I suppose intellectually as well, like a soldier."

"Your forté is more the emotional?"

"Spiritual. Voriah, she could be crippled and if that forwarded her salvation I wouldn't protest a bit!" Rachmiel swatted a snowball off course as it passed, so that it would only graze Martin's head instead of smacking him dead-on. "The body rots, the soul is eternal."

"That doesn't mean we should just let the demons trip them up and shove them down stairs," said Voriah. "Satan would maul every one of them if only he got the chance—tirelessly, Rock, he'd hurt every one of them."

"We can't be ridiculous about it, of course," Rachmiel said. "Some protection has to be physical, but not all of it. Despair isn't physical. Even lust is largely mental. He doesn't seem to be concerned with those, though."

"It's been one afternoon that he's acting like this." Voriah flashed to Alan's side and steadied him as he slipped on an ice patch. "Don't panic. Besides, anything he does is extra help. You can manage perfectly well even if he never touches her psyche." Voriah concentrated and helped Alan aim a snowball.

Katra'il flashed to Rachmiel and said lowly, "Check out the stoic."

Instead of looking at Tabris, Rachmiel looked at Elizabeth while Katra'il returned to Martin. She was unhurt by snowballs, although her coat was stained in two sprays of snow where she had gotten hit. Rachmiel winced as Kyle threw a snowball at his sister and it exploded into fine powder, and then he realized that Tabris had broken apart the snowball a micrometer away from contact with Elizabeth. She felt the blow because the air and the snow were moving, but no pain.

"Tabris," Rachmiel called to the angel standing at attention by a close tree, "you can't do that."

"Of course I can. God's permitting it."

"But," Rachmiel flashed to him, "if you do that she's not going to learn how to dodge them, just that snowballs don't hurt."

"Why should they have to hurt?" Tabris looked at Rachmiel darkly. "If I can keep them from touching her—"

"You can, but actions have consequences. If she learns to dodge then she can help protect herself, and the one time Martin throws an ice ball at her head and we miss, she'll save her own life."

Rachmiel punctuated this by changing the flight path of a snowball a degree so that it only grazed against her shoulder, and Tabris broke apart the projectile.

"Working together," Tabris said, "we're a perfect team. We won't slip. We can keep her perfectly sheltered."

Rachmiel felt the frustration welling up in his heart, and Voriah saw even from the distance that his eyes had widened and his breath had caught. He flashed to his side.

"The object of the game," Rachmiel said very slowly, with quite excellent command of his own voice, "is not to shelter her from every opportunity of pain, but to shape her into a creation worthy of being called a child of God. Pain isn't pleasant, but it'll make her grow. That's how God changes them. That's how He deepens their ability to love Him."

Tabris swung his head around to face Rachmiel. "What do you know about pain?"

Rachmiel recoiled. Tabris flashed to the next tree and watched Elizabeth grimly. Voriah forcibly flashed Rachmiel to the opposite side of the snowball fight. Miriael and Katra'il stayed silent.

Katra'il finally apologized.

"Forget it," Rachmiel said, locking his teeth. "God, send a message—I want Raguel to visit tonight as an arbiter."

Rachmiel stood smoldering by the others, his eyes on Elizabeth alone until he realized that Tabris' appearance almost radiated gloom, but when he looked over at him Tabris avoided his eyes and continued to watch Elizabeth.

That night, as soon as Elizabeth fell asleep, Raguel appeared and called Rachmiel and Tabris to him. He explained that he knew the details of the incident and that he wanted them both to listen to his opinion.

He explained to Rachmiel that Tabris had a vision of what a guardian angel was, what a guardian angel did, and the fashion in which he acted; that Tabris still was settling into his new role; and that Rachmiel must be more understanding.

Then Raguel turned to Tabris and said that Rachmiel had been Elizabeth's principle guardian from her birth, and as such knew better than any other creature what she needed. His word had to stand, and all his decisions about her had to be accepted. Raguel said that in this particular case Rachmiel was right and that Tabris had exceeded his proper boundaries as co-guardian.

"After all," Raguel said, "their spiritual growth is most important, even if it puts their bodies in danger. Even if they put themselves at risk of damnation, they must be allowed to grow on their own into the creatures God intended. We have to minimize our presence."

The pair stayed silent, Rachmiel sitting beside Elizabeth, Tabris standing by the door.

Raguel opened his hands, asking for their response.

"What is my purpose here?" Tabris asked, keeping his eyes carefully averted in the dark room.

"You're the co-guardian, subordinated to Rachmiel but still responsible for the care of Elizabeth's soul and body. Essentially, you're following the course of a regular guardian, and soon your insight into her heart will be almost equal to Rachmiel's."

"But if I have all the responsibilities of a full guardian, how can you justify—" Then he stopped.

"Raguel," said Rachmiel, "I have one comment, if you'll allow me to speak before you answer his question. I asked you to arbitrate precisely because I don't rank over Tabris. We are *co*-guardians, and our power will be equal with respect to her in a very short time. In the month he's been here I haven't once pulled rank, and for the next eighty years or so of Elizabeth's life I intend to do the same. I'm not giving orders. I want to reach an understanding."

Rachmiel looked away, his face flushed, his hand on Elizabeth's shoulder.

To Rachmiel, Tabris seemed like a black hole of emotion. The palpable coldness of his spirit penetrated Rachmiel, whose open heart frosted painfully at the touch but who forced it to remain open.

Raguel nonverbalized questioning, and Rachmiel returned an affirmation.

Raguel turned to Tabris with another question.

Tabris made no answer at all and Rachmiel struggled to look up at him, expecting to see the mahogany eyes ice-hard and his mouth tight. What he saw instead was a liquid gleam and trembling hands, and Tabris biting his lower lip. The two-toned angel nodded and then stood straighter, trying not to tremble.

"Tabris?" said Rachmiel.

"I'm all right," he said, his voice a bit too thin.

Raguel walked forward, but Tabris backed into the door. "Does it shock you that much," he said, "that he trusts you?"

"But I—this afternoon," Tabris said, "my best was wrong, and you trust—" He stopped and knotted his hands behind his back. "No, I'll be all right."

Raguel said, "Talk to me, please. I'm here to help."

"What do you want me to say?" Tabris asked, avoiding his eyes, the sheen of his emotional guards lying over his face and especially over the forced smile.

Raguel looked at Rachmiel, then at Tabris, and finally shook his head. "I'm not going to press the matter. But to get back to the other situation, Tabris, it isn't necessary to keep Elizabeth wrapped in a cocoon. Rachmiel was right in saying that exposure to the world will transform her into what God intends. Obvious threats to her well-being should be deflected, but be careful of being overprotective."

"Yes," he said, soldier-like. "I will."

Rachmiel could detect only the emotional void where Tabris stood, but Raguel turned to Rachmiel and the guardian refocused all his attention. "Rachmiel, I want you to be truly committed to this teamwork if that's what you want—no half measures. You can't override him the one time there's a serious disagreement, do you understand? And I want you to know that I think you're doing a very brave thing, Rock."

Flustered, Rachmiel smiled and looked aside. "That's not brave, it's normal. Who could subordinate someone just because he came second?"

Raguel smiled. "Can you two rationally discuss any problems that arise in the future?"

Rachmiel smiled with hope.

"We will," Tabris said.

They stayed up on the roof that night, looking together at the constellations.

Rachmiel nonverbalized that he needed to ask a question but feared that Tabris would become angry.

"All right," said Tabris.

"What happened with Sebastian?"

His mouth twitched. "What will knowing that do for you?"

"Well for starters, I might be able to help you avoid similar situations with Elizabeth. I could avoid comments that might evoke painful memories."

Tabris sighed. "I don't want to answer you, but I'll give you a reason why: I don't want to think I've caused you to be uncomfortable or self-conscious. Don't change your behavior. I'm not going to let any off-handed remarks offend me."

Rachmiel bowed his head. "But what about helping you?"

"I—can't say, really, but I'll excuse myself if I need to."

Rachmiel bowed his head again.

They turned toward the stars. Rachmiel pointed out one in particular and they waved to it. "A friend of mine guards that star," said Rachmiel, "and it makes her feel happy when I remember her."

Tabris laughed, and Rachmiel glanced up at the lightness of the sound—he wondered if he ever had heard Tabris laugh before.

The fingers of the wind lifted stray flakes of snow and blew them through the angelic pair. Tabris flexed his wings, spreading the feathers so that the cold reached through the matting to the skin underneath. He inhaled sharply, then laughed again, a much richer sound than before, as though it involved all his being instead of just his mouth.

"Have I ever told you," he asked, "how much I love the cold?"

Rachmiel smiled, meaning that he had guessed. "Where were you before?"

"A suburb of LA. Beastly temperature there—always sixty-eight and sunny. They have smog that could make an angel retch—the people breathe it just fine but their angels have to comb out their lungs every night." He shook his head bemusedly. "They like living there too. I'll never understand how six million people can congregate in one place so hot and crowded—it's the armpit of America."

Rachmiel reflected on a similar comment he had heard about New York City.

"That it's—"

"That's it," Rachmiel said quickly, smiling, intoning that there was no need to be graphic. "You were there thirteen years?"

"In suburbia, yes." Tabris tilted back his head. "Thirteen years, no snow. No cold wind. Nothing but room temperature and the slowly circulating smog. On New Year's Day they would make announcements like 'In 1991 we exceeded federal smog regulations on only one hundred seventy-one days.'"

Rachmiel squinted painfully.

"It was an improvement, too."

Tabris spread his wings and lay back in the snow on the roof, actually inside the froth without marking its substance.

Rachmiel suddenly began radiating nervousness, and Tabris waited while he actively manufactured the courage to speak again. "Tabris," he said at length, "how did you—"

"Snapped his neck."

Rachmiel nodded in emotional and verbal silence.

Tabris had his eyes closed, and beneath the snow his hands were in fists.

Rachmiel trembled, knowing he radiated tension but also resolving not to be curious. His angelic will was strong enough this time to conquer his natural inclination to identify himself with Tabris by asking hundreds of questions. He knew Tabris would realize that but could not help himself.

"Rachmiel," said the darker angel, "Rock, if they tell you I didn't love the kid, please, remember that I did. It wasn't that at all. Don't feel you have to tell anyone else—I'd even prefer you didn't. Just you remember it."

Rachmiel nodded, and Tabris arched back his neck looking at the moon. There was tension rolling off his skin, continually evident in the way his arms and legs were stretched full length, his wings spread so that they shook a little against the powdery snow. It was Rachmiel, however, whose eyes shone like black water.

"Tabris," he said, "I never doubted it."

They stayed quiet a while on the roof until Tabris rolled onto one hip and looked at Rachmiel with a slightly asymmetrical smile. "Thank you," he said.

10

THE NEXT MORNING RACHMIEL LEFT FOR A FEW minutes to help the guardian of the old woman up the road, and Unbridled came for a visit.

"Of course," said the demon, "my name is no longer Unbridled. It's Irony."

"Is it?" said Tabris. "Keep your distance, by the way."

Irony stood on the window sill while Elizabeth dressed across the room, prey to a sudden Tabris-inspired ten-year-old's quixotic fear of the window.

"She'll be a very attractive woman," said Irony. "Will you help her develop her physical potential?"

"No," said Tabris. "Her physical attributes concern me about as much as this conversation."

"You're too harsh," said Irony, sitting on the window sill so that his legs stuck into the room. "I remember when we used to have the most amazing conversations."

"And of all those, the only one that mattered was the one when you said you hated God."

"I understand—all the conversations about the intricate beauty of a flower become obsolete when one learns the true mysteries of life. Tyranny—now *that's* worth a conversation or two. The beauty of a flower is repugnant when one detests the brand name and the manufacturer. Do you still love this misbegotten world?"

Tabris sighed.

"You truly should give it up as a vain pursuit, before He breaks your heart with His cold eyes." Irony stood up, now on the inside of the room, but Tabris' eyes flashed, and he leaped back onto the sill again.

"Now," Irony said, "my purpose for coming—do you know where Rachmiel is?"

"Yes."

"Well, he isn't there. He's before the Tribunal asking to have you removed for Elizabeth's sake."

"Of course," Tabris said glibly. "He goes every night, right? And are you going to tell me now about his plans to hire a group of friends to rough me up if I stay too close to the girl?"

"Oh, be serious," said Irony. "I'm the ironic one, not you. Rachmiel's afraid you'll break her neck. He says he can't keep his eyes off your hands, and he can imagine you snapping the child's spine at any moment."

"I'm sure he said exactly that, *Irony*." Tabris grinned maliciously. "Now go."

Irony vanished. Tabris looked at Elizabeth, his eyes dark and obscure. He touched her limp red hair, then smiled. He approved of her outfit as she inspected herself in the full-length mirror and then accompanied her down the stairs to breakfast.

Word spreads quickly among angels. In fact, if one were to place them in human terms, angels would be the worst gossips imaginable. Particularly in the lowest choir, telling just one angel means the speaker has told every last citizen of heaven. The ninth choir is at times like one beast with a thousand heads, and it seems that information passes like a brushfire, almost without their willing it. Of course, if someone says specifically, "Keep this secret," or even hints at it the way Tabris did on the rooftop, personal revelations travel no farther. For the most part, though, angels cannot keep information to themselves because they lack bodies. Anything at the forefront of their minds is completely apparent, nonverbalized without effort and concealed only with considerable work.

Within a half hour of Sebastian's murder, every guardian angel on earth knew as much as the first angels on the scene had known—it was so disturbing to those first witnesses that the situation burst out of them almost volcanically, and the repercussions were felt throughout the planet. The earthly guardians lacked only the details, and those traveled hard on the heels of the emotional impact. The whole ninth choir had known before the end of the trial and had been awaiting the verdict hungrily. Raguel's tour of all the world's households to talk to the guardians had been necessary because everyone had heard already. Feelings ran high and turbulent—prevention of a mass recurrence had been essential and had actually been begun by other high ranking angels, including Michael and Gabriel, before Tabris' trial had ended. They had started with Sebastian's own household.

A human government would have hushed up the affair, admitting to it only if the news media made the unfortunate discovery. God's government lacks that option, and probably would not have exercised it anyway—they're too democratic.

This nature of angels (as though each were a sieve of information, each angel his own broadcast news network), has more good effects than drawbacks. When Rachmiel said he trusted Tabris, any angel even remotely connected with the affair knew quickly, and for a while some of the soft-spoken exchanges that accompanied Tabris like an invisible cortege were about that development instead of about what they thought he deserved. To Tabris, incidentally, they sounded the same since some of the emotions accompanying Rachmiel's trust were indignation and outrage, but he never visibly reacted.

Rachmiel grew flustered when he realized that his judgment could cause that much stir, and he wondered about the negative ramifications if he had told Tabris that he was not trusted, that he was under explicit orders, and that his opinions were overridden before consideration. One night while Tabris sat by the lake, Rachmiel confided to Voriah his terror that so many angels' opinions should rest on his own.

"But we trust your opinions largely because you're so levelheaded," Voriah said, "and you work closely with him all the time."

"But I'm not God," Rachmiel said, the strain and fear very present in his voice. "I can't see into his heart!"

Rachmiel's verdict stood, though, and Tabris' reputation began changing as more and more angels began attributing his long silences to vigilance. Spare incidents here and there began circulating the planet like trade winds, and although Tabris never made the comment he often reflected that his life was like a detested celebrity's on the cover of a supermarket tabloid. Angels still could detect his presence because of the emotional void when he entered the room, the distinct lack of an aura that not only was a spot of emptiness but actually absorbed some of the emanations of other angels. That emptiness had become his trademark. Not many other angels admitted that they trusted him, particularly the ones who knew him only by sidelong glances, but the household angels and some of the ones who worked with him on a daily basis began asking him to watch their charges if they were needed elsewhere. Precious few did, but at least he was not written off completely.

The grammar school lunchroom, for example, swirled with mixed opinions about this notorious two-toned newcomer. While the children stampeded toward the long plastic tables with their fixed benches or raced to the hot-lunch line, their angels would first take attendance and note only whether Tabris was in the room and if so where he was. The tremendous ceilings in the institutional green cafeteria provided much wing room for the guardians, who sometimes flew overhead, but in general they shunned the ceilings, which were decorated with the thrown open-faced halves of the hot-lunch version of the Same Old Stuff: grilled cheese. Grilled cheese stuck to the ceilings when thrown with enough force, and most of the boys (particularly the older boys), soon learned the trick of the toss.

Without looking upward, Elizabeth and Moriah sat together eating lunch. The girl so recently rescued from social grammar school exile, Moriah was chattering innocently and quickly. She had left half her sandwich uneaten while she talked, and her guardian was trying to get her to finish it even as she spoke about her mother's fight with her younger sister.

Standing alone against the wall a short distance away, Tabris watched darkly, his eyes narrow as he listened to the chatter. Rachmiel had glanced at him a couple of times and now watched Elizabeth uncomfortably. A part of him wanted to say to Tabris, *you can go—find someplace quiet!* but he refused himself. Tabris might take that as an open proclamation of distrust, and so short on the heels of his opening his heart to Rachmiel (though only a little), it might wound him deeply. The orange guardian realized how tightly he himself was holding onto God, and he knew that without Him probably the child discussions would drive him crazy too, although not as quickly as would most adult conversations of the same caliber.

Moriah's angel radiated disapproval—he had been nonverbalizing that and more ever since Elizabeth had first spoken to Moriah a week ago. He wanted Elizabeth and Rachmiel without Tabris. Even now, every so often, the angel flared with near anger and half-controlled fear which God had to help him calm.

Three older boys, sixth graders, were talking loudly down the table from the girls, and Moriah chose this time to finish her sandwich. Elizabeth took out her apple and said that she liked yellow apples more than the red ones, and then she began eating too.

Tabris suddenly changed his focus, and Rachmiel realized there was a demon present.

Usually there are many demons present in any gathering of humans. Among children the density is somewhat lower, but still they can appear, and at times God will order the angels to allow them to stay—either as a temptation or a trial for a person. In this case the demon had been "invited" when one of the boys began telling a dirty joke to the others, and therefore could not be driven away.

Rachmiel realized suddenly that both Elizabeth and Moriah were listening, not knowing that they should not be. Probably some time later that evening Elizabeth would ask her mother or brothers why the boys were laughing and then dwell on the answer for a while afterward—especially if her brothers explained it.

Rachmiel urged her to stop listening, but she had been captivated by the older boys' interest.

That was when Tabris said, "Elizabeth—there's Alan!" and she looked to the side of the lunchroom which Tabris had indicated, forgetting about the joke while she searched for her brother.

"Moriah," Rachmiel breathed.

Like most girlfriends, Moriah would share the joke with Elizabeth if it bothered her or she did not understand it. Tabris understood instantly and glared at the other guardian. "Tell her to ask Elizabeth what's wrong—now!"

The other guardian, clearly disconcerted, froze and almost resisted until Rachmiel amplified Tabris' desperate anger. Only then did he wrench Moriah's attention to Elizabeth, who was sitting up higher and scanning the crowd.

Rachmiel slumped forward with relief that Moriah still had been innocent enough for that to work.

Moriah was asking Elizabeth what was the matter.

Elizabeth explained that she had seen her brother from the corner of her eye, and they both looked until they saw Alan across the cafeteria. The joke was unfinished and forgotten to them.

To Tabris it was not. "You can't just say no," he said to Moriah's guardian, his eyes huge, his hands almost shaking. "You've got to give her something else to do—something good and interesting to take the place of what's bad and interesting. You've got to provide alternatives!"

The other angel's eyes had begun sparkling with mixed shock and anger. Tabris bent studiously over Elizabeth while Rachmiel looked at Moriah's guardian with a sternness unlike him.

The nearby angels were watching. Tabris made sure that a piece of apple which Elizabeth dropped fell neatly into the napkin on her lap.

11

INCIDENTS SUCH AS THIS HELPED TABRIS' REPU-
tation tremendously, and other guardians who had seen
them reported that his techniques, his power, and his
vigilance impressed them. By the time spring began coming to North Chittenden (admittedly around April) the
low hum of surprise had stopped accompanying Tabris
like a dark-coated secret service agent.

Rachmiel had grown very used to having Tabris
nearby at all times, even though Tabris might be as far as
five miles distant. Elizabeth, although completely unaware of his presence, benefitted greatly from it, and
Rachmiel often thanked God for sending Tabris to her.

The other household angels had been quick to discover the usefulness of an extra guardian, and now would
ask him to stand in without hesitation if they were wanted
elsewhere. Tabris had found this awkward at first but
soon got used to standing in Kyle's bedroom or walking
with Bridget. He learned once again that different people
need different sorts of care, that Bridget needed help
walking while Connie needed the energy to continue
working, and John needed approval. Elizabeth required a
lot of nurturing attention which Rachmiel applied instinctively—he had, after all, been made for her and she
for him, the two paired together in the mind of God
since before all creation.

Tabris found himself wondering at times what he
had given to Sebastian without thought that another angel would have found awkward and perplexing. How had

he and Sebastian interlocked, like one machine with its gears perfectly meshed?

Those thoughts upset him, and he immediately changed the subject every time he considered the boy. Usually this happened when he was with some other angel's charge, and the inner struggle remained for the most part inner.

Anyone could guess at his thoughts, however, and since angels are magnificently intelligent (seeing God, they can't really be anything else), their guesses would most often be accurate. Even demons could observe him for a long time and surmise what happened during those quick and quiet moments of agitation. Particularly Tabris' former friend, who went by any number of names at any given time, seemed to have made a career out of piecing together details and delivering them in the most disturbing manner at awkward places.

He appeared with a bright grin while Tabris stood in for Mithra watching John Hayes, who as usual was working at made-work in the basement. Earlier Mithra had appeared to Rachmiel and Tabris while Elizabeth read her English assignment and had asked if one of them could temporarily replace him.

"Which one?" Rachmiel had asked.

"Either," Mithra said. "I'm needed elsewhere."

"Tabris, you go," Rachmiel said. "I want to see how the story ends."

Tabris had flashed into John's office, standing like a soldier at the windows—narrow rectangles at shoulder height. A minute later his brightly smiling fallen friend had appeared, rubbing the smooth skins of his palms against one another.

"I see you're pleased?" said Tabris.

"This oh-so-smug grin means one thing, Tab—you're being sacked!"

"Like the Vandals sacked Rome?"

"No, as in fired. Mithra took Rachmiel's place and Rachmiel went to Raguel with a formal complaint—you desert Elizabeth far too easily! He says you wouldn't be fit to guard the contents of a locked safe, but he doesn't want to hurt your *feelings*, poor thing, poor little Tabris."

Tabris looked at John, working at his desk, working away anger at his wife and children, and his eyes narrowed.

"Oh, I know," the demon chuckled, "that you think Rachmiel couldn't be that deceitful, but you're not special, you're not the only one who can fake pleasure when you're really filled with anger!"

Tabris regarded John intently as he worked, being productive instead of going upstairs to talk to Connie or apologizing to his mother.

"Ask Rachmiel," drawled the demon. "He can't lie yet—not the way you can."

"Shut up, all right?"

"You *believe* me, don't you? Well you're shrewder than I thought, picking the first time I tell the truth to begin believing me!"

"Get out!" Tabris whirled. "I'm sick of you and your incessant prattling!"

"I'll be quiet," said the demon. "I'll just stay and we'll watch John together, and then when Raguel comes to haul you away, you can curse God and come home with me."

Tabris had his arms crossed, and again he watched John intently pour all his frustration into his papers behind a locked door in the wood-paneled basement office.

"Tab, if you haven't prayed for five months, how can God still love you?"

"Go—away."

"How can he? He's rigorous, He has standards and you're falling below those regulations. Don't work, don't eat. Publish or perish. Sink or swim. You're failing in every department, you jailbird! How long until He says 'Poorly done, you wretched servant. Enter into flames today'?"

Tabris drummed his fingers against his elbow.

"Come with me now," said the demon. "Jump ship before you're forced to walk the plank."

Tabris called his sword to his hands.

"No need to be violent," said the demon. "Should true angels be this short-tempered?"

Tabris said, "Yes."

"Doubt it."

Tabris drove him off then, a combination of will-power and spiritual steel. He stood against the door afterward, his arms crossed again, his breathing very deliberate, his sword sheathed at his side. He hardly reacted when Connie knocked on the door and John told her he was too busy to talk.

Hadriel entered the office—rather, he spoke to Tabris from the other side of the door as though there were no door. Hadriel was shaking, having given Connie too much of his energy. "Tabris," he asked, "can't you get John to let her in? She's very upset."

"I can tell," Tabris said, averting his face, deliberately constructing a mask from his will. He regarded John. "I'll try, but I'm not Mithra. Do you know where he is?"

"He's back with Elizabeth."

Tabris almost started shaking then himself, but instead he forced himself to craft a perfectly symmetrical smile. "With Rachmiel?"

Hadriel was so beside himself with strain that he completely missed the warning note in Tabris' voice. "No, Rachmiel went somewhere else, that's why Mithra didn't come."

Tabris glared angrily at John, unfairly so but the man did not notice anyway. "Why don't you go get him, Hadriel? Recall Rachmiel. Then you go take the afternoon off and I'll stay with Connie."

"Are you sure?"

"Please," Tabris said, making his deep eyes deeper still, as though filled only with concern. "You need the rest. I can give Connie access to my energy, and you'll be able to recuperate your strength and help her better once you've returned tonight."

Hadriel nodded, shaking with relief while Tabris returned upstairs with Connie.

"Connie," he said as she walked to the sink to let her pent-up tears mix with the steam from the hot dishwater, "Connie, I'm giving you the energy from my heart, as though I'm a spiritual battery, and for now it's yours. I apologize that it's tainted."

Then Tabris began empowering her heart. When Josai'el appeared, he was standing by the door with his eyes closed and his breaths painfully deep.

"Tabris," she said, "Connie is—Tabris? What's wrong?"

He opened his eyes with slow difficulty and smiled tightly. "Not much. What about Connie?"

"Bridget's upset because she thinks Connie will break all the dishes if she keeps slamming them into the sink. What's the matter?"

Tabris smiled with a perfectly executed tremble. "Connie saps the energy from you, you know that. Hadriel had almost collapsed—I don't know how he does it every day. I don't know how *she* does it, either, now that I think about it."

Josai'el nodded. "Do you need help? I'll get Rachmiel."

"No, don't. I'll live." Tabris tightened his arms and straightening his legs, then looked down at the no-wax floor while Connie stared out the window. "How is Mithra doing?"

"Fine. He's with John, trying to convince him to come upstairs and talk to her, but it's hard. He's been doing this habitually ever since they were married."

After a moment's hesitation, Josai'el left the two-toned angel alone with Connie and his own thoughts, alone with his torn hopes that Mithra would bring John upstairs for Connie's sake or that Mithra would not for his own. As time wore on it became more apparent that John had made a good retreat into the basement and would not be reappearing any time before dinner.

Just as Tabris had predicted, Connie drained most of the ready energy from him, leaving nothing extra for thought or for dwelling on inner wounds and the sense of betrayal. After a while his face acquired the glassy shine Hadriel's often did, and any angel who saw the distant and pained look assumed that Connie was too great a drain on his resources. That night at dinner Tabris said nothing, standing behind Connie's chair and staring only at her hair. He managed to last until seven that night without looking at either Rachmiel or Mithra.

Miriael came for him when Hadriel returned vastly recovered, and forcibly took him out to the lake. Rachmiel was there, and Miriael left the pair together.

"Elizabeth?" Tabris asked, his eyes averted.

"Miriael cast a Guard over the room—she's protected. You need the help more. You're exuding a black cloud of fatigue as though you just wish the whole ordeal were ended."

Tabris reflexively gripped his heart, wrapping it with his will the way a man will apply a tourniquet to a bleeding limb.

"Don't do violence to your soul," Rachmiel said, putting an arm over Tabris' shoulders, but he stiffened and twisted from the touch.

"Tabris?" Rachmiel asked.

"Could you leave me alone?" he said, turning away his face. "Please, it's been such a difficult day. I want to be alone."

Rachmiel's heart had begun radiating stung pain, so powerful that it met with the pain inside Tabris and burned all the open wounds.

"I came out to pray with you," Rachmiel said, his voice cracking.

"Your concern is noted and appreciated," Tabris said, "but I want to be alone."

They stayed wordless, Tabris tense and Rachmiel stunned, until Rachmiel flashed back home.

Tabris looked at the still surface of the lake, like a sheet of glass warped by an occasional ripple. He clamped his heart shut against the pain in the distant house with a two car garage and an office in the basement. Then, fully shielded, he said, "God?"

He trembled, keeping his privacy locked in huge plates like armor around his emotions. "God," he said again, retreating even further from the surface of his soul into the darker depths of a nature he might have corrupted, locking each door behind him in the long spiraling labyrinth that mazed its way into the vulnerable core of his being. Battering tides warred at the outer defenses, easily able to overpower him but withholding their full strength.

Tabris clenched his teeth and forced himself to lie back on the ground, to close his eyes.

"I wish," he said softly, "I really wish, God, if You love me, that You would annihilate me and end it."

But God did not strike Tabris as he lay on the new grass, and in the morning, when the red sun arose, Tabris forced the wide look to disappear from his eyes and returned to the house, to Rachmiel.

Rachmiel had fled Tabris and flashed directly to Voriah.

"Rock!" Voriah had cried, "my goodness—what happened?"

Rachmiel had almost collapsed, reeling with emotion—hurt, anger, confusion, rejection—and he was crying the way angels cry, simply releasing the emotions without channeling them at all. No tears were necessary, but if there had been real tears then Rachmiel's friends would all have gathered and not left him alone for the next month; tears are rare and indicative of nothing less than spiritual calamity.

The household angels had gathered, though, and Rachmiel slowly calmed as they absorbed the stray emotions that lingered in the air, lending him their inner peace to copy and then return, and slowly he found strength again.

In the course of that much nonverbal contact, the entire situation by the lake had become known.

"We should demand that Raguel transfer him," Katra'il said.

"No," Rachmiel said, still leaning against Voriah. "I'm all right, don't call Raguel."

Katra'il's hair and eyes shone with a harsh white light. "But he's got to be a part of the team here!"

"Our household isn't some ready-made structure that all of us had to fit when we arrived. The team changed for each of us." Rachmiel tried to stand on his own and was unsteady for an instant until God supported him. "We'll have to adjust for him, that's all."

"He'd better do some adjusting for us, too," Katra'il snapped.

"He's been through a lot," said Rachmiel.

"Oh, you're great!" she said. "You're like the puppy that wants to please its master the more it gets beaten. Just because your name means Compassion doesn't mean you have to be walked on by every half-demonic swine who thinks he can use you as his personal doormat! He murdered his own child! Rachmiel, he killed a twelve year old boy!"

Rachmiel had backed into Voriah, who said, "Kat, you're not being fair."

"To Tabris? Tabris arrived five months ago and has done nothing but sulk, and my guess is that in the next eighty years he'll sulk his way through three households and any friendships he's fortunate enough to gather along the way. Don't look at me that way—you can't trust him! He's two-toned."

Josai'el whistled sharply. "You're condemning every angel with two-colored wings!"

"Good!" Her wild eyes flashed. "See if I'm wrong! He'll move on Elizabeth soon, and then where will you be, Rock?"

She vanished, and Rachmiel started shaking.

"Hadriel, do go stop her," Josai'el said, at which he immediately left. She looked around at the others before continuing, her long limp hair burnishing her round eyes. "Do any of you feel the same?"

Mithra, Miriael, and Voriah nonverbalized that they had their emotions under reasonable control.

Josai'el moved closer to Rachmiel and touched his hands. "Rachmiel, do you want him removed?"

"No. I just want—" and he felt himself starting to break apart again so he paused and touched Voriah with one wing, "I want to know why he's so upset. I want to help him."

Mithra said, "You think it isn't just having had to empower Connie?"

"There's something more. I felt like he was angry at me."

Voriah leaned forward, touching Rachmiel's arm and communicating that without Tabris nonverbalizing anything all intuition was pure speculation.

Miriael paced, and then volunteered to go to the lake.

"No," Josai'el said. "Give him a chance to be alone—it's what he wanted."

Miriael's eyes narrowed. "What he *said* he wanted. He might have just been sulking."

"I wouldn't call it that," Rachmiel said.

"I'll offer to spar with him," Miriael said. "It's been a long time since we did that, and I'm sure it would rouse him if he's feeling depressed."

"On one condition," said Josai'el. "That you wait for him to return to us first."

A nonverbal blow struck them all. "What if he doesn't return!"

That was Mithra, and they all looked at him. "He's really upset," he said, "and all afternoon he's been dampening conversation, his eyes getting darker, and all the lines deepening around his mouth. This isn't depression—there's something drastically wrong!"

"He was fine in the morning," Rachmiel said.

He and Mithra locked eyes. "Before we left him with John," Rachmiel finished.

"Great," Mithra said. "John's silent treatment spread to him."

"What would John want?" Josai'el asked.

"To be alone for a long time, but secretly he also wants people to come after him, to make him feel important when they knock on the door and beg him to come out. There's a lot of power the family gives him by allowing him to manipulate them like that."

Josai'el nodded. "Then as best as we can, it's business as usual. We won't tell Tabris about this conversation, we won't go after him, and we certainly won't mention what he did to Rachmiel. Can you handle that?" she asked him, her eyes becoming worried. "If it's too much strain . . ."

"No, I'll hold together," he said. "There's a part of me that wants to Guard the room against him, but I'll manage."

"Pray about it," Voriah said. "I'll pray with you."

The group dispersed then, Josai'el to talk to Katra'il and Hadriel, Voriah and Rachmiel going to Elizabeth, and Mithra and Miriael returning to John's room where the two talked quietly between themselves.

Hadriel stayed on the opposite side of the room while Katra'il paced. Her eyes shone brilliant yellow, and her hair danced with that angry light.

"I can't believe they're letting him stay, and Rachmiel just lets him walk all over him," she continued, repeating everything she had been saying for the previous five minutes. "And Josai'el just lets it continue!"

"Katra'il, these are *Divine* orders."

"Oh, you're no better," she said, pivoting on the balls of her feet to walk in the opposite direction. "He's making a mess out of the household."

Hadriel watched her, each stride perfectly executed, deliberately placed on the carpet. Her face hardened and softened alternately as she passed through the starlight that made its way in through the bedroom window. Suddenly she flashed to Martin, where he sat on his bed reading a comic book. Smiling gently, she touched his hair, breathed onto his shoulder, and then lay back on the blankets.

"Hadriel, he took a boy like this, and he *killed* him."

"I know that."

"But . . . I don't understand. Don't you know what that means? Martin has my whole heart. God told me to guard him, but I'd be here anyway. Even if He told me I could go away, I'd stay. I love Martin." She sat up and looked at the boy's blond hair, his hazel eyes. "I wish I could show you the interior of his soul, Hadriel. He's exquisite. Every part of him, it calls to me. The things he does have his signature on them. I love watching his mind at work at a problem, trying every angle in the search of a solution."

"Do you think Tabris didn't love Sebastian?"

"He must have hated him," she said. "I'll bet he resented the boy, that he wanted to be free and couldn't leave while it was expected he would stay. You see how much time he spends away from Elizabeth."

Hadriel leaned against the book case. "Why don't you ask him that?"

Katra'il laughed curtly.

Hadriel had an odd gleam in his eyes, a gleam that reflected the starlight, the light from the overhead fixture, and somehow managed to reflect time itself. "Katra'il, are you afraid of him?"

"No!" she snapped, then paused and regarded Hadriel more closely, studied the glassy shine of his eyes.

"What I'm wondering," he asked slowly, "is why you've reacted so violently to having him around."

"Because he's a killer."

"No, because then all of us would be angry. I want to know about you."

Hadriel paced now, thinking, and Katra'il also went deep inside herself to study her own mental machinery.

"Maybe," she whispered, "maybe I'm afraid that if he could do it, I might too."

She looked down. Hadriel moved closer. "But you love Martin."

"I think he loved Sebastian. And I've seen the way he looks at Elizabeth—as though he has to remind himself not to love her too much. If he feels this way about her then he must have loved Sebastian."

She leaned against Martin, lighter than the air he was breathing and therefore undetectable. "But why did he do it? And if he did it, then I might too!" She looked up anxiously. "Do you think that's why I'm so upset?"

"Possibly," Hadriel said. "I think that's what a lot of angels are feeling."

She looked at her hands. "Do you think I should apologize to him?"

"I don't think you could do it without causing more problems than you'd solve."

"That's true." She looked again at Martin. "Do you think I'd ever, you know—"

"I don't think so. Then again, no one ever thought Tabris would. I tend to believe, though, that if you don't let emotions build up you'll be fine. You seem to be able to express yourself well enough."

Katra'il chuckled. "Too well. I'm afraid, though, that—well, I know I'm capable of almost violent outbursts, and I'm naturally sarcastic. What if one day, in a blind rage, I do something horrible like that to Martin?"

Hadriel sat on the carpet. "What would make you that angry?"

"Sin."

"Right. But you wouldn't kill him if he were deep in sin, because that would send him to Hell. You'd have to wait for him to repent, and after that you'd have had time to think it over, which means that you wouldn't be so impulsive. And anyway, you'd be too glad he repented to be violent."

Katra'il chuckled. "But why did Tabris—"

"He's different, more pensive. He's more a watcher than a doer. He might mull over his anger long enough for the child to repent out from under him, and then when he'd be ready to act the child would be safe."

Katra'il sighed and leaned back against the wall. She locked eyes with Hadriel.

"You're okay," he said.

Josai'el appeared in the room, and Katra'il bowed her head. "I'm sorry," she said.

"Has Hadriel calmed you?"

"Significantly. I don't think I'll have a problem again."

Josai'el nodded, her straight hair falling forward over her shoulders. "Well, you're definitely calmer. Hadriel, I might send you out to talk with the rest of the world's guardians."

Hadriel smiled and nodded shortly.

"He doesn't know about my reaction, does he?" Katra'il asked.

"No. Just make sure it doesn't happen again, even out of his presence." Josai'el's mouth tightened. "Don't mention tonight's incident at all, especially how angry you were, but also his treatment of Rachmiel. Can you handle that?"

"I can," Katra'il said.

Josai'el nodded and left the room.

Tabris returned to Rachmiel like a knight wearing armor that shone—his eyes held a quiet gleam, and all his movements were deliberate and stiff.

Rachmiel felt like a liar as he greeted Tabris, but God strengthened him and reassured him that saying hello to someone toward whom he felt anger was not a lie if he did it for Him. Relief dawned over Rachmiel at that, which showed in his eyes, but Tabris either did not notice or did not comment. "How is she?" he asked.

"Fine."

"Good."

Then Tabris left the room. Rachmiel sat tremulously at the end of the bed. He stretched out full length beside Elizabeth and purred, "Wake up, Sleepy. Please, wake up." He closed his eyes. "Elizabeth, I need you awake now. For me, please."

The girl sat up and yawned, then looked out the window. She smiled around the room, and Rachmiel felt her newly awake sensations flooding into his spirit, the early morning stiffness in her arms and fingers, the head rush as she stood up and her vision darkened momentarily. Tabris had said that this was not a usual development in children, but it was all Rachmiel had ever experienced. The slack relaxation of sleep drained out of her body as she breathed deeply and walked to the window. The guardian smiled, his eyes transforming their color into rich crystalline orange. He had felt her morning sensations for ten years, and he knew the whole routine well by now. The moments of most intense connection between his soul and hers came when she had just awakened and had not yet closed her mind to God. He shivered when she prayed just after waking, when God touched her heart and Rachmiel felt that fingerprint etched into his soul for the rest of the day. Most mornings, however, she simply arose and got dressed, and that was all right too. Rachmiel could feel the general swirl of her thoughts while she made her first morning steps.

Still lying stretched out on her bed, still with his eyes closed, Rachmiel fell in love again with the brightness of Elizabeth's soul, adoring the strong clarity that rivaled the purest mountain brook or the most piercing sunbeam. He focused his soul to look at God through hers and smiled hugely as he watched grace become magnified when it passed through her heart.

He had focused so intently on her that he almost jumped when he heard her voice, and he did jump when he realized the words were not spoken.

"God," her prayer had sounded in his heart, "Grandma says I have a guardian angel all my own. Can you say 'hi' to her for me?"

Rachmiel hardly cared that she had just called him a her—gender is like a suit of clothes to an angel, easily altered when necessary. The fact that her thoughts had sounded in his head had not confused him either—God had simply forwarded this prayer the way He did all her prayers. What astonished Rachmiel was the fact that Elizabeth had spoken to him at all. He sat up staring, then said, "Hi back, Sweetie."

She began picking out her clothes, and Rachmiel gaped, watching with such fascination that he did not recognize the emotional void signaling Tabris' return until the other angel spoke.

"Did you just hear—"

Rachmiel nonverbalized utter joy, and he beamed brilliantly. He reached into Elizabeth's imagination, the farthest he could penetrate into her thoughts, but found her very intent on only her clothes and getting dressed. "It's over for now," he said, a little sad. "She might never speak to us again, but that's more than most angels get in all their charges' lifetimes!"

He smiled at Tabris, who looked away, but for once Rachmiel did not feel the rebuff. "I felt it too," Tabris said. "I'd have thought God would only let you hear it."

Rachmiel frowned, a clear rebuke, and nonverbalized, *Co-guardian*. Then he laughed out loud. "That was great. Ten years from now I'm going to have to remember that, when she's sinning up a storm, and I think there's no gratitude in this job."

Fully dressed now, Elizabeth had begun forcing the brush through her hair. Tabris watched her intently, as though he were checking her before he left, but then he stayed in the room.

"You can return if you want," Rachmiel said, seeing the hesitancy.

"No, I'm her co-guardian, remember? You can't get rid of me that easily, not if God says I'm going to stay." Tabris laughed, a tight, forced, tin-sounding feat. Then his eyes narrowed and he regarded Rachmiel piercingly. The orange-eyed angel nodded, glad—but with one hand tight in God's.

12

AS TABRIS VISITED THE LAKE ONE NIGHT, RACH-miel spoke to Voriah in Alan's room. The moon had risen but was obscured by cloud cover, and the angels glowed softly to make seeing one another easier. In their light, the posters of airplanes and basketball players that lined the walls seemed to take on an appearance of being half alive. The hamsters in a cage in the corner were trying to attract Voriah's attention, chittering so loudly that Alan stirred and Voriah had to bless them to make them quieter.

"Tabris did something strange today," Rachmiel said, sitting on the desk that Alan had left covered with pencils and paper. It was the only disarrayed part of the room, and he would have felt uncomfortable sitting on a floor not strewn with clothing.

Voriah shrugged.

"Stranger than that. While Elizabeth was at school. All the other guardians were silent. You know how they tend to get quieter when he's around."

Voriah rolled his eyes, nonverbalizing, "He's an emotional black hole."

For an instant Rachmiel stilled, but then Voriah relented a little. Rachmiel leaned forward and touched Alan where he slept beneath extra blankets.

"What are his dreams?"

"Nothing right now, he's not in REM. Come on, tell me about today. I'll behave."

Rachmiel looked up, reluctant for the simple reason that he hated hearing others maligned when they had no chance for self-defense. If he had been human, he would have wrung his hands. As an angel, he excused himself to check on Elizabeth.

Voriah followed him to the girl's bedroom. "Rock, I'm sorry. You know that whenever Tabris comes into a room you can tell he's there by what he *doesn't* nonverbalize. No, let me tell you, you're with him so much that you've gotten used to it, but think about how we feel. You know how the rest of us have an aura. Well, we can tell he's around because he dampens everyone else's—we just feel this emotional vacuum arrive in the room. That's why he stops conversation."

Rachmiel grudgingly agreed in his mind that an emotional black hole was in fact an apt description.

You see! exclaimed Voriah's eyes. "Now tell me that story."

Rachmiel and Voriah returned to Alan's neater room. "Elizabeth learned fractions today, and she had a hard time understanding what they were. Music is more her specialty, although I suppose math plays an important part there as well. She'll be a great piano player if she applies herself." Voriah smiled, and Rachmiel started laughing. "I'm sorry, I'm in love."

"How can I be annoyed when I'm the same way?" Voriah asked. "I haven't cast any stones at you in the mad-about-your-charge department."

Rachmiel grinned, and he met Voriah's eyes for a long friendly moment.

"She didn't understand fractions," he said, "so Tabris . . . taught her."

Voriah's eyes snapped.

"He showed her, in her mind, what it meant to have a fraction. He conceptualized it in a way she understood. I can't explain it, but that's what he did."

"I've helped Alan understand new concepts," said Voriah.

"Not like this. I tried helping her understand too— he just reached in and *taught* her. He kept saying her name, that he knew she knew it, and suddenly she did." Rachmiel radiated amazement.

Voriah thought for a while, on such a central level that Rachmiel could not feel the surface thoughts spinning in his mind.

"He's new," Voriah finally said. "She's not used to him yet, not enough to start ignoring him as totally as she ignores you."

"Maybe," Rachmiel said. "I think it was his technique. All the other angels were wondering what I would do—they kept staring at me as though he were going to kill her too, or else make her insane. Making her insane might have the same spiritual effect as killing her."

"Right," Voriah said, "mortal sin to him and the end of spiritual growth to her. How *did* you react?"

"I thanked him. What else could I do? He's taking his responsibilities very seriously."

Voriah rolled his eyes. "I didn't catch that," Rachmiel said, a little upset.

"He's like the British honor guard—he's very intense. He hardly talks unless you ask him to. He never defends himself when other angels stare."

Rachmiel nodded and sat down. "So what can I do?"

"Not much," Voriah said. "Don't be critical, I guess. Ask leading questions without prying. Follow your nature—empathize."

Rachmiel said, "How can you empathize with an emotional black hole?"

While Rachmiel sat considering his words, Voriah's eyes began to swirl. For a moment Rachmiel failed to notice how the white and blue color spun in Voriah's eyes, but then he felt the changed presence in the world, now not Voriah so much as Him.

The guardian bowed in the presence of the Lord, channeled through Voriah who had been possessed by God after giving permission to be used as a temporary mouthpiece. He would not remember any of the conversation after God released him.

"My Lord?" asked Rachmiel.

"Compassion, son of Love, will you serve me?"

"Always," said Rachmiel. "What should I do about Tabris?"

"Be patient," said God. "He needs your strength for now, the knowledge that he can rely on you and trust you when he has to. You must put yourself on the line for him. Someday, you will have to love him."

Rachmiel turned visibly colder, his eyes simultaneously widening and hardening.

"I know that will be difficult," said God, still speaking through Voriah, "but work with me. He isn't past the danger yet. You have good cause to fear for his safety."

Rachmiel closed his eyes tightly.

God agreed that the prospect was awful and painful. "If you go through pain, though," He added, "you might help to save him."

"I'll suffer in exchange," Rachmiel said eagerly.

"This isn't a trade," God said tenderly, correcting Rachmiel's theology a little. "Your pain will be in your love for him, when you've found it, and until then the pain of empathy and helplessness and the yearning to help. I know you would suffer for him, but only One could suffer and repair another on that merit alone."

Rachmiel nodded and then Voriah was back in his spirit, shaking his head to clear the fuzzy aftershocks of God's possession.

"Did God answer you?"

"Yes—I'm going to go back to Elizabeth's room."

"You look like you need the support," Voriah said. "Let me come with you. We'll pray together."

They went to the bedside of a sleeping girl who understood fractions and had no idea what divided spirits watched her while she slept.

On the first clear Saturday of spring the Hayes family had a picnic. The boys played frisbee in an open area with their father, and Mithra watched the way the frisbee spun as it traveled, how that spin helped it to become more dynamic and to travel further than it could have otherwise. Connie and Bridget were setting up the food on a wooden picnic table with chipped red paint, with flakes of fallen paint covering the pale shoots of grass growing up around the legs. Elizabeth read a book under an apple tree.

Tabris had walked off a little distance from the others so that it was Rachmiel beside Elizabeth, reading over her shoulder to make sure she extracted the right information from the words and was not exposed to any offensive material.

Miriael asked Tabris to spar with him for a while. He agreed, and the pair began fighting as though they were Michael and Lucifer, eternally locked in combat, each deadly serious in expression.

Miriael's charge Kyle began roughing up his younger brother Martin, but neither Miriael nor Tabris seemed to notice. Elizabeth worked harder to concentrate on her book.

The pair circled again before resuming their fight. The harsh sounds of spiritual metals scraping against one another echoed off the hillside, and the death-like intent of each angel radiated for miles around. A few angels turned up in battle armor to ask if they were needed.

They fought hard, so much so that Kyle and Elizabeth became agitated, restlessly moving about, aimlessly looking for something to do to burn off their energy. Rachmiel tried to calm Elizabeth, but that would only have succeeded in making her depressed, so instead he channeled her energy into a desire to learn to play frisbee.

"Should we stop them?" asked Hadriel, but Josai'el told him to let the pair finish their duel.

Very quickly, however, it became apparent that the pair were evenly matched, that they might well fight for an hour before either made a slip in judgment which would cost him the battle. They knew each other's styles by now, and to some extent they were able to anticipate each other's moves. Victory probably rested in risks and unpredictability, but neither seemed interested in taking chances, just in dueling. With one hand on Elizabeth's shoulder, Rachmiel realized that winning was not the object of this match. These two loved to combat for the sake of combat itself, and if one won too quickly that would be a shame. At that point, Rachmiel finally understood the concept of the stationary bicycle or the treadmill.

Josai'el had managed to calm Kyle somewhat, her crystalline eyes large in her thin face as though she were already planning a reprimand for Miriael about his carelessness. Rachmiel had better luck with Elizabeth, naturally a more sedate personality, and simply encouraged her to continue playing with the frisbee.

While Mithra watched keenly, Voriah cheered on both participants.

The fun ended immediately when three demons arrived to investigate the commotion. Tabris and Miriael clashed with them instantly, driving them away with their mere presence—as battle-warmed and fierce as they looked, the demons fled after only token resistance.

Josai'el thrust herself between the pair before they could tangle with each other again. "Miriael, look at Kyle!"

The warrior angel's eyes rounded, and he trained his gaze on the boy for a moment before nonverbalizing self-horror and sorrow, his open admittance that he had not thought the boy would react since he was already involved in frisbee.

"And Tabris," Josai'el said, turning to him, "Elizabeth is very receptive to you because she's so young—look what it's done to her."

Tabris remembered how Sebastian's mother had needed to refrain from wine and certain medications while she was pregnant because of the tiny life growing inside her, and he realized that he was in the same position. His gaze lowered and did not lift even when Rachmiel touched his shoulder. "There's no problem, Josai'el. I was steadying her."

"Rachmiel," she said firmly, her long straight hair framing her stern eyes, "you were having trouble."

"Not overly much," he said.

Mithra chuckled, and Katra'il looked at Hadriel.

Tabris breathed deeply. "No, she's right. I apologize. Sparring while Elizabeth was awake was very unprofessional. I won't do it again."

Josai'el nodded, but something in her eyes signaled her discomfort, and Rachmiel wondered if reprimanding the pair had been the best course.

The guardians grew calm for a while, for the most part talking among themselves. Katra'il called her guitar to her hand the way Tabris and Miriael had summoned swords to theirs and she began playing Pachelbel's Canon in D. Hadriel and Mithra formed a light sculpture, calling up a solid block of light and then spinning it as though it were pottery on the wheel, except that wherever they touched it the light changed color and shape. Rachmiel sat close and watched the sculpture progressing, always changing as it spun, and once he even extended his own finger to graze the outside, leaving an orange swath behind. Tabris stood by Elizabeth, who had calmed substantially and returned to her book.

The family was ready to eat, and they gathered at the picnic table. The angels bowed their heads and pulled their wings in closely while John said grace for the family and then burst into chatter of their own while the children began squabbling over how many hot dogs they deserved and who got the only can of grape soda.

Tabris walked away from the noisy confusion, his eyes drawn toward the crowns of the trees where birds had begun building or rebuilding their nests. He was about to turn and point out a certain nest to Rachmiel when tremendous power washed over the field, and all the angels gasped when Christ appeared. Tabris lay prostrated at His feet, trembling and tense.

"My Lord," said Josai'el, which the other angels said also, except for Tabris who said nothing.

Jesus' eyes were golden, but sharply so as he regarded the two-toned angel before Him. Rachmiel had moved closer on the assumption that any matter involving Tabris perforce involved him, but the cold glare of Christ's eyes shocked the angel named Compassion. Jesus sensed his fear and looked at him with a smile and all the love the angel remembered. He melted momentarily until he realized that Christ was angry, and justly so, at the one guardian ever to have broken the one written law.

"Tabris," He said.

The coldness in the Divine voice made Rachmiel's spirit twang like a violin's string that was too tight and snapped, and he imagined how it might feel to be on the receiving end of such controlled wrath.

Suddenly Voriah stood beside him, supporting him. Tabris, at Christ's feet, had made a nonverbal obeisance.

"You haven't expressed any concern about Sebastian," said Jesus.

Tabris shuddered, drawing his wings tighter over his head, his knees closer to his chest, his forehead harder against the ground.

"It's time you visited him."

Tabris protested so strongly that Rachmiel cried aloud "No!" before he even realized he had spoken. "He's not ready!"

Jesus looked at Rachmiel, and Tabris said, "I won't."

Rachmiel dropped to his knees, partly from habit and partly from weakness. "Please don't force him," he said. The tension inside Tabris was so great that his teeth almost chattered, and Rachmiel continued pleading, almost babbling. His heart was awash with Tabris' nonverbalized fear, with the pain sent sloshing through Elizabeth and back up into Rachmiel, although the loss was too inexplicable to cling to her, and mercifully she only conducted it without feeling it. Though more innocent than she, Rachmiel had the capacity to experience such heartrending grief for what it meant—the loss of everything considered valuable, the near loss of one's self, the scare of having everything but God torn away. What he reacted to by babbling Tabris responded to with silence.

"My Lord," he said suddenly, "let me go instead."

He held his breath then, and he knew Tabris had done the same.

"Please," Voriah said, and Rachmiel realized then that he was kneeling, "spare Tabris for now."

The other angels asked as well, and Rachmiel could feel Tabris' gratitude, but not that so much as surprise and sudden fear at the actions of his friends. Rachmiel registered the fear, but had no idea why loyalty frightened Tabris until he realized that if he fell now he would be harming more than just himself. Reaching through Elizabeth, Rachmiel gave strength to him in the way Tabris had given strength to Connie, and it was received reluctantly.

Jesus said, "I'll let Rachmiel visit for now, but Tabris, eventually you'll have to face him."

Tabris nodded from his prostrated position. "Thank you."

"Tonight I'll send a messenger for you," Jesus said, looking at Rachmiel, His eyes changing color to the orange-gold of honey. He smiled so that Rachmiel could meet the gaze and fall headlong into the love God had prepared just for him. "Thank you, Rachmiel," said Jesus.

This bewildered him, and his eyes flushed the deepest purple a sunset could paint the sky. Then Jesus left them.

The family was eating potato chips and pretzels, talking about the NCAA basketball tournament and other important things.

13

THAT NIGHT, ALMOST AS SOON AS ELIZABETH HAD gone to bed, a messenger angel came for Rachmiel. Tabris was deliberately out of the room. The white-winged angel locked eyes with Rachmiel.

"We haven't really spoken since this afternoon," Rachmiel answered. "I don't know how he feels about this."

The angel frowned, scornful, as though thinking that any angel who did not love his charge was not worthy of his species.

Rachmiel looked down nonverbalizing confusion—he had no idea if defending Tabris would breach his confidence. "But if he didn't love him," Rachmiel said, "I think he would have gone immediately."

The angel flashed him out of the room to a grassy field. In the distance across the flat land there stood two figures, and they approached.

"The angel with Sebastian is Casifer," said the messenger while they walked. "He's been given charge over the boy's upbringing until he enters the complete Beatific Vision."

"So he has to finish growing up here," Rachmiel asked, "in Limbo?"

"Right. He's happy here, and there are others here who were killed before their completed development, so he has plenty of company." The messenger looked up at a bird that passed overhead. "He knows about Tabris, and he knows Casifer isn't his real guardian, but we haven't told him Tabris' name yet."

"I understand." Rachmiel could envision the mutual misery that the boy and Tabris would share if Sebastian were able to repeatedly summon Tabris while the ex-guardian refused to respond.

"He's at a normal level of growth for most twelve year olds," the messenger added.

As the boy continued advancing toward them, Rachmiel gasped when he saw Tabris!

It had to be Tabris, only it wasn't—he was much younger, his spirit not weighted with the experience of ages. Where it counted, though, the resemblance struck Rachmiel deeply. Physically he looked different—shorter, more stocky than the lithe and iron-hard form Tabris wore naturally. The boy's movements were still awkward and his bearings in that adolescent off-balance that Rachmiel had seen come and go in each of Elizabeth's older brothers. It was the soul of the boy that resembled Tabris exactly, as though God had photocopied the angel, reduced him in size, and inserted him into a human frame.

The boy's eyes glistened with the same depth Tabris' did, and he kept his face under the same rigid control. Rachmiel felt uncomfortable, having lived with Tabris for five months and now being confronted by this imitation, like a great-uncle seeing his grandnephew and remembering his own long-dead brother. The mannerisms, the bearings, the tight and dark look about the hands and eyes, they were all Tabris.

"Hello, Sebastian," said Rachmiel, almost stammering.

"This is Rachmiel," said the messenger.

"My guardian?" asked the boy in disbelief.

The messenger shook his head.

"He and I work together," Rachmiel said.

"I thought Jesus was going to invite him to come."

"He sent me instead," Rachmiel said, glad of the slightly ambiguous pronoun.

He realized then how redundant his position was, since any other angel to Sebastian was still not Tabris. The messenger departed, and Rachmiel looked up at

Casifer, whose bright eyes welcomed him with green warmth. This angel practically exuded kindness, and Rachmiel felt glad for Sebastian, accompanied by this warm and generous soul. Casifer and Rachmiel had worked together on occasion, and since their first assignment they had been friends because after becoming close angels stay that way—unless one falls. Casifer's white wings lifted and touched the tips of Rachmiel's orange feathers. Then they hugged angelically, more an exercise of the soul than of the spirit form, and Sebastian watched with interest as their hearts coiled about one another momentarily.

"How did you do that?" he asked.

Casifer explained the process, and Rachmiel smiled with renewed gladness for Sebastian, who had a truly kind angel for a teacher. Casifer too seemed very pleased with the opportunity to substitute, and then Rachmiel remembered that Casifer's one regret in all existence had been that he never would be the guardian of a human being—God had revealed that to him during the early years of human existence, when Casifer had seen the bonding between angel and charge and had grown eager with anticipation. This was very close to the actual thing, and Casifer certainly was taking Sebastian that seriously.

Rachmiel watched Sebastian's first halting attempt at a spiritual hug, smiling as the boy managed only to meet Casifer, not actually to grasp the other's soul in return. Casifer laughed kindly—a laughter still tinged with the shock an angel feels at finding he can love a human child so strongly. Rachmiel knew that self-surprise well. At times he still felt it when he looked at Elizabeth as she read a book or played a sonata on the piano.

When they began walking, Rachmiel realized how much he missed Heaven. Limbo resembled it exactly, that same barely sloping terrain, the distant mountains with their jagged peaks and brilliantly white snow caps, the air so clean it could mesh with his own essence and remain tinged with his spirit for a few minutes after he left a place. Limbo was, in actuality, only the outer layer of Heaven, although the earth itself had been the outer layer until the event which angels call the Mistake. It was in Limbo that aborted lives such as Sebastian's could complete their development into full souls, and usually these souls were accompanied by their guardians. For obvious reasons Sebastian was not, although for a moment Rachmiel wondered why keeping Tabris and Sebastian together was such a bad idea.

Sebastian asked questions—about his parents, his friends, his dog—but Rachmiel admitted he had no idea how any of them fared. Sebastian nodded, then shrugged and started talking about all the things he had learned in Limbo, how he and Casifer had gone rafting down a stream, not as exhilarating as when he was alive since he had no body and no adrenaline, but still fun. He talked about sitting alone by a lake and reading aloud for the lazy pleasure of hearing his own voice. He showed Rachmiel how he could pronounce a few halting sentences in the angelic native tongue—Glossolalia—but admitted that the preferred mode of speech, nonverbalization, was beyond him except for a few straightforward emotions such as happiness or sadness, and even then they were not under his control.

Casifer made a complex nonverbalization to Rachmiel then, that as a human Sebastian expected to be in control of what he said and did not say, that he thought he could nonverbalize happiness when not actually feeling it. Rachmiel smiled, realizing that someday he would have to teach Elizabeth the same, that in God's light no thoughts were shameful and all could be broadcast without fear or embarrassment, that the soul did not need to be cloaked and hidden to protect itself from the horror of knowing and being known.

Sebastian grimaced. "I can almost understand your nonverbalizations," he said, "but they're so complicated."

A language without grammar, Rachmiel reflected. Humans had invented verbalizations making it easier to lie.

"But angels have a language too," Sebastian said.

Casifer informed Sebastian that there were several angelic languages, and each had its place.

"But all are coupled with nonverbal affirmation," Rachmiel said. "Demons use the same tongue, but they remove the nonverbalizations from the communication."

But Tabris had done the same, Rachmiel realized.

Feeling Rachmiel's shock, Sebastian welled up with concern, and Rachmiel covered quickly by congratulating him on a perfect instance of nonverbal communication. Sebastian laughed out loud, looking with an asymmetric smile at Casifer, who nodded with a grin of his own.

Sebastian leaned on Casifer's arm and looked up at the sky, resting his head back against the angel's wing. "Tell me about my guardian," he said.

Rachmiel paused.

"Please," Sebastian said. "I, I want to know about him, what he's like, if he's—the type of things he likes, what he's doing now . . ."

Sebastian might or might not have realized how many questions he had asked nonverbally, but innocent as he was, all his questions had risen to the surface and bombarded Rachmiel at the same time.

"Right now, he's back at home guarding my charge," he said slowly, trying to decide what was worth saying and what was best not said. "He's her co-guardian. Her name is Elizabeth Hayes, and she's ten."

Sebastian looked down at his hands, and they were small hands.

"Yes, I trust him," Rachmiel said, supplying the hollowness of his voice with the actual feeling from his heart, because that at least flowed deeply. "We work well together, and Elizabeth responds well to him."

"Does he love her?"

"I think so—guardians pretty much have to love their charges. We see God in you so strongly."

"So you love her too?"

Rachmiel did not have to speak this time—the word *dearly* would have been redundant.

Sebastian closed his eyes and slumped heavily against Casifer.

Rachmiel would have answered the nonverbal question that Sebastian was pumping out continuously, but he honestly did not know if Tabris would want him to reveal the answer—and in this language without grammar it was hard to pin the boy's sense of abandonment to the present or the past. Sebastian's feelings were not the only chronologically ambiguous ones, either. Tabris had said that he had loved the boy. He might not still.

Sebastian changed the topic deliberately, so deliberately that Rachmiel could feel the effort his innocent soul had to expend in order to accomplish what he did not want to do, and they spoke about a few inconsequential matters. God let Rachmiel know that he should leave, and the orange-winged angel explained that Elizabeth was going to wake up soon.

"Will you come back to visit me again?" asked Sebastian with bright eyes, a lot like Tabris when he was on the brink of a painful moment.

"If you'd like," Rachmiel said.

The sheen vanished from the boy's eyes, replaced with the deep mahogany that wrung Rachmiel's heart. "I would," he said. "Very much." Sebastian tried to affirm this nonverbally, and Casifer smiled at the effort the boy extended—it felt contrived but Rachmiel knew it was actually an awkward attempt to mimic something that ought to have been happening naturally, and soon would.

"I'll come again soon," Rachmiel said, and he gave a promise with his heart.

Sebastian flashed a lopsided smile at him just before he left.

Tabris was lying full-length next to Elizabeth when Rachmiel returned, one of his two-toned wings spread protectively over her like an extra blanket. The night had grown chilly, and he was warming the air around her body, then keeping the warmth trapped beneath the sheets.

"Did anything happen while I was gone?"

Tabris said, "No," and Rachmiel nodded, glancing into Elizabeth's soul to make sure all stayed sinless. She was dreaming about cotton candy, and he laughed. Listening to the music of Rachmiel's voice, Tabris guessed at his activity and closed his eyes.

Rachmiel emitted a field of tension, and Tabris stretched out, forcing himself to do the proper thing. "You met him?"

Rachmiel nodded, his closely tucked aura had changed to one of extreme eagerness, worry, and excitement. Tabris decided not to respond, and instead asked, "Is he enjoying himself?"

Rachmiel nodded again.

"Who's staying with him?"

"Casifer."

"He'll be devoted. He never had a charge of his own." Tabris looked back at Elizabeth, his heart ringing like a large bell in a tower, but he controlled himself. "I was wondering if you would return before she awoke."

He could feel Rachmiel's inner gasp even without seeing the purple flash of his eyes. Rachmiel could not understand the deliberate lack of concern—the change of topic. Reserve he might have been able to fathom, but apathy made no sense at all.

"I know you like to be the one who wakes her," Tabris continued while watching Rachmiel out of the corners of his eyes. "I can't imagine a morning when she awoke without you once calling her Sleepy. She'd be disoriented all day. I'm no substitute for the personality who's been faithful all her life. Of course, you can't substitute for God either."

"No, God is far more important to her well-being," said Rachmiel. "His grace is more pervasive than our presence."

Tabris, like most people, knew that the trick of changing the subject when talking to angels is to change the topic to God. No angel can resist. God is an obsession for celestials, both fallen and unfallen. The fallen will curse Him whenever they can, the way a recently divorced man will insult his ex-wife every time she comes up in conversation, even if by pretending to forget her name, and will dwell on the pain of betrayal in his solitary moments. Unfallen angels love God so much that to them every moment is like the first moment a boy falls in love—every instant in Heaven is like a first kiss. A boy will daydream about his first love, talk about her to his family and closest friends, write her name in the margins of his notebook. Tabris had ushered Sebastian through that first euphoria, and the similarities had surprised him. All innocent love is alike. Because of its naivete, the first crush seems ridiculous to adults who have lost tears and sleep to broken love, but the angels' First Love never will never desert them. Experience has not dimmed the light in their hearts, and the silver frame of their memories has not tarnished. Similarly, for those angels who fell, the disillusionment never vanishes because no new love comes to replace the First: what they spurned was Love itself.

Rachmiel talked excitedly about God, and Tabris watched, the words making no visible impact on him. He did little more than nod, but that was all the encouragement Rachmiel needed.

Tabris realized that he had lost the firstness of his love of God by betraying Him, and he turned perceptibly paler as he listened to his co-guardian, but this time Rachmiel missed the change, and his voice did not waver to indicate any concern. Thinking deep inside himself—something Tabris had learned to do only recently—leaving his appearance unchanged while his soul practically convulsed on the inside—he realized that he was probably the only angel who would have been able to listen to Rachmiel unaffected.

But God, he thought, *you know I love you, don't you?*

No answer penetrated the outer shell of Tabris, and he rose again to the surface of himself.

"I guess I should wake her now," Rachmiel said. "Sleepyhead, it's time again."

Tabris saw the warmth in his eyes, an angel waking his chief delight while wrapped in God's love like a soft blanket, and he nearly sobbed in desperation.

14

THAT DAY ELIZABETH DECIDED TO TAKE A BICY-
cle ride. It was the first really pleasant spring afternoon
that she had to herself, so after church she went into the
garage and fought with the lawnmower, the garden hose,
six folding chairs, and a bag of fertilizer until she had
secured the release of her bicycle. Then, after assuring it
she had meant no harm by the long-term abandonment
occasioned by winter, she pumped up the tires and
dusted off the seat cover.

"Maybe I shouldn't go," Tabris said to Rachmiel.

"Don't be silly. I thought you loved to fly!"

"I do, but—what does this have to do with flying?"

Rachmiel nodded eagerly, his eyes brilliant orange
in anticipation. "You fly a little above and behind her,
that's all. Didn't Sebastian ever ride a bicycle?"

Apparently his visit with the child and Tabris' reaction to it had loosened Rachmiel's tongue somewhat. He
had never before mentioned Sebastian in casual conversation.

"Sebastian rode a bike," Tabris said. "I'd rather not
go."

"Do you want some time away from Elizabeth?"

Tabris' eyes popped. "No! No, it's not like that at
all." He shook his head to dispel the memory of a demonic voice like a zephyr winding its way through his
mind. *Rachmiel went to Raguel with a formal complaint—you
desert Elizabeth far too easily! . . . You're not the only one who
can fake pleasure when you're really filled with anger.*

"Tabris?"

The two-toned angel shook his head, almost violently, as though he could dislodge the memory from
where it clung to his spirit.

Rachmiel moved forward with concern. "Please tell me what's wrong," he said. "Was it that I mentioned Sebastian?"

"No—leave me alone," Tabris snapped. "I'll go biking with you. I'll stay with Elizabeth."

Rachmiel stepped backward. Elizabeth, unaware of the two angels, hopped onto the bike and pedaled down the driveway. Rachmiel helped her to catch her balance as she wobbled to a start, and Tabris guided the tires over the loose stones where the driveway met the main road.

Rachmiel emitted emotions almost randomly, and Tabris shook his head. "Look, I apologize. I was hasty."

"But I don't want to cause you any problems. I'm sorry I mentioned Sebastian." Rachmiel's eyes were as huge as fists. Tabris deliberately looked away and called to a honeybee in the path of Elizabeth's bicycle to make it rise higher into the air so she could go under it. "Tabris, I'm really sorry."

"The only thing you should be sorry for is sin, and there's no sin involved, is there?" But even as he said that he thought about Rachmiel and Mithra lying to him, running to Raguel, and his eyes grew glassy.

Rachmiel whispered, "What did I do, Tabris?" and Tabris knew immediately with that sharp cut of a confirmed rumor that Rachmiel had betrayed him after all. He said nothing, trying to both collect his thoughts and follow Elizabeth while she biked under the high sun. Demons could lie, but they told the truth when it was worse. This was worse.

Tabris had an irrational impulse to condemn himself outright and let Rachmiel bear the blame for all eternity, but his heart shuddered at the thought of losing whatever of God remained in him, of surrendering his whole personality to Satan's ravening claws, and he closed his eyes against the pain.

"I'll get someone else," Rachmiel was saying. "I'll get someone to watch Elizabeth, and we'll go to talk somewhere. Tabris, whatever I did, let me explain it."

Let me explain why I went to Raguel and demanded your removal.

Tabris was wearing armor—he had hardly realized when his clothing's fabric had stiffened into leather and metal. He felt the weight of the sword harnessed against his hip. "Rachmiel, shut up! Don't patronize me!"

"Rock!"

Voriah's frightened voice rang over the hillside, and Rachmiel turned even as Tabris realized the trap and reached for Elizabeth. A demon shot across the road through the spokes of her tires and tripped her. She cried aloud as the bicycle flipped and she was catapulted over the handle bars.

Diving down to protect her from being hurt, Tabris suddenly pulled back.

Rachmiel flashed beside her instantly. She was sprawled stunned on the ground, her arm scraped, her forehead cut badly and blood pouring over her right eye and cheek.

Tabris blazed in pursuit of the demon, catching him within the minute, blindly enraged and thrashing him to no end, so far from reason that he hardly realized when the demon lost cohesion. He sliced him into four pieces, scattering him in the different oceans, knowing even then with grim desperation that the demon would recover soon, and that Elizabeth had been hurt anyway.

When he had finished, standing on an ice floe in the Arctic, Tabris realized more and more as he calmed down that he had to return and face Rachmiel.

One heartbeat later he realized that no, he had no need to return—he was much further than five miles from Elizabeth now, and he felt no dizziness, no numbness. That probably meant he had been released from service. He was free to do as he pleased.

He could go wherever he wanted, as far as he desired from the girl who sat on a dusty road sobbing because he had hesitated. Hesitated needlessly. Tabris could go to the farthest planet, bury himself in a distant sun, and even enter Heaven to present himself before the Lord.

He returned to Rachmiel.

There were a few more angels there than before. Elizabeth stood up, and, fortunately, someone who had been driving by in his pickup truck was bandaging her forehead. It was a shallow cut despite all the blood, Tabris realized with relief. The stranger had already offered to drive her back to her parents' house. Tabris looked around, tested the emotional waters, and realized that Rachmiel was really, really angry.

He almost flashed away, but Rachmiel turned to him.

"You creature! What were you doing? I thought you had her, and then you backed off! What kind of guarding is that? Better if you'd just let her fall—for the Lord's own sake, then I'd have gone after her, but you left her unprotected the first time she really needed you!"

Tabris stepped backward, but Rachmiel continued pressing him. The other angels glared with the same coldness, their faces and their eyes set like iron. He shook, looking about as though to escape, but he knew they could follow. They could keep him from Elizabeth, they could keep him from running. He began shaking, but the rage in Rachmiel's face, the red of his eyes darker than any sunset Tabris had seen in all time, pierced him like a spear, and he panicked. He squirmed with the need to explain what he had no right to.

He gasped for breath, almost choking. "I didn't—"

"That's right—you didn't! You didn't grab her, you didn't cushion her, you didn't do a blessed thing! You're great at deflecting snowballs—why are bicycles so difficult for you?"

"Because I killed Sebastian on his bicycle!" Tabris shouted. "Is that what you wanted to hear? Sebastian was riding his bike and he fell off, and as he hit the ground I broke his neck! I got scared that I'd do it again—all right?"

Rachmiel had changed completely—from irate guardian to very scared friend, and Tabris vanished from the circle of angels, leaving behind the distinct feeling that he wanted no pity.

When the other angels moved closer, Rachmiel realized how badly he was trembling.

"Was he serious?" asked one. The words were redundant—they knew he was serious, but that outburst from someone normally devoid of emotion had stunned them all.

"Rock," one of the angels said, "you'd better go to him. We'll stay with Elizabeth for now."

Rachmiel looked around and knew that he had to go, despite his fear. He breathed deeply and flashed himself to wherever Tabris was.

He had expected to find himself by the pond. He landed instead in Elizabeth's room. Tabris lay face down on the bed, and Rachmiel suddenly understood that even though he had gotten inside, the room was Guarded.

He remained silent for a few minutes, the long seconds dragging one after the next like a seventy-five car freight train at a railroad crossing, a progression that seemed to loop into itself and recycle endlessly. During that time Rachmiel realized that Tabris was face down but not in tears, and that he was not looking up because he wanted not to confront his admission.

Rachmiel sat on the bed and laid one hand on Tabris' shoulder.

"Rock—"

Rachmiel shushed him, but not with his mouth. Putting his other hand on Tabris' other shoulder, he leaned closer so that their heads were touching. Closing his eyes, relaxing, he discarded his anger into God's ready hands and poured his peace into the hurt angel stretched at his side. Their breathing deepened together, their spirits relaxing to the same degree, the throbbing grief in Tabris gradually lessening until Rachmiel could absorb it into himself and place it beside his anger in the hands of God. Then, two angels bereft of their separate pains, they remained before an all-seeing Father who extended His comfort to them.

Tabris closed his heart when Rachmiel embraced that comfort, and the guardian wanted to pry him open until God stopped him. While he met God in a quiet room in his heart, Tabris left Him standing by the front gate.

The Lord put reassurance into Rachmiel and sleep into Tabris, so that when the orange-winged guardian stood, Tabris lay unconscious and limp on the bed.

Numbed, he leaned against the wall, blinking rapidly until Connie entered the room carrying Elizabeth. She was accompanied by Hadriel and one of Rachmiel's friends. The friend looked at Tabris with mixed fascination and eagerness, and Rachmiel realized wearily that every guardian in the world would receive a full report before sunrise tomorrow.

"You can go," Rachmiel told him. Hadriel was watching Tabris with the same interest and revulsion, but neither he nor Rachmiel nonverbalized or intoned anything about the sleeping angel. Elizabeth's mother was putting the child to bed, telling her to sleep for a while. There were fresh bandages on her forehead and knees. She lay in bed for a few minutes after Connie left, and then Rachmiel put her to sleep.

Hadriel had remained. "Guard the room. Josai'el wants to talk to you."

They went up to the roof, the bright structure of Josai'el's Guard glimmering in the sunlight over the whole of the house, ready to repel any demons who might try to take advantage of this meeting time.

All were assembled—the whole household except for Tabris. Hadriel bowed to Josai'el, nonverbalizing that Tabris was sleeping.

"He and Elizabeth both?" asked Katra'il.

Rachmiel nodded, his eyes heavily purple.

Josai'el gestured that Rachmiel should sit, and he took a spot on the ridgepole. His eyes had not yet stopped traveling from face to face.

"What exactly happened?" asked Voriah.

"He let Elizabeth get hurt," Rachmiel said. "I got angry. That's all." He looked away. "I don't want to discuss it. It's too close. I'm sorry."

Within a day or so the household would know the complete story anyway, not from him but certainly by word of mouth: from Rachmiel's visit with Sebastian to what Tabris had revealed about the bicycle. He knew they would learn, and at the moment he had no desire to teach.

Voriah's eyes had paled to the color of shallow water.

"I'll be all right," Rachmiel said. He returned to Elizabeth's room where the girl dozed fitfully beside Tabris. Putting her into a deeper stage of sleep, Rachmiel noted with appreciation how Elizabeth and Tabris had cuddled against one another, as though they were consoling each other for a common loss.

Well, he thought, *in a way that happened. Tabris lost his son, and she lost*—Rachmiel paused—*her husband?*

He staggered to his knees and gaped at the pair, souls perfectly fit into one another for their differences in the way he and she were bound through their similarities. Sebastian and she would have met somehow, probably in college, and married. Ten years down the road, Elizabeth would have been embraced by the charge, not the guardian, and Tabris and Rachmiel would have met on neutral ground, on easier terms.

Does Tabris know? he wondered, and God answered no to his unprayed prayer—Tabris had no idea. He thought he was with the family because they were such a strong unit.

In fifteen years, probably, Elizabeth would be held in another man's arms, and she would tell him she believed that they had been made for one another before all time. The man would run his hands through the waves of her hair and assure her that God always had wanted them together.

What about the children? Rachmiel wondered. If Elizabeth and Sebastian were supposed to have children, would she still be able to have them? Could the father be so easily substituted? Or would she perforce be infertile?

God calmed Rachmiel's heart. He explained that His plan was not a projection into the future, not a long list of occurrences that might or might not take place with a single goal at its end. Rather, God had designed a dynamic scheme with a general destination: not a script with words written in advance for hired mouths so much as what goes on in a kindergarten class when children play house. Elizabeth could still have children. Tabris had altered the Divine plan—he had not destroyed it.

Rachmiel looked at Elizabeth and Tabris, both sleeping to escape their wounds, although sleep could never heal an angel since injuries are inflicted on their souls and healing requires a conscious act of the will.

He moved closer and touched Elizabeth's cheek—she was so young and already robbed of a husband. He saw how well her soul meshed with Tabris'—no mere coincidence any longer in Rachmiel's mind—and he realized how many people had been hurt. Chiefly Sebastian but also Elizabeth and her unconceived children, the boy's parents, his friends. Rachmiel's sunset-colored eyes flickered to Tabris again, and around his heart he could feel anger coiled like tight wire, straining him with its magnitude, and the disgust Rachmiel was feeling began radiating from his body in little rings. In her sleep, Elizabeth moved.

"He widowed you, and then he injured you as well," Rachmiel said. "He doesn't deserve—"

He caught himself then.

God blossomed like a flower in Rachmiel's heart. *I love him,* God said, and Rachmiel curled up by the bedside with a small cry, the coo of a wounded bird. "I'm sorry," he said, feeling the remorse acutely in his heart and needing the words to ease the pressure. "I'm so sorry. I need your help."

Rachmiel opened his angry heart to God, who gave him a new understanding of Tabris, a renewed compassion, a fresh spirit, a glance that gave him a small view into the angel's heart before closing the door.

Rachmiel's eyes bugged, then he said "Let me see more!"

"That's for Tabris to do," said God.

Rachmiel tried to hold in his mind the intricate curves, the dark twists of a conscience that had opened itself and then found to its horror that it had lost the most important thing it could—the second, actually. It only *thought* it had lost the Most Important.

Rachmiel suddenly realized that he and God were in the same position, knocking at the outer gate of Tabris' heart while the inhabitant remained inside, huddled in the back of his closet. While God could see through the barriers, however, Rachmiel could not. He had seen the reclusive figure inside only once, a momentary glimpse this afternoon when he had emerged, showed his wounds, and then retreated.

Rachmiel climbed onto the bed, keeping one hand on Elizabeth while touching Tabris with the other. "God, he's so fascinating. He looks peaceful now, but it's only the relaxation of his guard. Before he wakes he'll get tense again."

"Work with me," said God.

"I'll try." Rachmiel sighed. "But how can I love someone the way you do? Sometimes I look at him and all I can remember is that he murdered someone completely at his mercy."

God touched Rachmiel's heart, not to force him to love but to remind him that He could reach inside.

"Will you help me to say what I should?" Rachmiel asked.

"Of course," said God, filling him momentarily with His Spirit. "I made you—let me play you."

"Always." Rachmiel leaned forward and touched Elizabeth's hair. "Thank you for her."

"Thank you for you."

Rachmiel smiled, his heart linked to God like a child who finally catches the sunbeam he has been trying to grasp all afternoon. He felt his soul warm in that uncreated light, and he continued watching the two sleeping souls.

15

ELIZABETH WOKE LATER THAT DAY, A LITTLE STIFF in her knees but for the most part recovered from her fall. She stayed inside the house, partly at Rachmiel's unheard request since he felt reluctant to leave Tabris alone. She sat in the slanted rays of the three o'clock sun to read for a short while, but when the pages failed to excite her, she tossed the book onto the bed and walked downstairs to the piano.

Ruffling through the sheet music until she found a piece she knew well—after three years of piano lessons there were a couple—Elizabeth wore a strangely serious look. She set up the pages before sitting at the Steinway upright that both her father and grandmother had used for their own lessons. She played idly with the keys for a few minutes, then practiced six notes of a warm-up before finally losing patience with the routine and unceremoniously beginning the piece.

Chopin had always excited Rachmiel, and his excitement had increased exponentially when Elizabeth had come along and heard the same things he heard in the music. Almost as soon as humans had begun making music, Rachmiel had begun struggling to comprehend this language, the way notes could embody emotions, because angelic music is not like human music. Human music is fraught with struggle, with imitation instead of incarnation. Angels can play notes that are what they represent, whereas humans only can reference common ideas. Each species envies the music of the other for this reason. Chopin had haunted Rachmiel ever since the music first had caught his attention, and during the man's lifetime he had often shadowed him, trying to discover where his store of power came from, where his finesse originated, and toward what he was driving. After the man's death he had asked him, only to find that sometimes the questions are more powerful than their answers, and many artists never know the motivation behind their work.

Elizabeth had not yet heard the great questions, since she was young enough to see in all life only answers. Sin obscures the answers to pain, and as yet she had not obscured her outlook.

She began the piece, making occasional mistakes, but the work became more dear because of she who played it. Rachmiel watched as her heart embraced the notes, ensouled the piano, and her fingers worked the keys automatically except for when she had to repeat the notes she had missed. She turned pages almost without realizing as she played, closing off the exterior thoughts to concentrate, eventually concentrating so hard that she was not thinking about the music at all, just producing it.

Rachmiel fell in love, his heart brimming the way it could only for Elizabeth, always for her. He embraced her, breathing deeply and tumbling into her headfirst so that his spirit resided inside her body, and he allowed his form to move in tandem with hers as though her hands were gloves over his that moved his fingers—and then he too could play Chopin. Pictures sprang to his mind, odd notions, and the love of God exploded like fireworks within him. Innocence was playing the questions that free will had raised, that reckless independence had been unable to answer, but she knew all along where the answers lay. Only Elizabeth could embody the music as she was doing, answering with the easy security of childhood all the irrevocable choices that adults know they have to make and already have made. Rachmiel could share that purity with her. He answered with the same words, the same childish confusion at the claustrophobia of adults when they realize that they have cut off most of their options and have to press forward or else be lost utterly.

Then Rachmiel slipped away into Elizabeth, because as long as she was occupied totally by the music he could release himself to the special guardian-charge bond that linked their souls. They temporarily united, her fingers more secure on the keys while he played. He was more amazed at the wonders of God while she saw the world through the view of a child.

Then Elizabeth stopped playing. He separated before she realized he had ever been inside her heart.

Rachmiel knew why the author of Genesis had said that the sons of God had fallen in love with the daughters of men—there was no sexual attraction there but rather the attraction of the awestriking beauty of an untarnished spirit that accepted God and the world as it was, making no unnecessary demands on either Him or the world or herself. What the union of a guardian angel and his charge would produce would be a courageous heart, a sensible mind, an intense devotion, and above all a saint. Anything else would be redundant.

Elizabeth sorted through the music for a few minutes and then put it away, turning on the television and deadening any contact Rachmiel might have had with her. Although he was disappointed, he sat beside her and tried to share her interest in the moving pictures, but found them flat and stale, almost maddening to his spirit, so after a few minutes he closed his eyes and prayed.

Then God played music in his soul. Not Chopin.

16

CASIFER CAME DURING THE NIGHT TO BRING Rachmiel to Sebastian. Reluctantly, Rachmiel accompanied him to Limbo, only after making certain that Voriah would summon him the instant Tabris or Elizabeth awoke.

Sebastian greeted Rachmiel with a strong hug—the spiritual kind. Rachmiel congratulated him on how fast he had learned.

Smiling, Sebastian reminded Rachmiel of Tabris that one night on the roof. The good feeling fled, though, when he thought of the angel lying face down on Elizabeth's bed, cuddled protectively around the child. He remembered when she had climbed into bed for the second time that day, at nine o'clock, and Tabris had reached for her in his sleep, touching his head to hers and laying one wing over her small sleeping body.

"You're not pleased?" Sebastian asked.

"I am—you remind me so much of your guardian."

Sebastian's face tightened as he finally placed the unhappiness that had shadowed Rachmiel the way smog clung to Los Angeles. "If I'm upsetting you, you can go."

"I'll have to go soon anyway—Elizabeth is going to wake up, and I want to be there."

His smile must have been contagious, because it was reflected in both Casifer and Sebastian.

"I know you think it's cute," Rachmiel said lowly. "So does he."

Casifer laughed. "I wake up Sebastian when he sleeps—you didn't know that, did you kid?"

"No."

"He has to sleep?" Rachmiel asked.

"For now, yes, but not on a regular basis. He's still growing."

"I sleep less the longer I'm here," Sebastian said. "In Heaven, I suppose I won't need to sleep at all."

Rachmiel remembered Tabris.

Casifer's heart jumped, nonverbalizing concern. Sebastian caught the feeling, but he had not felt Rachmiel's momentary flash of worry, and so remained silent while Rachmiel compacted the whole incident into one pellet of information and sent the whole emotional dart to Casifer.

Casifer turned to Sebastian. "You were on your bicycle when it happened?"

The child nodded.

"I should have trusted his concern," Rachmiel said.

"You had no idea." Casifer frowned then, his eyes darkening.

Rachmiel nonverbalized reassurance as best he could, and added that God was watching Tabris now.

"If my guardian needs you," Sebastian said, "maybe you should return."

Rachmiel nodded, his eyes darker than sunset, closer to dusk. "I would like to stay," he said. "I'm sorry."

"It's all right."

"When angels sleep," said Casifer, "it's an indication of trauma—it's always for spiritual recovery, as a last-ditch means of saving oneself from a complete emotional breakdown."

"It just postpones the problem," Rachmiel said. "Angels don't dream, so we wake up in the same condition in which we went to sleep. Humans sometimes sleep and feel better, but if an angel falls asleep angry he wakes up angry."

Sebastian nodded. "How will my guardian wake up?"

"Probably sad," Rachmiel said. "But sometimes, now especially, I feel I don't know him very well."

Tabris awoke instantly, his sword in his hand and his ears straining after what he just had heard.

"Tabris," came the hiss again.

"Irony, I'll destroy you."

"I have a new name now. You can call me—"

"I'll call you Condemned-by-God," he gasped, standing, arcing his sword around the room. "Go away. Leave me!"

"Please," said the voice, and Tabris realized it came from no single source—as though the walls and the carpet were speaking. "Come with me. What use is this family, that little anchor? She has another angel to take care of her, one who is actually capable of loving her. Come with me."

"No. This is where I belong."

"You belong with Sebastian," said the walls, but the carpet responded, "even though Sebastian hates you."

"I've been transferred."

"At Sebastian's request. I was at the trial."

"Then allow me to correct you. I was there too. Sebastian made no request of the sort."

"It was internal," said the desk.

"Then how do you know?"

"The boy told me himself when I visited."

Tabris screamed, flinging himself into a corner and slicing with his sword until the tip met with resistance and dragged the demon into the open.

"You'll leave him alone!" Tabris said, his eyes black, his face utterly tense, his teeth locked and gleaming in the night. He pulled the demon by his neck so their faces were inches apart and the demon's breath brushed his lips like the last humid breeze before a summer storm. "You'll leave the both of them alone!"

"So will you soon! Rachmiel's with Sebastian right now, gathering ammunition, collecting evidence—"

"Shut up!"

The demon kept babbling despite the wild look in his eyes, or perhaps because of that. "They talk about you—why do you think Rachmiel didn't tell you about his visit?"

"I didn't ask," Tabris growled, still gripping the demon by the throat but relaxing his hold somewhat.

"That's playing right into his desires. He wants that and makes you think he's reluctant to probe the wounds. Could he really keep it secret if that wasn't what he wanted?" The demon gasped for air and Tabris loosened his hold some more. "He's afraid you'll discover. Sebastian hates you, you know. Your Tyrant wanted to arrange a meeting and have some sticky-sweet forgiveness scene, but Sebastian's mad and he made Rachmiel mad too. They're conspiring now. Sebastian's asking that you be retried. That's why your bond to Elizabeth is looser. Rachmiel wants you to be able to leave at any moment with no shock to the girl."

Tabris glowered. "You're lying."

"I'll go on. Raguel heard Rachmiel's complaint, and he's watching you closely. He showed up to see what had happened when you knocked Elizabeth off her bicycle—"

"I believe that was you, dear."

"—and he saw how angry Rachmiel had gotten, so he went home to reconsider the wisdom of placing you with a girl so close in age to Sebastian. They say it's dangerous, that when she begins to sin constantly you'll punish her with one hug too many, the way you did Sebastian. Raguel's investigating a new bond, one with an adult who's already got one foot in Satan's doorway, and you'll be transferred if you make one more false step."

Tabris smiled.

"It's my duty to warn you. Tabris, I'm the only one you have left!"

"You're lying. You're only friends with yourself, and I have God. Even if every other angel in creation conspired against me, even if Sebastian condemns me in effigy every night before he goes to bed, I still have God." He smiled tightly. "No one can take away that consolation."

They looked one another in the eyes for about ten seconds before the demon cracked up. "You're good. You almost convinced me there, but you've never believed that. If you had then you'd send me away when I come, but you want me around. When two liars get together and know they're lying it's an awful lot like truth, and you need that reality. I realize what you're doing. You're covering all the bases, but God doesn't share. He never would—I should know. He'll settle for nothing less than subsuming your whole will. Rachmiel's happy doing that, he's happier not having to think, but you—you can't let Him drown you that way even though once you thought that was best. It'd be untrue to your nature, to your name—Free Will."

Tabris breathed deeply.

"I wasn't lying," said the demon. "Rachmiel was mad. Sebastian can't forgive you. Raguel's been investigating the case. And Rachmiel has asked that you be transferred because he can't guard you *and* Elizabeth."

"But you're a liar. I can't trust anything you say."

"I say enough that you know is true that you can trust me for the parts you don't—and if you were damned for believing a lie you know it wouldn't hold."

Tabris glared darkly.

"Look, you're chained now, a bird with its feathers clipped. Come with me, be like me. I'm Unbridled. Now my name is Windswept. You can truly be Free Will, if only you'll come."

Tabris closed his eyes. "No, I won't."

"But Free Will—"

"I'm exercising it now, by refusing you. I chose once—*irrevocably*. You're not God to me, you're not that special to me, not half so awesome or breathtaking. You don't have the power to make me gasp with the radiance of infinity."

"But if the only reason you love God is for the things He gives, then give up now. That isn't enough for Him. He's insatiable. He'll want you to love Him for what He is, not for His marvelous deeds."

Tabris smiled in perfect symmetry. "The way He loves me?"

"I wouldn't say that—He claims He loves the essence of His children and not their deeds, but I know better. I was condemned for the things I did."

"But you used your actions to corrupt your essence."

"And you didn't? You murdered a child. All I did was refuse to bow."

Tabris turned aside. "I don't know—there's a difference somewhere, in the heart I think. You wanted separation. I wanted . . ."

For the next moment they both stayed quiet. Tabris shook his head fiercely, letting go of the demon and looking at Elizabeth.

"What did you want?"

"I don't know."

"Did you get it?" Windswept chuckled in sing-song. "Be careful what you ask for . . ."

"Be quiet. Go away."

When Tabris said that he felt the spiritual emptiness of the room minus one demon. Windswept had taken his hatred of God with him. Elizabeth had grown restive, and Tabris watched her sullenly. "Go back to sleep, little lady. It's four A.M."

Suddenly he looked around for Rachmiel.

Tabris spread his wings and flew to the roof, but Rachmiel was not sitting on the ridgepole to take a head count of the stars or find God's name on the clouds that drifted high overhead. The zephyrs heralding spring called to Tabris, cool and welcoming to his hot heart, but he folded his wings and dropped down again through the roof, through Elizabeth's room, into the living room.

Hadriel and Katra'il looked at Tabris when he alighted. "How are you?" asked Hadriel's eyes.

"Awake. Where's Rachmiel?"

Hadriel and Katra'il shrugged, and Tabris flashed to Voriah in Alan's room.

"Tab!" he exclaimed. "You're awake!"

"For a while now. Where's Rachmiel?"

"With Sebastian. I'm sorry I didn't realize you'd gotten up. I was supposed to call him when either you or Elizabeth did, but Alan was having frightening dreams and I felt I ought to stay with him."

"That's fine," Tabris said. "Alan should come first—hopefully I can take care of myself." He smiled his amazingly balanced smile. "You don't have to call him. I'll watch Elizabeth until he returns."

Tabris reappeared in her room, then paused and set a Guard on the walls, layering them with his will to repulse Windswept if he were to return, as well as any angel who wanted only to talk to him.

Sitting on the edge of the bed, he looked down at his hands. "I've forgotten how to do this. Help me?"

For a moment he thought about Christians returning to their churches after long absences: wondering which shoulder to touch first in the sign of the cross, which pages to turn to in the hymnal, and then realizing as they looked around the pews that no one cared, least of all God. They had come home—no one would complain about the muddy shoes on the front hall carpet.

"Please," Tabris whispered, "help me," and he struggled to open the locks on his heart, very aware of the distance between God and him. The tension built in his heart for several minutes, and finally he stopped in frustration.

The instant he slackened his concentration, Christ appeared. Tabris flung himself to the floor, prostrated.

"Tabris," Jesus said, standing amidst the clutter of Elizabeth's room, "Tabris, don't be afraid."

"But how can I? Please, please," he gasped, "don't force me. I'm not ready."

"I am, though," Jesus said. "Call me. I'm waiting for you."

Tabris shivered uncontrollably, afraid to look up even after Jesus had gone. His whole form shook with cold that penetrated his spirit, his bones, his fingers. It hurt him and made tears spring to his eyes.

Josai'el called to him from the other side of the Guarded wall.

To deny he needed help would have been pointless, as well as a lie, but Tabris wanted no part of the sympathy Josai'el would give. Only reluctantly did he let down the Guard and allow all the household angels inside, except for the conspicuously missing Rachmiel. Josai'el held him while he sat upright, and Hadriel, Mithra, and Miriael joined her. From the living room Katra'il cast a Guard about the whole house, and Voriah went to find Rachmiel.

"He's still weak," Miriael said. "There was a demon in here recently—I can feel the stain. The rest of you go, I'll take care of him."

"The presence of the Lord was here too," said Hadriel.

"Probably a battle," said Miriael. "The rest of you should go."

Rachmiel arrived just then with Voriah and he forced everyone out, including Miriael. He helped Tabris to stand, and when the two-toned angel had his balance, he let him stand on his own.

"You were attacked?"

"That was what woke me up before you returned. My demon friend. He attacked Alan first to keep Voriah from coming."

Rachmiel nodded, recognizing a typical pattern of demonic attack. "Are you going to hold together?"

"I suppose."

Rachmiel nodded, the resolution shimmering off his skin not to pry for details.

Tabris looked away. "You were with Sebastian?"

Rachmiel nodded.

"You don't tell me about him."

Rachmiel's eyes popped, and he nonverbalized that he was complying with what Tabris wanted.

"Or were you hoping I wouldn't ask?"

"What would you like to know?"

Tabris laughed tightly, as though he were on a stage acting. "I can't ask that. But what do you think of him?"

Rachmiel's smile deepened into his face, as though he were delighted even with memories and was glad for the chance to share them. "In some ways, he's exactly like you."

"Which ways?"

"Oh, his eyes for the most part. They're exactly like yours: dark, quick, mysterious. And his face is very similar, very much under control. He laughs just the way you do. Well, the way you did that night on the rooftop."

Tabris walked to the window and looked outside at the moon-dusted new grass. "What about his hair?"

"It's dark like yours."

"And his hands?"

"Small."

Tabris flashed in front of Elizabeth's mirror, then concentrated so that he reflected.

"Tabris!" Rachmiel exclaimed. "What are you doing?"

"She's asleep," he said, visible for once in both the human and angelic planes of existence. "She won't see me."

Rachmiel had his hands over her blue eyes, staring at Tabris even as Tabris scrutinized himself before the mirror. "My eyes," he mused, studying his own face, looking into the mirror closely. "And my facial expression. But dark eyes like mine?"

Rachmiel's own eyes had grown as round as tea saucers. "Yes."

Tabris laughed, a dry sound that slipped into Rachmiel's soul like a machete. "Well, he's just like me—our souls are alike. Of course we'd be the same after he died. I should have known. I should have realized."

"Tabris?"

"He hates me."

"I—I didn't—"

"You don't need to ask him, I've explained it. He doesn't want to know about me because then God will force the issue and make him forgive me. He wanted me to meet the boy for that reason, didn't He?"

Rachmiel nodded quietly.

Tabris shook his head, looking again into the glass. "My eyes. So he looks just like me." He chuckled. "I suppose I deserved that much."

"What? Tabris, please don't play like this. Talk to me."

Tabris made himself invisible again, no longer reflecting from the mirror, reflecting only from Rachmiel's pink-tinged eyes as he met his gaze. "It's all right, Rock. You're okay. Stay strong. Keep visiting him. Just don't talk to me about it."

Rachmiel nodded.

"I don't want you to tell me the things he says," Tabris said. "I don't want it because I'm afraid to hear the truth and you shouldn't have to lie. I couldn't deal with it if you lied to me."

"I'd never lie to you," said Rachmiel.

Tabris shook his head.

"Tabris, when did I lie to you?" The guardian's eyes had flushed crimson, trembling. "Tell me!"

"Not now. I'm shaking." He looked aside. "Please, let me go."

Rachmiel nodded quickly, and Tabris vanished.

17

TABRIS FLOATED ON THE PERIPHERIES OF HOUSE-
hold life for the next few days, not staying for long in any
one room or with any one angel, saying nothing and
becoming more than ever what the others called an emotional void. He communicated with no one, except for
one night when he sparred with Miriael for the full nine
hours Elizabeth slept. They had traveled to the tundra of
the Arctic for the match, and the slippery terrain provided a new twist to the play.

Both had taken wounds nine hours into the match,
but no single one great enough to make a victory. They
each had shortened their swords, and Miriael had called
a knife to his free left hand.

When they grappled in close for a moment, Tabris
suddenly found the knife in his hand, slashed at Miriael's
throat—and missed.

Miriael's eyes flashed angrily, and he threw Tabris to
the ground, flinging his sword away into the snow. "What
is this—are you playing to win or not?"

"I am," Tabris said, sitting up and gasping out a
white cloud. "I was—I don't know." He leaned forward,
dropping his head down between his knees. "I'm sorry. I
tried. But I couldn't."

Miriael sat facing Tabris, still angry but forcing himself to listen. "I'm sorry," Tabris said, breathing deeply to
clear his mind and begin making sense. "I could have
won, but I flinched. I couldn't slit your throat."

"Because you broke Sebastian's neck?"

Tabris nodded.

They sat quietly. Tabris looked up with a smile that inhabited the right side of his mouth more than the left. "You're very direct."

Miriael grinned hugely, kicking a little snow in Tabris' direction as though to say that straightforward-ness cut through a number of difficulties. "You're not offended by that, are you?"

"No. You know anyway." Tabris lay backward so that the snow rose up on all sides like a wall. "It's so odd, feeling that my darkest secrets are known everywhere."

Miriael frowned.

From where he lay looking up at the sky Tabris could not see Miriael, but he had felt the negation. "What about me don't you know?"

"Your whole psyche. You're difficult to understand. You worry Rachmiel."

"I know. But he's gotten a lot less curious lately."

Miriael's eyes flashed.

"Or else more controlled, you're right. The effect is the same, at any rate."

Tabris sighed. "Let's just wait here until they wake up at home. I don't want to return yet."

Casifer came to Rachmiel when Tabris began his match with Miriael. He bowed, his heart commending the guardian to God. "God said you were alone," he said. "Sebastian wants to see Elizabeth."

Rachmiel smiled. "Please, by all means." Then he paused, thinking about how Sebastian and Elizabeth should have been married, but God assured him that the visit was a good idea.

Casifer left and returned with Sebastian, who looked around open-mouthed at the room. "Wow! This is great. I haven't been back to the world at all before now, seri-ously."

"I'm sorry your first visit to earth has to be a mess," Rachmiel said, indicating the small pile of clothing on the floor and the books scattered everywhere. "I'd have inspired her to clean if I had known you were coming."

"It's no problem," Sebastian said. "Is this Elizabeth?" He walked closer to the little girl in the bed. "She's adorable, Rock. No wonder you love her."

"Come here," Rachmiel said. Putting his hands over Sebastian's eyes and concentrating, he showed the boy her soul as he saw it—a pastel swirl of grace and mercy, of compassion and powerful love, quiet understanding and untainted faith. Innocent as only a ten-year-old girl can be innocent.

Sebastian whistled. "Are all our souls like that to you?"

"Everyone is different," Casifer said. "Your soul would have sharper colors, more contrast, but yes, without sin you're all that beautiful."

Just then Voriah entered the room and startled visibly. Abruptly the rest of the household had crammed into the bedroom.

"Sebastian?" said Josai'el.

"Hello," said the boy, a little bit startled but good natured about being the center of attention. "I'm here to meet Elizabeth."

Voriah gave him the spiritual equivalent of a handshake, a milder form of a hug. "Glad you could come. Rock, he looks just like Tabris!"

"Tabris?" said Sebastian.

"That's your guardian's name," said Casifer.

"I like the sound," Sebastian said, then looked back to Elizabeth. "She's remarkably innocent for a ten year old."

"You were quite innocent until you were twelve," said Casifer.

Voriah had excused himself, and Rachmiel felt his throat a bit tighter than he liked. "Have you visited your parents yet, Sebastian?"

"No. This is my first trip down."

"Let's go for a while."

Casifer looked concerned. "That might be painful. It's three hours earlier there. They might not be sleeping yet."

"I'll be all right," Sebastian said. "Please, I don't know when I'll be down again."

"You can stay out all night." Casifer nodded as though he were forming the idea even as he spoke. "Let's visit a few other places first."

"Rachmiel, you come with us," Sebastian said. "And your friend too, the one who told me my guardian's name."

Rachmiel looked to the head of the household.

"I'll watch Elizabeth and Alan," Josai'el said.

Rachmiel smiled. "I'll get Voriah and we'll catch up to you."

Sebastian and Casifer vanished, and Rachmiel went to Alan's room.

"I made a big mistake?" said Voriah.

"You mean the name? I guess so." Rachmiel sighed. "He'd have learned it soon enough anyway. They've invited us to go on a mini world tour. Josai'el said she'd watch the kids."

Voriah nodded, and they flashed to meet Casifer and Sebastian, landing on the top of the Statue of Liberty in New York Harbor.

"You're joking," Voriah said. "All the world to visit and you chose New York?"

"I've never been here," Sebastian said. "Where would you suggest?"

"Australia. It's as far from New York as you can get and not have to float."

"We could go underwater, though," Sebastian said. "Let's do that. Let's go under the ice floes in Antarctica."

"No," Rachmiel said. "Let's not."

"Antarctica is a continent," Casifer said. "It isn't floating. You can't swim under it."

"We could try the Arctic circle," Voriah said. "That would be interesting, and it's just as cold."

"Would it be too cold, though?" Sebastian grimaced. "I want to see some fish if we go underwater."

Casifer volunteered to share a place he knew well, and they flashed from Miss Liberty's shoulder to a coral reef on the bottom of the Pacific. At first it was a frightening experience for Sebastian until he became used to not needing to breathe. He met several species of fish that no living human had cataloged. Multitudes of watery life swam directly toward the three angels and the premature saint, seeking God in the dark waters, sensing His presence but failing to find it. The lightless currents flowed through the foursome, who expanded their other senses to compensate for blindness. Something like sonar filled them, an instinctive understanding of the location of everything that lived and moved in the small radius around them. They appreciated God's presence among them, pointing out with silent understanding how God had filled the oceans so much more than the land.

When Sebastian indicated that he wanted to leave they flashed to the cliffs in Washington State overlooking the Pacific. The dark horizon offset them as they glowed softly at the edge of a sheer drop which plummeted to a small strip of rocky beach caressed regularly by the waves. Overhead the stars glittered. Already dry, they smiled at each other and projected their own wonderment and inner peace.

Voriah suddenly chuckled. "I'll bet Elizabeth dreams of fish."

"Swordfish," said Rachmiel with a light laugh. "Look at the moon. This place is so majestic, with the sky so clear and those sitka spruces towering upward like the slats of a picket fence. This is just the most amazing world."

Sebastian breathed deeply. "Isn't it, though? I'm sorry I left it so soon. There were so many places I could have gone, so much I never did. I'd have climbed mountains and gone deep sea diving for real. Now I'll have to wait until afterward, when this earth is destroyed and the new one created, but I don't think it can be the same."

"It couldn't be that much different," said Voriah. "Probably, it'll be even better."

"I would have been able to decide for myself if I'd done them here first."

Sebastian leaned against Casifer, suddenly looking very much like the adolescent boy he was and not like a reduction of Tabris. "I'm sorry, I'm talking against your friend."

"It's the way you feel," Rachmiel said. "No one said Tabris was justified. In fact, neither did he."

Sebastian looked at Voriah and Rachmiel with tears in his eyes, but Casifer could not see them the way Sebastian was standing, and the boy managed to keep them out of his voice. "Maybe I'm being evil, but I haven't forgiven him yet. I'm still angry at times."

"It's all right to have those feelings," Rachmiel said. "You've been wounded. Feeling angry isn't wrong. Now that you recognize your anger, though, you're pretty much bound to work at forgiving him."

Sebastian nodded sullenly, agreeing that he ought to do the work even though he clearly did not really want to succeed.

"Pray," said Voriah. "Pray for the grace to want to forgive him, and if that's not easy then pray to want to want to forgive. God will take over if you let Him. I'll even pray with you."

Sebastian's eyes brightened. "You would? Could you pray with me now?"

Casifer sat and guided Sebastian down so that he was sitting in his lap. Rachmiel and Voriah joined them on the rocks while Casifer locked his arms around Sebastian's waist, becoming an angelic seatbelt. Casifer opened his heart and joined with the other two angels so that their souls formed a triangle, a strong fortress of grace around Sebastian that would focus his prayer and enable him to open his heart as well.

"Don't expect immediate solutions," Voriah was saying softly. "Just open your heart and invite God inside. Once He's in, He'll make whatever alterations He wants."

Sebastian breathed deeply and then closed his eyes to make a conscious invitation to God, one all the angels could feel, but they also knew he had kept his heart locked tight.

"You're trying too hard," Voriah said in a low tone designed to guide without startling. "Relax. Trust Him. He's not going to hurt you. He made you."

Casifer had let go and was rubbing Sebastian's shoulders while Rachmiel opened his own heart to the Lord to show by example.

"Relax," said Voriah.

"I'm trying, Coach, but it's tough."

"Then let's stop. There's no need to rush."

Rachmiel felt God run out of his heart like water flowing back to the sea from a rocky New England shore.

Sebastian sagged limply against Casifer. "Why is it so difficult to pray? As a kid I prayed all the time."

"This is different," Casifer said, rubbing Sebastian's hair in a slow and rhythmical circle. "You're not just asking God for a favor—you're asking that He actually enter your heart and see every part of your soul from the inside, as clearly as you see it and not as ready to accept excuses. Worse, you're asking Him in to see a flaw, and you're afraid. Maybe you don't want to forgive Tabris yet. Keep trying, though. God will come in as soon as you let Him."

For a long time they stayed on the cliff, Sebastian eventually lying on his stomach, his cheek against the grass that had managed to find a foothold in the seemingly solid rock and grow despite constant wind and scarce nourishment. He listened idly while the angels talked about a few different topics, all of which interested him and would have been even more interesting if he had understood more, and he lay drowsily until he asked the time and discovered that it was late enough that his parents would be sleeping. Casifer flashed to Los Angeles and back and told them it was time.

The four arrived in a dark bedroom, and Rachmiel suddenly found himself fighting his lungs to continue breathing air that was dense with pollutants. After a moment he had recovered, though, and was able to look around and distinguish the square shapes of the furniture, the bed, and the couple cuddled against one another beneath the blanket.

"Hi, Mom," Sebastian said. "Hi, Dad."

The two guardians of Sebastian's parents greeted him instantly, then said hello to the angels accompanying him. Reintroductions were made, and a few nonverbalisms explained what each was doing nowadays.

"How is Tabris?" asked Sariel, the angel who guarded Sebastian's mother. She smiled with concern and curiosity, raking her hand through the short blond waves of her hair. "He's never visited."

"He's surviving," Rachmiel said. "Until a short while ago he wasn't permitted to exceed five miles or else he'd probably have come, but I think he's happy with us."

Voriah was smiling. "Doesn't Sebastian resemble him?"

Right now, Rachmiel thought, when he's staring at his parents as though the five of us were long gone, he really does.

Sariel had squinted, and now shook her head.

"It's almost exact!" Voriah exclaimed.

Sariel looked at the father's guardian, who squinted and shook her head herself. "Not at all. There's a slight similarity, but not as close as some I've seen."

Voriah communicated confusion, as though doubting his own sanity.

Casifer nodded, also uncertain. "Rachmiel said Sebastian's eyes were exactly like Tabris'."

Sebastian had not yet registered the discussion taking place among the angels, most of it nonverbal anyway, and he moved a little closer to the edge of the bed. Casifer touched him with a wing tip, and Sebastian clutched tightly at the white feathers.

Sariel shook her head. "I was with him for thirteen years—we were even merged for the nine months of the pregnancy."

Rachmiel was looking at Sebastian carefully, and the other angels turned their eyes to him too. As though suddenly aware of their attention, Sebastian looked up from where he had knelt to touch his mother's face and smiled hesitantly. "How is she?"

"Doing better," Sariel said. "It's taking her a while, but she's recovering slowly. She started going to work again last month."

Sebastian nodded then kissed her cheek gently, as if he were brushing her skin with a rose petal. Sariel smiled softly, her mouth and eyes speaking simultaneously about euphoric gladness—Sebastian was saved—and the most heartrending grief a mother can feel, holding the lifeless body of her son against her heart and rocking him back and forth, crying into his limp hair and speaking to him as though everything could "be all right" when no, it would not. Sariel's heart projected a memory she could not control of a husband and wife sitting together on the couch, his arm around her, trying together to comprehend a completely senseless loss.

Sebastian walked around the bed to his father. "And Dad—how is he?"

"It hit him hard," said the other guardian, "and he still comes across daydreams he hasn't removed you from yet, and then he has to realize all over again that you won't be there."

Sebastian nodded, his mouth tightening.

Casifer nonverbalized sudden concern, and then both he and Sebastian were gone.

Rachmiel stayed still for a moment, and then met Sariel's eyes. "Thank you for visiting with us. I think it meant a lot to Sebastian."

"Let me come back with you," Sariel said, her eyes bright. "I'd like to see Tabris again."

Rachmiel brought them back to Elizabeth's room, but Tabris had not yet returned. "Where is he, Josai'el?" he asked, and suddenly he knew: still in Antarctica with Miriael. "Shall we visit there?" he asked Sariel as Voriah returned to Alan.

She assented, and the next instant they found themselves dusted with snow, about as far north as they could go without going south again. Bright whiteness surrounded them and made them squint until their eyes adjusted after so long in the dark.

"Tabris!" Sariel exclaimed, seeing him seated beside Miriael.

"Sariel?" he asked her, flashing to her and hugging her—more with his arms than with his soul. "I'm glad to see you again. How are you? How's the family?"

"They're all right. I'm fine. Rachmiel says he's taking excellent care of you," she said with a laugh like music. "I'm glad. I saw Elizabeth and she's just the sweetest little girl, and I met Voriah. You're in with a really solid household. How are you? You're looking strong."

Tabris smiled slightly, looking over his battle armor and his short sword by his side. Rachmiel startled to realize that this time the smile was genuine, and he wondered how often Tabris had smiled and fooled him into thinking he meant it. "I've been sparring," Tabris said softly. "This is Miriael, who guards Elizabeth's brother."

"The warrior type?" Sariel asked, her eyes flashing brilliantly. "You like to mock fight? We never did."

Not mock fighting, said Miriael's eyes. *This is to the death.* "Tabris won last the match."

Sariel hit Tabris lightly on the shoulder. "Take it easy on him, hot shot, you understand? We can't have you brutalizing your housemates. They might be valuable someday."

Tabris laughed, but Rachmiel could tell his eyes had darkened.

Sariel chattered aimlessly; Rachmiel found himself wondering if Tabris had gotten a word in edgewise during the entire twelve years he had been with her, how he had reacted to the temporary merger of their spirits during gestation, and if he had attempted to ask for help when Sebastian had become a difficulty to him.

"So you're doing all right?" Sariel asked. "I'm really glad. I've got to get going, to be with Ellen when she wakes up. I'll let you continue sparring with Miriael. Come on Rachmiel," and then they stood in a darkened bedroom in a Los Angeles suburb.

"Sariel?" asked the other guardian.

"I—I can't—" Sariel collapsed against Rachmiel, and the other angel rushed forward. "Tabris is so—he's different. I just looked at him and I knew, so I chattered at him. I was afraid that if I even stopped talking I would start *radiating* sadness. He's changed. He looks just like Sebastian does, they were right. Dark eyed, dark haired, face all tense, I couldn't believe it." Sariel closed her eyes as if she could wipe the memory from her mind, and Rachmiel squeezed her tightly while she poured all her pain into his waiting heart. "He was so different."

The other angel guided her to the bed and let her sit, holding one hand while Rachmiel took the other and touched her with his wings. "You must have been shocked," she said to Sariel.

Sariel shuddered.

"What did he look like before November?" Rachmiel asked, his eyes large and purple. "I've never seen him any other way."

The other angel responded for Sariel. "His eyes were bright, hazel actually, fading to green on the edges just like his wings. His hair was almost blond but it never quite got that light. The wings were a bright emerald green on the outside and a brown like rich honey on the inside. He laughed often, and his face was somewhat more relaxed than Sebastian's was today. He always had a stiffness to his bearing, as though he were a perfectionist about things like posture and movement, and he liked to watch a lot. He watched more than he acted, I guess. He was never particularly verbose, but when he was upset he would speak less."

"The opposite of me," Sariel murmured, and the other angel gave her a side hug. "He's all changed now. His eyes aren't his own—they're dark, darker than chestnut, almost black I'd say. Even his feathers seemed to have darkened, but I'm not sure if it was that or the general drabness about his whole spirit. He was wearing battle armor."

The other angel startled.

"That was my reaction too," Sariel said. "And his hair was a bit darker, or at least it didn't reflect the sunlight. He avoided my eyes a lot, but it might have been that he could tell I was upset."

Rachmiel had begun shimmering with self-disgust. "I told him Sebastian resembled him exactly, and I had no idea why he got upset."

"Hair, eyes, you pointed out those?" said the father's guardian. "I'll bet he got upset. He probably said nothing, right, and nonverbalized a whole lot."

"He said a lot," Rachmiel said. "There was nothing nonverbal."

"I don't think he nonverbalized even once," Sariel told her.

"That's odd," she said. "Even when he wasn't speaking, and that was most of the time, he was nonverbalizing in a steady stream."

"He's had a difficult time," Rachmiel said. When Sariel shook her head quickly, he ran his tongue over his teeth and then asked, "How was he as a guardian?"

The father's guardian whistled. "He was really good," Sariel added. "He kept the boy very well shielded all the time, and Sebastian stayed practically sinless until he was twelve. Then one day something happened, and Tabris became very grim. He stopped talking. We assured him that it happens to all children, that it wasn't his fault because the child had free will. Sebastian turned back to God after a day or two, but Tabris stayed quiet and sullen. No one could entice him to talk, and then one day he killed the boy."

Rachmiel looked down.

"It's very sad," the other angel agreed. "The changes you described, they're not good. He needs some sort of help."

Rachmiel volunteered nonverbally.

"Will he talk to you at all?" asked Sariel. "He's probably very particular about his confidants. What about that angel he sparred with—Miriael? Will he talk to him?"

Rachmiel shrugged.

"Only God knows what sort of outlet he has," said the third angel, her brown eyes dimming. "Maybe God put him with you because you're a good match. Probably it'll be you he trusts most—if only for Elizabeth's sake since her two guardians shouldn't be at odds."

Rachmiel looked aside, his wings shaking.

"Married?" Sariel exclaimed. "Sebastian and Elizabeth? Then it has to be you—you'll be as compatible as those two would have been."

Rachmiel winced. "He hasn't trusted me yet. The other day he accused me of lying to him."

"Where is he getting an outlet?" the third angel asked, racing past Rachmiel's pain in her attempt to identify Tabris'. "This is going to drive me wild. He couldn't keep so much pain locked away from everyone."

"Maybe he can," Sariel whispered, her eyes glinting fearfully. "He's got a very strong will. He could control his whole soul if he had to, and maybe he's done just that as a reaction. Maybe he wants comfort but no sympathy, or maybe he doesn't even want comfort. He knows he's wrong, and so does everyone else in the world. Has *anyone* tried talking to him?"

Rachmiel's mouth twitched. "Raguel, I guess. I've avoided the topic because I thought he'd bring it up if he wanted to discuss it."

The father's guardian snatched Rachmiel's hand. "I know it's difficult for you. You must be under so much strain right now, taking care of the child and worrying about Tabris, and trying to figure out what to do for both of them. I'm sorry—we've been forgetting that if you talk to him you'll feel his pain as acutely as he does."

Sariel hugged him too, and then they both looked at him with concern.

"I'm fine," Rachmiel said. "Commiserating is my nature."

"Compassion," said Sariel with a short nod.

"But you'll have a difficult time if you get him to talk," the other angel said. "His heart's pain will overwhelm you once you set it free. He always nonverbalized powerfully and precisely, and he might excise your heart if you're not prepared. We'll be praying for you."

Rachmiel felt his heart fill with questions.

"Some night when Elizabeth's sleeping, then do it," Sariel said. "If he breaks down, you don't want it to happen in front of her."

Rachmiel nodded, then stiffened. "I have to go back—she'll wake up in about five minutes."

The parents' guardians nodded, and Rachmiel left.

18

TABRIS ASKED PERMISSION TO TAKE THE NEXT night off. Reluctantly, Rachmiel agreed—reluctant only because he had hoped to have a discussion with him while Elizabeth slept. Despite Rachmiel's very clear disappointment (although Tabris had no idea of its cause), he left and found himself above the postcard skyline of New York City.

A crime for every streetlight, he thought, spreading his wings to hover with difficulty in the thin air. He felt himself almost coated with atmospheric grease that made him slippery in the sky and could boost his maximum velocity by almost a third of his normal potential. He shook his head to force himself to get used to the sky's consistency, angling his wings with great concentration to hover a while longer. The air burned his skin some, and his eyes itched.

"Do people really live down there?" Tabris asked God, not expecting a response. "This is proof of their belief in You. If they thought this was all there was, how could they stay in that filth?"

Vermont was too oxygen-rich for good rapid flight. New York was far too polluted, its air too weak to suspend a hovering angel who made himself semi-corporeal. Los Angeles had very dense air, but the oxygen mixed into that density was very sparse for this planet, although not as depleted as the air Tabris had found over Moscow and Berlin. In the search for the perfectly polluted city, only Reykjavík and Denver had answered his very specific criteria—Denver primarily because of its elevation and Reykjavík for its longitude.

For tonight, however, New York would suffice. For some reason the thought of Reykjavik made his heart pound, and Denver seemed too foreign right now. He sliced through the unbelievably sickened air and spun, no more than a green blur as he corkscrewed down the streets of midtown Manhattan. He skimmed the heads of New Yorkers who would not have seen him even had he been visible—they walked the darkened avenues with their heads bowed to watch the pavement.

Tabris approached the Empire State Building and made a ninety-degree turn to race straight up the side, skimming the silvery windows that reflected the lights from the traffic but not his image. He opened his wings as he passed the scalloped top floors and snagged the needle-thin broadcast antenna, spiraling around it until his momentum diminished and he slid down it like a fire pole.

"Almost," he gasped, "almost as good as LA."

Leaping from the top, he cannonballed down to street level, breaking out from the falling fetal position at the twentieth floor, flexing his back into a tight arch and opening his wings into a force of gravity that would have blown the feathers off a real bird. He spread his arms and laughed. With immense concentration and a pained expression on his face, he managed to pull up before plummeting through the cement, twisting to redirect his momentum and blaze along at street level.

The other angels glanced at him and ignored him. He went wild while they continued their normal courses, and he knew their eyes did not follow him while he streaked, a green-winged fury, through the corridors of midtown, between the tall buildings like rows of dominos that made the perfect playground for someone who wanted in his heart to be a child but instead had found the games far too real and the toys more serious than he had anticipated.

He circled the Citicorp building, knowing that if he slammed into it he could level that whole area of Manhattan—there was nowhere for a building that size to fall—and all of a sudden the resemblance to dominos was a very grim one indeed, no less grim because Tabris had no body to ram even intentionally into one of the skyscrapers. A crashing airplane or a sustained high wind would suffice too.

From there he rose higher into the night, soaring now, spreading all his feathers even down to the brown ones, and arcing on the power of his own momentum to whatever level he found just right for him tonight. Once he had mounted the cloud cover he turned east, gliding out over the unseen Atlantic, conscious of the silence and the lack of any other nearby angels. He could hear the rhythmic call of the water beneath, the song of a sea with her barely chained chaos, the destructive powers of an appetite that never satisfied itself on just the shores, as though all the seaboard was an hors d'oeuvre to sharpen her appetite for the tremendous expanses of rock between coasts. The sea must have thought the moon close because now the tide was high and reaching upward, outward, licking at the rocks with famished patience.

Tabris turned his head to regard the moon and thought, *I used to pray at times like this.* "What happened to me, God?" he asked, mocking himself even as he did so. He knew what had happened.

"I wish I knew," he said, aloud to ease the tension that could build up within an uncommunicative angel. "I wish I knew if I were really forgiven, if there's any point to continuing to struggle. I wish I could ask and be answered."

No one had heard him—no one but God, and Tabris knew his comments had been duly recorded in God's files as all such self-reflections must be. He folded his wings to fly at a lower altitude, leveling off at the cloud cover and then passing through the white mist, at times visible and at others not, so that his flight path was for the most part hidden.

In a minute or so he grew conscious of another presence.

"Windswept, show yourself."

"And do more than you've done?" said the demon from somewhere. "No, meet me halfway. Rise up ten feet."

Surprising himself by acquiescing as far as seven feet, Tabris looked out above the tops of the clouds which moved beneath his fine spirit like a water bed.

Windswept skimmed the surface and flew beside him, the tips of their wings nearly touching. He smiled, almost a kind smile if one could forget the condition of the soul which had dressed itself in that gentle appearance. His amber eyes, round and liquid, radiated gladness when at last Tabris met them with his own. The demon brushed away some of the hair from his eyes, moving the black strands back where the wind of his own motion could keep them in check for now. He looked around. "What a lovely night. It's a bit banal and lifeless, but that's what you mean by 'lovely,' isn't it?"

"I guess if you leave out the 'love,' that's just what it does mean."

"Ah, my favorite verbalist exercises his pun nature. You make my heart flutter when you do that. It makes me remember some really interesting moments when we still met on friendly ground."

"Whatever makes you happy," Tabris said, "even if those moments never happened."

"Please, don't lie. That only makes it worse for you. You're the one who wants so desperately to believe you're the good guy, remember?"

"I *am* the good guy," Tabris said, smiling brilliantly in the moonlight which was reflected against the cloud cover just beneath him.

"Please," said Windswept, rolling onto his back and sinking lower into the pillows of mist so that they rose up about him like a feather bed, "not now. Let's enjoy tonight. I miss just being silent with you, being together without talking, knowing that you're with me, knowing you. Let's go wherever the winds take us."

Tabris made no answer, and Windswept angled closer so that his left wing extended beneath Tabris' left wing. The demon arched his neck backward, sharply and audibly inhaling the cold. He closed his eyes tightly, then opened them and stared into the moon. Tabris looked up to that white wonder as well. "Isn't she beautiful? So round and misty, so distant. It's cold on the moon, Tabris, and alone. No one's there now—let's go."

"No."

"Please," Windswept said, sliding almost directly beneath Tabris. "Please—I want to—I need—"

The demon flung himself at Tabris, clasping him around the shoulders, gasping as he wrenched his body up and tangled his wings in the two-toned one's beating above him. Tabris pulled backward and flung the demon away from him.

"Please," Windswept gasped, suddenly changing to a more curved body, a female body. Her almond eyes glistened with tears. "I love you. I don't understand—"

Windswept realized the magnitude of her miscalculation then, that even if lust had been the only thing left of love in her, it would still have been the last thing Tabris would respond to. Only the fallen angels exercised their bodies that way. Tabris' revulsion had placed him clearly on the other side of the line.

"Leave me alone!" Tabris said. "You're damned and you want me condemned too! That isn't love! How could love destroy what it loved?"

"How could you kill a twelve-year-old boy?" she asked. "How could God burn the souls He built with His own fingers? I'm adhering to His nature—I want you to be really mine, and I'll make you lose yourself to have you that way, just as He'll make you lose all of yourself to be His. Is that love? How can it be love to own something so totally that it ceases to exist?"

"But that isn't love!" Tabris said. "That's all wrong! God is different. I know it, He has to be."

Windswept hovered upright a short distance away, not moving any closer for the moment. "But you love me, don't you?"

"I don't know, I don't see how I can, but I remember the way you used to be, and I loved that."

"I'll be that way again," she said. "I'll change my name to whatever it was before, and we'll start over. Let's be new once more. I'll be your darling, and we'll talk and laugh again. You'll respond to me, and I'll respond to you the way I did so long ago on the plains of Heaven, and this time when I leave you'll have to follow."

Tabris looked over one shoulder. "I would have to follow then. That's why I can't follow now. I'm not prepared to say no to God just to say yes to you."

Windswept's eyes flashed. "If it's my gender that's bothering you then I'll change again," said the demon, seeming like the voice of reason. Abruptly he was male again. "I did that to force the issue. You don't want me as I am, and you don't want me in some new sexual way, but you do want me. I'll be yours whichever way you want if you'll tell me how. I'm very flexible."

Tabris folded his wings and dropped through the clouds, plummeting blindly until Windswept grasped him around the waist and pulled him up into level flight again.

"You can't run from your own heart," he said. "Let me change my name—call me Sought. Better still, I'm Destination."

Tabris flashed away, but Destination joined him in a foreign field where the heather and wild flowers slept until next morning. Looking around, they could see for miles and meet only more fields, distant hills with gentle slopes, and darkened houses by a lonely two-lane highway, a straight gash across the land. "Tabris, you broke my heart when you refused to follow me into freedom. How can you cling to your tyrant Father now, after all He forced on you? He put you in a situation you couldn't possibly withstand and then blamed you for failing. This whole probation business is just an excuse to make your damnation worse when it happens. He's justifying His malice to all the little worms like Rachmiel and Mithra. They'll never question Him, not if He's seemed to be merciful at first."

"Shut up," Tabris choked. "Look—maybe I am trapped. Then wait for me. According to this ineffable plan of yours, I'll have to foul up sooner or later; and then I'll give in to you, anything you want, because nothing will matter any longer. Then you could batter me from one end of time to the other and that couldn't be worse than being betrayed by God." The word *Daddy* remained unsaid, but the emotion trembled just behind the closed shield on Tabris' eyes.

Destination smiled wickedly, as though momentarily lost in thought, then brightened again and looked up into Tabris' dark eyes. "Do you mean it? When you fall, you'll be mine again?"

"*If* you were right, yes." Tabris closed his eyes. "But you're not. If you really believed my damnation was inevitable you wouldn't be working on me. You'd be waiting. You're scared that I do have a chance at full restoration, and you're jealous."

"Please—I'm hurrying God along, that's all." Destination lay back to look up at the moon. "Do you think He cares what you do?"

"Yes."

"Have you asked lately? I don't think so. He won't respond to your prayers. In fact, He'll go against them. I'll bet that in a few days He orders you to visit Sebastian. Then you'll come gladly to me, if only to avoid facing the kid."

Tabris shook his head.

"It's both or none. God and Sebastian or nothing. He'll push it."

"Maybe."

"Definitely. The kid hates you anyway. Has Rachmiel given away his secret yet?"

Tabris nodded.

"About going to Raguel or about how the kid feels?"

Tabris looked away, nonverbalizing the latter.

"So you haven't lost it," Destination marveled. "Rachmiel said you had." Tabris looked up with a frown in his eyes. "Nonverbalisms. Rachmiel said you never make any, that you lost your capacity for higher emotion when you fell."

"Why do I doubt that?" said Tabris. "Could it be that Rachmiel never passes judgment on anyone's thought processes—hardly even on actions? He might say I never nonverbalize. He'd never speculate on the reasons why."

Destination tossed his head. "My point was that you hadn't lost the capacity. Maybe you haven't lost other capacities either. The capacity to love me, for example."

"If only you hadn't lost the capacity to be loved," Tabris said, giving a mock sigh and a wry smile, "what fun we'd have."

"Don't talk nonsense. God loves us all, remember?" And then Destination chuckled. "I hope He loves you just as much as me. Not as much as I, no—I'd hope He loves you far less than I do because then you'll stay as you are. He only messes with the things He loves when they get His attention. But if He loves you just as much as He loves me, then we're going places—or at least you are. You'll be sent to me! Sooner or later He'll try to possess you, intellect and soul, and you'll recoil. It's in your nature."

"Now who's talking nonsense? I submit to God all the time."

"So much that you find it difficult to bring yourself to pray, impossible to open your heart. It's in your eyes, that soul-starved look I thought I'd only see Below. Tell me, if He loved you wouldn't He give you what you needed before you asked? Wouldn't He enter your heart to rescue you, invited or not?"

"You're not making sense," Tabris said, smiling crookedly. "You say He wants to possess me, but then you say He won't act unless I ask. That's a contradiction right there."

Destination sat up, deadly serious and with grim eyes. "He wants you to do the asking so you'll be more dependent, Free Will! He engages in a type of torture, making you suffer if you won't submit and engulfing you if you do. He's created a game we can't win!"

"Not by your rules, no."

"Not by any! We've been created by an infinitely powerful child! Someone who loves breaking His toys just to see what they can't withstand, and to make it more fun He's rendered the toys indestructible and self-aware—the only course *left* is utter despair because once you're aware of the situation all you can do is see the entrapment!"

Tabris sat up. "If I don't correct you you'll think you've won, so give me five minutes. Be silent and listen. No nonverbalizations either.

"God didn't create us merely for His entertainment," Tabris said. "He does test us, but only to make us stronger—to show us just how strong we are. But He made us to need Him, to need His power and His love. He does want to help, but we have to ask first, and then He'll come to the rescue. That makes us dependent, but it's a good dependence, one that's more necessary than psychological. He designed us that way, but His every action leads us toward making ourselves rationally independent and worthy of being called His friends."

Destination's eyes flashed.

Tabris glared. "*Your* independence was just perversity. We have to be reasonable about it. You can't prove you have free will by refusing to do anything you haven't thought up yourself."

"But you haven't answered my complaint—that God wants to subsume the things He's created. *That* was how I asserted my will—by staying independent of Him."

"But in 'subsuming' us, as you call it, He actually heightens our individuality, making us more precise in our abilities so that we each can achieve our full potential."

"All 'holiness' is the same—a reflection of the same mirage!" Destination said.

"On the contrary, all evil is the same—all liars lie the same way, all brutes bully the same way. No one can tell the difference between Hitler's behavior and Stalin's and Napoleon's. But look how different Francis of Assisi is from James the Apostle or Paul from Peter! And you," Tabris said, glaring with disgust, "your whole personality is gone. I remember what you were, and it isn't what you are now. You lie like the rest, you sneer at anything that disagrees with you, you call any authority but yourself tyranny. That's not your potential personhood! You're not independent—you're degraded!"

Tabris huffed.

"You're so cute when you're mindlessly reciting," said Destination. "You act as though the Almighty *needed* your defense when I'm sure He does not."

"You just don't listen, do you?"

"The way you listen to me, Tabris. Except that I know you're lying to me to convince yourself of your position. I can hear the pain in your voice, the forcefulness that comes from self-doubt. Like those pro-choicers, always screaming in crowds to shut out the tiny voices in their hearts that say they're wrong while the pro-lifers stand praying quietly in little groups at the clinic doors. They rant just the way you do because they've convinced themselves they're right and now they're too afraid to back down. They've got too much invested. And I hear the same thing in your voice. You want to convince yourself that everything's going to be all right. That's okay, we all do that. But you should know when to give up. You can't spout theology forever. You'll slow down someday and realize just how pathetic it is."

"No," Tabris said. "Slowing down is what opens the rift and makes us think we're learning the truth. Things seem different from the other side. You're looking at the world in reverse, so that right is left. You're explaining the way you see God once you've decided you hate Him. I'm holding on because I don't—I couldn't lose that love. It sustains me. And if letting go means adulthood, then I'll remain a child."

Destination bit his lower lip and looked away. "I can't bear to see you in bondage. If you came to me just once, you'd learn how He really is. It's a pain that changed me forever, a betrayal so complete that I could never return to Him again. I grew up, and I'm better off knowing the score and alone in Hell than full of gaiety in Heaven but deceived every instant. Suffering causes growth, and I've grown."

Tabris trembled, but then felt his mouth saying, "Why is growth necessarily good?"

"Because it is. You yourself said God wants us to grow."

Tabris' eyes flashed. "But you want no part of God—you think all He wants for you is pain and struggle."

"This is different," said Destination, his gaze flickering from Tabris to his own hands. "It's—it just is. He can't lie about everything or else He'd be totally unbelievable."

Tabris leaned forward, touched Destination's shoulder. "Like you."

"I'm not pathological. I know every time."

"So now God isn't all-knowing either." The two-toned angel lay back on the hilltop, looking up at the stars through the remarkably clear dome of the atmosphere. "Growth is good, you're right, but not all kinds of growth. Trees and vines get trimmed to keep them growing in the right direction. That makes them better for bearing fruit. We grow through experience, but not every experience is good or necessary for proper growth. And pain isn't always a bad thing—it makes us deeper, better able to appreciate peace when we come across it." He took a deep breath, then sat up and met Destination's eyes. "What you call growth is separation from God, but it isn't really growth—you're making yourself more shallow, cutting off different capacities, modeling yourself to minimize what you are so that God's presence will be as limited as it can be. That's not growth, that's amputation."

Tabris closed his eyes with a warm feeling, a good feeling, in his stomach.

Destination burst out laughing, a forced sound and not as immediate as it usually was. "You're good. You deserve an Academy Award."

"I'm glad you're in Hell."

"I am too. Come join me."

"In God's name, go away."

Suddenly silent, the hill country stilled as though it were a tomb, until the insects began once again to call to each other. Tabris sat alone. Bowing his head, he said, "Thank you, God," and felt a muted response somewhere in his heart, as though the Lord were thanking him in return.

"You're the one who gave me the words," Tabris said. "I know I'm the one who let you, but let's leave it at my thanking you for now. Please."

He felt God turn his mind toward Rachmiel, a gentle reminder of an orange-winged guardian with sunset colored eyes who waited for Tabris' return. Although the push in his mind was very gentle, it made Tabris shudder because of all it touched—the wounds still were raw in his heart, and he still felt uncomfortable letting anyone, even God, see the convoluted interior of his soul.

"God," he whispered, "I feel so grimy inside."

God's Spirit refrained from telling Tabris just then that He loved him anyway—it would have shattered him completely.

Tabris looked at the lonely moon. "I suppose I should go back, right?" and God agreed, so Tabris stood and looked around once more at the hills before flashing to Elizabeth.

He was tired, and he knew he would not have the energy to close himself as tightly as he normally could. If Rachmiel wanted to, tonight he could extract all the information he wanted. He returned anyway.

19

RACHMIEL FELT TABRIS' PRESENCE BEFORE HE saw the two-toned angel, and he leaped to his feet from where he had been sitting in the center of Elizabeth's room. "I'm back," Tabris said unsteadily, his voice shaky. "Easy night?"

"I've been praying," Rachmiel said, his heart pounding and nonverbalizing for whom before he realized. Tabris obviously tried not to react. "Where did you go? You look drained. Was it that demon again?"

Tabris nodded, straddling Elizabeth's desk chair in reverse so that his chest was covered by the backing like a wooden breast plate. Rachmiel took that as a sign not to move forward and immediately discarded any plans for having an open-hearted discussion tonight—that would not be fair. Already Tabris was emanating a stray haze of emotion, a far cry from his usual emotional vacuum and a signal that his guards were weakened. "If I can help you with the demon," Rachmiel said carefully, being as precise as possible, "maybe by fighting him, just ask. I'm willing."

Tabris nodded, focusing on Rachmiel as intently as if he had trained his binoculars on a foreign spy. Rachmiel turned and looked at Elizabeth, asking God for help as he did so. He would have smiled at the little girl, but the effort to put on appearances might have made his wings shake.

"We do have to talk," agreed Tabris, and Rachmiel's spine stiffened—he'd had no idea that he had nonverbalized anything at all.

"Not necessarily now," he said. "You're hurt."

Only after he said the words did Rachmiel realize how true that was, and he turned quickly.

"That's why I said it," Tabris said, avoiding the gaze even before it focused on him. "God said you need the talk, and I'm willing to do it now while my defenses are lowered."

"That's not fair to you," Rachmiel said, almost shaking himself. "I won't—I just can't."

Tabris looked up, and Rachmiel caught a stray flash of sincerity, of terrified need that had made too many realizations in too short a time. Tabris felt like a child all alone in a very large empty room with a high vaulted ceiling, and Rachmiel could sense that smallness, the loneliness which wafted from his soul like bright ribbons but left his skin raw and sensitive underneath. The two-toned angel met Rachmiel's eyes and the guardian nodded. "All right. I'll try."

They looked at each other, and finally Tabris said, "I'm sorry if I'm hurting you, but I'm not going to hold back, all right?" Rachmiel gently nonverbalized permission to say anything he wanted. "I said that you lied to me, and I meant that."

Rachmiel nodded. "What did I do?"

"You went to Raguel on your own."

His eyes popped.

Tabris gripped the chair tightly. "Mithra came to us and asked one of us to sub for him. You told me to do it, but five minutes later Hadriel said Mithra was with Elizabeth. You lied to me. You went to Raguel."

Rachmiel's whole form refused to obey him, and he sat as still as though he had turned to gelatin. He was unable to meet Tabris' eyes because the two-toned angel looked only at his hands. The guards around his emotions were vibrating almost violently, and Rachmiel could have grabbed the nonverbalizations with his soul, they were so strong. He did not.

"And you've been asking to have me removed. Raguel came when Elizabeth fell off her bicycle, and you were angry. You asked to have me removed, and he immediately slackened the bond between Elizabeth and me. You've been colluding with Sebastian to gather evidence to remove me from Elizabeth."

Tabris looked down farther, so that his head hung between his shoulders. "I—I can see why, but Rock, Rachmiel, how could you—how could you lie to me?" With a small gasp he put his head onto his arms, and Rachmiel flashed to his side. "Please," he gasped, "please don't lie now."

"I never lied to you," Rachmiel said. "Not once. Mithra left and returned that one time, and I never asked Raguel to remove you after you arrived. The bond is slacker because you needed the range, and you've proven your loyalty. I wasn't getting rid of you. I've gotten angry, but I've never wanted you gone. Please, Tabris, it's okay."

Rachmiel felt Tabris exerting a massive effort to regain control. The emotions stopped leaking from the chinks in the wall around his heart.

Wrapping Tabris in his wings, Rachmiel held him tightly. He rocked him gently, the way Elizabeth's mother still rocked her occasionally.

"The kid," Tabris whispered, "he does hate me, though."

"I don't know—he's trying to forgive you. He's trying to pray."

Tabris was shaking like a kitten in Rachmiel's grasp, and Rachmiel was suddenly frightened that his arms would be wet with the tears of an angel who always tried very hard to keep everything bottled inside his heart. "Easy," he said. "I'll listen. I'm here."

A momentary flash escaped Tabris' mind—that demon with eyes bright as amber—and abruptly he understood where Tabris had found an emotional outlet. Rachmiel gripped him tightly.

"Enough of what he said was true," Tabris said in a shaking voice, "that I started believing all of it."

"Don't believe any. I wish you'd come to me sooner."

"But Sebastian—"

Tabris choked.

"He's working on it. He's trying to forgive you, but it's hurting him. He needs time."

Tabris cuddled closer to Rachmiel as though the orange wings could shut the world away from him, hide him from Sebastian and block the memory forever. Rachmiel squeezed him. "If you met him he might find it easier."

"No," Tabris said. "Not until God forces me, I won't. I can't. Don't you see?" and he began quivering violently. "Don't you? I watched him from when he was tiny and innocent, such a precious baby, and I kept him sinless for so long, but—but then—"

Rachmiel cooed, an odd but decidedly angelic response, nonverbal reassurance of his presence that simply told Tabris he remained strong, he understood, he cared. It had effect instantly. Tabris began calming, his head dropping a little against Rachmiel's chest.

"Tabris," the guardian whispered, "don't speak now. Don't think about it. You deserve better than this, better than to be completely hysterical when you tell me what happened. Wait a while, wait and make sure you really want to tell me. I can wait. This is too much like a trash novel—let's wait a while and make it literature."

Tabris chuckled and Rachmiel relaxed. He let the two-toned angel sit up a little, looking at Elizabeth and seeing that she had grown restless in her sleep. "Go to her," Tabris said. "Put her back in REM. I didn't mean to disturb her."

"No problem," Rachmiel said, flashing beside her and laying one hand over her eyes. "She'll be dreaming again soon."

He heard Tabris gasp as unseen power took form in the room, and he dropped to his knees.

"Relax," said Jesus. Rachmiel stood up and, turning, noticed that Tabris had prostrated himself completely. He did not raise his head even when Jesus addressed him.

"Tabris," Jesus said, "I'm taking you up on your offer."

"You are?"

"You said you wouldn't go to Sebastian until I ordered you, so I'm ordering you. I want you to visit him tomorrow night."

Tabris' heart groped for Rachmiel's. "My Lord," Rachmiel asked, "may I go with him?"

"Yes. Casifer will be there too. My suggestion is that you go someplace interesting, such as a rain forest, or off the planet entirely, just to keep him occupied and give him a chance to get to know you."

Tabris nodded. Something nonverbal escaped him, anticipation and tension, fear but also relief.

"It'll be difficult," Jesus said, "but you can manage. You should try to pray before you go."

"Will you tell Sebastian or should I?" Rachmiel asked.

"I will," said Jesus. "Rachmiel, will you join Tabris in prayer before tomorrow night?" The guardian nodded. "I'll be with you too, Tabris, just ask for me," Jesus said. "And thank you for speaking today on my behalf."

"I tried," Tabris said, and Rachmiel could almost hear his tight smile.

Jesus laughed. "Thanks to both of you," and then He vanished.

Tabris rose tentatively and looked at Rachmiel with worried eyes.

"You're taking it well."

"It had to happen eventually." He looked at Elizabeth. "She's all right now?" Then he walked to the window and looked up at the moon hanging in the sky with its impossible weight and white glory. "I went to New York before, and that's where I met the demon. He started playing theological Ping-Pong with me, but the Spirit spoke through me and managed to confuse him. That's why I think it's funny that He thanks me. It's not like I did any of the work."

They stood beside each other in the white light from the window, looking at the moon. Quietly Rachmiel extended his heart to God in thanks for the opportunity to speak with this enigmatic angel.

"Should we pray now?" he asked.

"Not yet," said Tabris. "Let me think first."

20

THE WHOLE DAY BEFORE VISITING SEBASTIAN, Rachmiel exerted his will with strength he might have felt himself incapable of earlier. Tabris needed him to be strong now, needed him not to nonverbalize to everyone in exultation that he had let him see a little into the mazy interior of his soul. Both he and Tabris moved about more lightly, but no one asked why and both managed not to explain the change. Rachmiel also noted in relief that the other angels did not seem to know about the alteration in Tabris' appearance, so Sariel had not spread the word about that.

In the car returning from school, Rachmiel suggested that the angels pray together, and Voriah agreed quickly. They quieted, and one by one they opened their hearts to the Lord—Rachmiel, Voriah, Hadriel, Miriael, and Katra'il. Tabris breathed deeply and faked it.

Beside him, Rachmiel touched him with a wing tip and nonverbalized his presence, but Tabris resisted. With his eyes closed, Rachmiel grabbed tighter to God's heart, and in return God gave him strength.

Elizabeth would go to bed at nine and would probably be asleep by nine-thirty, at which point Casifer would come to escort them to visit Sebastian. Before that happened, Tabris had to pray and Rachmiel had to know a few things about Sebastian's childhood, how a guardian as brilliant as the one Sariel had described could suddenly do the worst thing possible in terms of spiritual development. His need was not as pressing as Tabris', but it might help if Rachmiel understood the dynamics when guardian and protege met face to face at last.

The thought of the young boy meeting the cold eyes of his once-guardian and seeing no love there made

Rachmiel shudder—the love had been buried many layers deep about six months ago under sheets of denial and strips of pain. Love had been replaced by fear and mistrust and shame—mostly shame, Rachmiel realized, and mistrust of others' reactions alloyed with a large amount of mistrust in himself. Tabris had learned to slow his reaction time just because he doubted his own responses. Rachmiel had watched him often enough to know how he operated, and he had learned quickly to shoulder all the work if the protection required actual contact with Elizabeth. Tabris could handle projectiles and insects and fractions, he could keep Elizabeth from hearing what she should not. If she needed to catch her balance, though, or if she were walking in the dark, or if she stumbled and fell—dealing with those situations was Rachmiel's job, unsaid but understood all the same.

Rachmiel's mind contained a portfolio thick with observations on Tabris: the way he walked, the things he avoided saying, the way he watched Elizabeth from time to time, and the distance in his eyes when she shone most beautifully. From these odd moments Rachmiel had pieced together an inadequate portrait of the two-toned angel. Inadequate, but accurate. There were blank patches in the colors between the lines, but the lines were in place all the same.

Before Elizabeth had gone to bed, while she still lay propped on her pillows reading, Tabris said, "What do you know about me?" He had cast a light Guard over the room, enough to prevent eavesdropping.

"You mean about Sebastian and you?"

"Right. No need to duplicate information."

Rachmiel's spirit grew tense, eager. "Well, for starters, you were an amazing guardian to Sebastian. You gave him the best protection imaginable." Rachmiel smiled. "You kept him practically sinless until he was twelve."

"Do you know what that sin was?"

Rachmiel shrugged. "Sebastian never told me, but after what you said to Josai'el, I'd guess he stole something."

"You're quick. It was a tape of some pop rock singer."

"And you got him to turn back to God within a few days, but it upset you greatly."

Tabris nodded, leaning back against the wall and smiling dryly, an off-balance curve that Rachmiel knew was not forced. Rachmiel continued. "Your fellow guardians told you not to worry, that there was nothing you could have done to prevent it since Sebastian had free will, but you felt guilty anyway."

"That's close," Tabris said. "What I really felt was this incredible sense of failure, that a guardian as powerful as I am could have let my own child steal a tape from a music store. And I lost some of my sight into Sebastian's soul—that happens to all of us when they sin. It'll happen to you too. When Elizabeth sins, we'll stop being able to see all her soul's beauty."

Rachmiel grimaced, looking down. "That doesn't reflect on us. It hasn't on Katra'il or Mithra."

"They're not top fifty in their choir, though." Tabris' eyes narrowed. "That's definitely a type of spiritual pride. God made me the way that I am, after all, but it galled me that lesser angels could do a better job, even if their jobs were easier. I had to be better—faster, stronger. So one day Sebastian proved he had free will, and three days later I proved the same."

"How did it happen?"

"You tell me."

"On a bicycle—you said that already. Sebastian hit a rock and went head over heels, and you didn't break his fall."

Tabris closed his eyes and leaned back, wrapped in pain. "Rock, Rock, you always want to believe the best. You're forgetting—I *killed* him. We're not talking negligent homicide. This was murder. He went over the handle bars, and I had my hands around his neck to keep him from being paralyzed in the fall, and then, just as he hit the ground—I broke his neck." Tabris moved his hands in a sudden snapping motion. "Just like that. And I stopped, and I realized—Lord. I stopped thinking then, standing over his body until two angels came and carried me away, chained me, and brought me to the tribunal. Casifer came and lifted Sebastian's soul from his body and brought him to judgment." Tabris had grown very pale, and he shook his head slowly. "You know the rest, I suppose."

Rachmiel paused. "But—had you planned it?"

"No. Actually, that's how Raguel released me. He said I hadn't meant it. I did mean it—just not for too long before it happened and not too long afterward. I really did regret it instantly, but by then it was too late to change the action. If I could have resurrected him I would have, but I couldn't. I was too stunned to do anything. I didn't know what to do."

"You didn't run?" Rachmiel asked.

Tabris laughed—a painful sound. "Where would I go, Rock?"

"That's true." Rachmiel looked at Elizabeth. "I think I would have run, though."

"It was such a shock," Tabris said, "that I don't think anyone could predict his reaction. You might cry. You might just start laughing insanely. Once you leave God nothing is sane any longer. I just stopped moving because I was afraid that . . ."

Tabris wrung his hands together, swallowing convulsively.

"Go on," said Rachmiel.

"That if I did anything else, God would . . . You know 'fight or flight'? I did that but stopped in the moment of decision, like a deer in the headlights of an oncoming car. Justice was bearing down on me, and I could feel the Doppler effect of it; I knew it was coming closer, and at the same time I didn't feel anything at all."

Rachmiel ventured to ask the question vibrating in his heart. "But . . . why did you do it?"

Tabris' eyes flashed for the first time, as though he had been about to grab the guard tight around his heart again. "That doesn't matter. It's done. What matters is what happens from here."

"But—"

"It's not important," Tabris said, his voice tense. "Knowing why can't change matters."

A few moments passed, during which Rachmiel sat in shock, afraid that he might have made Tabris unwilling to speak further.

Elizabeth looked at her clock and was about to close the book when Tabris said, "Not yet, it's a good book, it's worth losing sleep for it. You'll finish it by ten, and that's enough sleep. You're not tired."

Elizabeth returned to reading.

Rachmiel's mouth twitched, but of the two souls in his care Elizabeth's was suddenly the less jeopardized. "So," he said, still somewhat hesitant, "you would try to do it differently if you started again?"

"But isn't that the whole point?" Tabris asked. "I'd do the same—we'd all make the same choices if we were returned to the first moments. Damnation and election weren't subjected to chance—as if had I been facing west instead of north I'd have been damned. That's why it's so horrible a thing to contemplate. Rachmiel! They made a fully knowing irrevocable choice that they'd have made no matter what else we had done for them beforehand. Every step of the way was their own choice, each building on the next to whatever conclusion they were writing for themselves! And—Rock, I'd have done it anyway. I know it. Not that I was right. Not that I wanted it. No, no, oh, that was never my intention. I haven't lived an instant since without regretting it in every part of my soul." He shuddered, gripping his arms to his sides. "Every minute, whenever I see Elizabeth and feel that rush of camaraderie when she smiles, I remember: I killed my own son! How can I ever be happy again? How can I laugh when I should be crying every instant at my own stupidity—one evil moment! God!" He doubled over, shaking so wretchedly that Rachmiel grabbed him, cuddled him, folded over his curled body. "How can I love this girl and protect her when I murdered the one I should have defended at all cost?" He gasped, tearing away from Rachmiel and flashing to the upper corner of Elizabeth's bed, by her head. She had lain down on top of her book, but neither angel noticed.

Rachmiel extended his heart.

"How—" Tabris pressed closer into the corner. "How can—"

Rachmiel leaned forward, and Tabris pulled back again so that the orange-winged guardian felt forced to retreat. "Tell me, please. If you're asking how God can love you, He does. You're still His. And we've forgiven you. How can we hold bound what He's loosened?"

"But how can I forgive myself?" Tabris asked.

"I don't know," Rachmiel said. "That's tough. That's always hardest."

Tabris looked up, his eyes still wide but his mouth no longer as tight. "Isn't it, though? I mean, I deserve Hell."

"But there's mercy too."

"That makes no sense. I can see Him being merciful to humans, to others, but to me it seems ridiculous. I should have known better. Rock—I'm an angel! We don't get second chances."

"You did."

That was more a nonverbalization than spoken. By now Elizabeth had gone to sleep.

Tabris looked at his hands.

"Don't dwell on it," Rachmiel said, suddenly near.

"I killed my own son."

"You regret it."

"That makes it worse—if I thought it right at least I could live with myself."

"In Hell!"

"There's that," Tabris said. "I didn't lose God's love, even though I lost everyone else's."

Rachmiel protested nonverbally. Tabris looked up with a very powerful dare in his eyes, a nonverbalization complete with emotional and syntactic components.

"Not everyone," said Rachmiel, his voice shaking.

"Name," Tabris said, "one."

Rachmiel quivered.

"When you can, tell me," Tabris said. "I shan't wait with held breath, I assure you."

"Don't be that way," said Rachmiel. "What about Sariel?"

"That's good—any angel who guards a person who knew Sebastian would be angry because of the unnecessary grief I've subjected his charge to in the aftermath, the questions about how a good God can permit senseless tragedy. I felt it when Sariel visited. She was fascinated by the spectacle but repulsed by me. Like a horror movie. I'm a side show. And her compatriot there in LA probably tried to 'solve' me, like a thief cracking a safe."

"Please," Rachmiel said, "don't speak."

"You see," Tabris forced himself to laugh, but it was tight, "you'll pity me, but I don't deserve pity, or compassion, or mercy. I don't worry about love—that can only come from one Source for the rest of my life. I might hide my emotions, but I'm still sensitive to everyone else's. I still feel all the small exchanges, the mistrust, the debates, the hushed chastisements . . ."

"I'm sorry."

"The anger. The guardians are far less understanding than the ones who never guarded. The opposite of what you'd expect, Rock—the non-guardians imagine it must be horrible to guard, the guardians know it's the most rapturous feeling imaginable short of seeing God. They don't understand how I could have done it. I look at Elizabeth, and I don't understand it either."

He launched from the corner and lay full length on the bed, across and through Elizabeth. "Tonight I get to meet the soul I slaughtered. Dark eyed, like me."

"I'm so sorry, Tabris. I didn't realize you weren't dark eyed by nature."

"He's not either. He's angry, and it clouds him."

"Are you angry?" Rachmiel asked, his eyes round.

"No—just unforgiven." Tabris rolled onto his back and laughed tightly again, like a man insane. "I wish I had an out, a type of suicide that would end in annihilation. But I wouldn't use it. I'd just want to know I could. There's pain here, but there are other things too. Cold nights, polluted cities, occasional chats with the Creator. Those make the dry in-between times worthwhile. Remind me of them after I've met Sebastian. I'll need a cold night over a polluted city then."

"Would you settle for a chat with God?"

"If He'd consent to chat back," said Tabris, lying with his head dangling over the side of the bed and his wings dropped back so that his feathers touched the carpet. "The cities are always there—distant, sullen, throbbing, tense—and the people have arranged it now so that pollution we'll always have with us too. Prayer is remote and far between to me. Opening those rusted hinges is hard work nowadays."

Rachmiel volunteered.

"Thanks," Tabris said, turning his head and smiling upside-down. "I'll remember that."

Just then, Casifer arrived. The two angels stood up, Rachmiel touching Elizabeth and calling Voriah to the room to assume guardianship.

"Not yet," Tabris said. "Bring Sebastian here."

Rachmiel understood a little of the concept of *home territory*, and decided that Tabris needed whatever assurance he could sift for himself. Casifer vanished. Rachmiel had time to nonverbalize to Tabris what a human might phrase as "good luck" before he returned with the boy.

21

SEBASTIAN STOOD NEAR CASIFER'S WING AS though he might dive for cover in an emergency. It seemed that Casifer was his guardian and not the angel he faced across the room.

"Sebastian," said Tabris.

The boy nodded. "Tabris."

The tension showed on every inch of the boy—his soul was emitting streamers of fright, fear, hope, rage, and need. Facing him, Tabris had become such an emotional vacuum that Rachmiel found it hard to believe that only ten minutes earlier he had been nonverbalizing complete syntactic units.

"How are you doing?" Tabris asked, human in his conversation for now. They all could see how Sebastian was doing: he was upset. Tabris smiled, very forced, but Rachmiel realized that the boy did not know him well enough to figure that out yet. "I trust Casifer's taking remarkable care of you."

"No one's remarked so far," said Sebastian, which surprised Rachmiel as well as Casifer. The boy's dark eyes had locked onto Tabris, and the two seemed mirror images of one another. Rachmiel looked at Casifer and saw him struck by the similarity of guardian and charge. Resemblance was normal—near identity was not. Probably, Rachmiel realized, if Sebastian had grown older and done all the things God had planned—or even things God had not—he would have completed his development into a very different soul.

"Where had you intended to go?" said Casifer, his hands obviously under very willful restraint not to reach out and touch the boy's shoulder.

"Any place is fine," Rachmiel said. "The Lord suggested something exotic, like a tropical rain forest, or even off this planet if you want."

Sebastian had his eyes locked on Tabris. "Whatever you three agree on," he said, "that's all the same with me."

Casifer looked at Rachmiel, who nonverbalized *I honestly don't think it matters.*

"Rain forest," Casifer said. "We'll save the planets for some other time."

The four of them landed in South America. Casifer began immediately to point out all the varied types of life, the different adaptations each one had made to better suit its environment. There were plants at ground level that had learned to survive with nearly no light even though its lack stunted their growth, and bugs that had learned how to burrow underground to escape the birds. Overhead there were birds whose beaks had changed shape over the generations to better open whatever seeds they could find. Rachmiel and Tabris followed them, tourists in this darker and leafier part of the world. Tabris made a very forced nonverbalization, that this place made him wish for open sky and flight, that the damp heat of the air felt mildly oppressive to an angel who used to race down the side of the Rockies and then glide as far as he could across the Great Plains without moving his wings, usually clearing Kansas and sometimes Missouri.

Rachmiel nonverbally reassured him.

Sebastian turned around suddenly and squinted.

"You're having a good time, kid?" asked Tabris.

"I've never seen a place like this."

"You don't need to tell me," Tabris said, torn between tension and a smile, and his soul seemed more like an emotional black hole than ever before. Rachmiel wished Tabris would release his control somewhat so that he could feel whatever Sebastian and Casifer were nonverbalizing.

"I mean even after I was alive." Sebastian looked at them with his head aslant and his mouth in a perfect imitation of Tabris' forced smiles. "I've been undersea and in a couple of spots on earth since then with Casifer and Rachmiel, and . . . who was the other angel, the one I called Coach?"

"Voriah," Rachmiel said with a laugh.

"He gave you lots of advice, kid?" Tabris' eyes sparkled.

Sebastian shrugged and turned back to Casifer.

They walked for a while, content to wander aimlessly along the detritus-covered ground. Tiny animals crept close to the group, and Rachmiel stopped walking to crouch low and hold the small ones in his hands. Casifer turned and smiled, his eyes rounding as Rachmiel stroked a tiny bird who sang to him eagerly.

"Those two are a lot alike," said Sebastian.

Tabris nodded. "I think so. *Rachmiel* means Compassion."

"What does *Casifer* mean?"

"That name isn't so obvious. As best as I can understand, he's the angel of solitude and tears, and the angel of temperance. Do you remember the movie *Wings of Desire*? The second angel was supposed to be him."

Sebastian smiled. "It was wrong."

"Very. Try explaining that to people. For the most part they just use us for our names, not for who we are or what we've done. We're portrayed as extremes or mere facets of God's love. We're brushed off as ineffectual or else we're gods—that's so backward." Tabris shrugged. "I'm sorry. I shouldn't be preaching to you."

Sebastian caught the hastily retracted nonverbalization. "You can teach me also."

"Maybe." Tabris smiled, a forced smile. "Is there room enough? I think Casifer's done a better job than I did."

Sebastian trembled, but shook his head and avoided responding.

Casifer and Rachmiel rejoined the dark-eyed pair and they continued meandering.

"Would you like to hold a bird?" asked Rachmiel.

"If it's possible," Sebastian said. "Won't it fall through my hands?"

"You're as corporeal as you want to be, to a point," Casifer said. "You can hold a bird if you want, or you can completely discorporate. We'll have to practice your control over that sometime."

Sebastian's eyes flickered to Tabris, but only Rachmiel caught the gesture. Tabris was narrowly regarding Casifer. Sebastian looked back. "Yeah, I guess."

"The next time a bird flies to us, it's yours," Rachmiel said.

Tabris and Sebastian walked in silence until Casifer turned around with a small red bird in his hands and slipped it gently into Sebastian's cupped palms.

"He's so light," Sebastian said. "And he's soft!"

"Stroke his head," Rachmiel said. "Aren't his feathers smooth?"

"They are," Sebastian breathed, his face as radiant as if he were staring into a spotlight. "Does he trust me?"

"You're from God, how could he not?" asked Casifer.

Tabris was standing to one side, and Sebastian turned to him. "Would you like to hold him?"

"No, but thanks. He looks happy in your hands."

"But he's so special," Sebastian said, "how could you pass him up?"

"Because he's so special—I want you to keep him."

Sebastian's hollow look tightened Rachmiel's stomach. The boy looked back at the bird. "Tabris. What does your name mean?"

"Free Will."

"But how is an angel's name supposed to reflect who he is? Does Rachmiel *have* to be compassionate?"

Casifer answered, "Some angels didn't adhere to their natures and fell—you know that. Our names express our natures."

Tabris looked like he was about to thank him, but Rachmiel stepped closer.

"How does your name express your nature?" Sebastian was still looking at the bird nestled in his hands. It had begun pecking at his fingers.

"Our potential is the highest expression of what our names mean," Casifer said. "In some respects, our names *are* us. Your soul has a name too, and eventually you'll discover it, but that's a long personal journey you'll make through time. Angels are given their names. Humans earn them."

Rachmiel touched his orange feathers to Tabris' green ones.

Sebastian let the bird fly away and then looked up. "Let's keep walking."

"There are mosquitos under these leaves that are the size of thimbles," Casifer said.

"Thank you for sharing that," said Tabris.

"The only place they grow bigger is New Jersey," Rachmiel said quickly, his eyes glistening so that Sebastian would realize the "statistic" was not to be trusted. "In New Jersey, mothers have to chain down their baby carriages or the mosquitos will carry off their infants."

"You read this in the *Weekly World News?*" asked Sebastian.

"If it's printed in a newspaper then it has to be true," Rachmiel said, then smiled. "Insects are far more impressive when you're incorporeal and can't be bitten, stung or infected."

Tabris said, "Dragonflies are awesome either way." It was a calculated sentence.

"You like dragonflies?" asked Sebastian. "I love them—they're beautiful! I remember one landing on me once, and I was so happy I hardly breathed for two minutes."

"I remember calling over a dragonfly and then trying to get your lungs to work before you passed out," Tabris said, laughing with real emotion behind the sound. "I was glad you liked them because it meant you'd spend less time running away from them than the other kids."

Sebastian had a queer look in his eyes, as if he were struggling inside, which had to be the case, Rachmiel realized. He was faced with someone too similar not to forgive, and yet he had been hurt so deeply that forgiveness seemed impossible.

"Are you getting tired, Sebastian?" asked Casifer.

"Ah, somewhat," said the boy. "Actually, if we might, can we pray for a little? I mean, I think I've seen a lot of really new things, and I want to assimilate it all."

Rachmiel had a good idea what these really new things were, and certainly Tabris knew, too—the boy was practically transparent. He had a very angry core overlaid with sensitivity and newness, trust and mistrust, love and uncertainty.

"We could go to the lake," Tabris said.

"I was thinking of that cliff by the ocean in Washington State, if that's okay."

"That's fine," Tabris said, and Rachmiel felt the nonverbal stirrings within—it really was okay. Then they stood on the clifftop, overlooking the pounding force of the ocean.

Tabris closed his eyes, extending a nonhuman sense to touch the waters: fierce, formless, dark, deep. Behind him he sensed the straight spruces standing in rows like pikes on a rack. On the other side of Rachmiel and Casifer, Sebastian had touched the sea with a decidedly nonhuman sense he had recently discovered. The ocean beat the shore with the regular rhythm of a pumping heart. The smell of salt permeated the air, and Tabris inhaled it deeply.

Rachmiel spread his wings halfway and opened his heart, reaching out his hands and waiting to feel God's touch in return. Then, as the tension in his heart increased, he almost vibrated with expectancy until God's fingertips brushed his. He pushed forward, taking God's hands in his own, grasping and pulling himself closer until God's heart had completely enfolded him and he could dissolve the walls about his will and allow God into all his thoughts—a flooding so intense that for a moment Rachmiel scarcely existed as a separate creature.

In that moment, Rachmiel reached out for Sebastian and helped him to let down the fences he had established to stay self-contained. The boy cringed in fear, but Casifer gripped his hand, and Sebastian allowed Rachmiel to dissolve the walls.

What overwhelms an angel can destroy a human, which is why human prayer is difficult. Sebastian experienced close communion with God, deep love, and very minute awareness of God's presence in all the world. When angels pray they meet God on His own terms, but human beings must have God come to them. Sebastian was surprised to find God within him as well as everywhere else, as though every living cell glowed with its mitochondrion and all living things were impressionist paintings formed by brightly glowing dots. The sea shone like a small sun, and the cliff was speckled with brightness. The angels gleamed as single units, not outlines or points so much as shafts of light arcing upward toward God while glowing tendrils laced them to each other and to the surrounding world. Even the rocks glittered with a distinct outline to Sebastian's hungry eyes.

God asked if there was anything Sebastian wanted. Rachmiel and Casifer felt the request, a young boy's plea for the love of his near-father and for the strength to want to forgive someone who had hurt him very deeply.

Tabris had felt the blossoming of the three hearts beside him, although God had shielded him from the boy's prayer, and he clenched his teeth.

Reaching for his hand, Rachmiel realized that Tabris would refuse, but he had to try anyway.

Tabris did refuse. Keeping his eyes closed and feeling the praise and amazement from the three at his side, he stood in silence that God did not compromise by piercing.

They stayed that way for a while. Tabris managed to lose himself by thinking, by restraining his heart completely—at least until Sebastian left. *Then*, he continually promised himself, *then I'll break down. Then I'll cry. If I have to I'll cry for weeks. I need to cry, but not now.*

To open his heart to God, he knew, would be to shatter in pieces where he stood, in front of Sebastian and Rachmiel and the new guardian, overlooking the salt water that rammed itself ceaselessly against the coast to swallow all the world's stone and smother it in formlessness. Like tears, Tabris realized. Tears do the same when angels cry.

Lucifer had cried before falling—cried the frustrated tears of a jilted lover or of a favored son who had pampered himself until he had forgotten how to work. He had cried when asked if he loved his Father long after he had forgotten to care for anything but himself. He had stood shaking with rage at the order to bow before an enfleshed creature, even one Divine. He had screamed in anguish, in rage, in jealousy that someone could supplant him as God's first son, even if that one were a son Begotten and not made.

Tabris had been distant then, but every angel had heard the cry, the protests, the denial that God could ask something so demeaning from someone so powerful. All the angels had heard then, and Tabris remembered the fright of realizing what Free Will really meant: it meant he could take back his hand, could say no, and could follow his own plans instead of Another's.

If I break apart now, he wondered, standing at the rocky edge of the vertical precipice, *will I fall like Lucifer? Are tears an angel's method of despair? And would the despair be unjustified in my case?*

Rachmiel, the angel with eyes the color of sunrise, turned to him and took his hand, the brilliant red and purple swirl of his eyes saying that God had made Himself present in Rachmiel's spirit, possessing him with permission to use the body for a little while, and Rachmiel would have no awareness afterward when God let go.

"Not now," Tabris said, and the swirl faded even though he refused to relinquish Rachmiel's hand. He needed that strength, at least.

Sebastian had begun shaking his head in near disbelief, but the two angels Casifer and Rachmiel had already
made the transition from that ecstatic state and were able
to ease him down to normal levels of perception.

"I could have stayed there forever," Sebastian
gasped.

"When you're capable, you'll have that all the time,"
Casifer said. "That's the Beatific Vision. Angels have that
level of awareness and higher."

Tabris smoldered, staring darkly at Casifer.

Sebastian's mouth opened. "And you can still func-
tion normally? What's your prayer like?"

"We meet God soul to soul, not just face to face,"
Rachmiel said. "It's a more total union. Most humans
would explode with that kind of experience."

"You'll develop as time goes on, so your capacity will
deepen and your endurance will become greater," said
Casifer. "When you're ready, God will take you into
Heaven for good, and then the experience will be easier
on your mind—and eternal."

Rachmiel watched what happened next, and
watched helplessly: Sebastian realized that if he had been
allowed to live to his full development he would have
entered directly into Heaven—but more than that, the
suffering he endured in life would have deepened his
capacity to hold the Vision far beyond what he saw now.

The anger rose for an instant before Sebastian could
control it.

"Thank you for visiting," Rachmiel said, speaking
forcefully to get Sebastian to concentrate on him and not
on Tabris. "Will we visit again soon?"

"God willing," said Casifer, holding Sebastian's hand
tightly.

"Thank you so much," Sebastian said smoothly, his
voice so much a parody of Tabris' that Rachmiel fought
himself not to wince or close his eyes. The boy had no
idea that Tabris could do the same thing, and Rachmiel
felt as though he had a truly unfair relationship to this
child as well as a new perspective on Tabris' defense

mechanisms. "I'll look forward to seeing you both again," Sebastian said, giving a spiritual hug to Rachmiel and Tabris although Tabris' was somewhat more clumsy. Then they vanished, returning to Limbo.

22

TABRIS STOOD STRAIGHT FOR A MOMENT, THEN turned to the ocean.

Rachmiel extended his heart. "Are you all right?"

"I—I'm thinking . . . No, I'm not all right." He bowed his head. "I'm not, and I won't be ever again."

He dropped down to sit on the edge of the cliff, swinging his legs so that his heels hit the loose stone without knocking any free. Then he inched forward.

"Tabris, don't do that," Rachmiel said, touching his shoulder. "No jump from the heights can kill you."

"No, it's the gesture that counts. One plunge to the rocks as though I can leap away from it all. At times I wonder if immortality isn't a curse. It certainly is in hell. One mistake and I'm wearing a scarlet *M* for all God's creation to see. And the child is so unbelievably angry I'm surprised he can control it. He radiates once in a while, seismic rings that rattle out from his heart and strike me with as much regularity as a pulse. And sometimes, when I do something that reminds him that he's dead, the rage erupts, but then he pulls it back just before he releases it all."

"Just like you." Rachmiel sat beside him on the ledge. "He's trying hard to keep himself bound so tightly that no one can tell what he's feeling. But he's young yet. He doesn't have your control. He slips."

Tabris bent forward and put his face down in his palms. Shuddering, he said, "I didn't teach that to him. He learned it on his own. It's innate."

"Tabris, is he ashamed and that's why he hides his feelings?"

Tabris fell forward onto his knees and gasped. "Rock, please don't push it. I'm so close to losing it now. Don't talk."

"You think he's ashamed."

"God!" Tabris shouted. "God, please stop him!" He flung back his head and stared into the sky. "Don't let him—"

"Maybe you need to let go, just once. It's unreal to try to deny that much. If you're ashamed, tell me. Cry if you have to. It's all right."

Tabris flashed back ten feet from the edge. "Look, I can't, not here, not now. I want to be private, alone, so that if I do cry I'm on my own. You wouldn't have to see me—to see what—"

He fell to his knees and buried his face in his hands. Rachmiel curled over him and held him gently, pouring the ease out of his heart like an offering of wine or water, being present the way a mother will say "shh" to a frightened child.

"To see what your soul is like when it's not clouded over?"

Tabris struggled to escape Rachmiel, whose arms held strong and tight around him. He fought to get his head up, to leave this orange-feathered cocoon that was shielding him from the outside world but trapping him with himself. "Please, I don't want anyone to know, but everyone does, they all see me and remember that I wrapped my hands around a boy's neck and snapped it as he hit the ground. And I'll never be the same. Not with you, not with God, not with—"

He broke off suddenly. Rachmiel gripped him tightly, almost surprised at how Tabris had lost his strength, and definitely frightened by the muscles that had turned as soft as jam. "Not with Sebastian?"

"Or with me."

Finding a little strength, Tabris sat up to lean against Rachmiel, laying his head against the other angel's shoulder.

Rachmiel waited to feel the first of the tears on his shoulder, and he rocked Tabris easily. "But you haven't lost Sebastian completely."

"I lost his trust. Without that the rest is worthless. I loved him more than I love Elizabeth—I loved him more than *you* love Elizabeth, for crying out loud! But in his best interest I sent him to heaven too soon and I lost him forever. One mistake! One—and I lose everything!"

He quieted momentarily, long enough for Rachmiel to say "You didn't lose everything."

"You're hinting at God's love like a good little angel. He's losing patience too." Tabris lifted a hand to his eyes and found to his surprise that there were no tears. "I hurt Him also. I lost His trust along with the rest. He doesn't answer me any longer, even when I do call, and I'm—I'm slowly falling out of love with Him."

Tabris grabbed Rachmiel tightly, looking out over the western waters, still gasping with the dry heaves of a tearless cry. "I know it's unorthodox, but could you ask God if He still loves me?"

"Did you ever read of the prodigal son?"

"The older son didn't kill the younger son when he repented. I did." Tabris sat up and away from Rachmiel, but he pulled him back. "The younger son gets the fatted calf. The older son gets chewed out."

Tabris looked up at the stars overhead. "Look what I've done to myself—I can't even cry any more, I'm so used to keeping a hold on my emotions. Look at me—the pearl of great price smashed, the five hundred talents buried, it's all the same. The wise virgins spilling out their extra oil and burning it. It's me. I accepted a gift from God and flung it back at Him."

"But maybe you're not all these things you say. You're the younger son in as many ways as the older, and in a lot of ways *you're* the pearl that God finds, and *you're* the talents that He invests and multiplies."

Tabris shifted a little to lean more completely on Rachmiel. "How can you say that?"

"I believe He forgives."

"Only if you're human. Lucifer was never forgiven."

"He never asked."

"Neither did I."

Rachmiel grabbed Tabris tightly, as though he were afraid he would be snatched away by a sudden wind. "Why not?"

"Because I deserve this—the Vision stripped away, the difficulty in prayer, the hatred of that child, the righteous anger of all my friends. I could never ask to be forgiven because I can't balance all the scales."

"But God can."

"No. He can't make Sebastian do all the things he was supposed to, to fulfill His plans in the way only Sebastian with his background and personality could have done. Imagine if Mary had said no to Gabriel—would he have gone door to door? No one could have mothered Jesus just the way she did. Sebastian can't develop his soul as he ought to have. He'll never get married, have children, go to college, hold a job, you know. And his children's plans have been frustrated because they won't be his children any longer. And what about the woman he should have married? Will she be able to marry and have kids anyway? And what about her new husband, who shouldn't have married her but someone else instead? The repercussions are infinite."

"But you're speaking as though there hasn't been another untimely death in all creation."

"Not by a guardian."

"Well, no." He rocked Tabris slowly, very aware of the tension caused by unshed tears even though he was calmer. "But in human terms, life goes on anyway. God's plan is more dynamic than we imagine. He created us with free will—don't you believe He took that into account? We aren't cast in roles."

Tabris made no protest, but he had grown tense. "His parents, his children, though—he's not there any longer."

"The children are hypothetical anyway. His parents are surviving. And his wife—don't worry about her. She'll be fine."

Tabris yanked away and stared at Rachmiel, who nonverbalized, too late, a retraction.

"Try not to overreact," he suggested, his eyes almost closed.

"His wife?" Tabris hissed, jumping to his feet. "Elizabeth? And you didn't tell me? How long have you known?"

"About two weeks. Don't be upset. She won't—"

"But Elizabeth! I've done so much over the past six months to keep her safe and not hurt her in the slightest, and now—and I hurt her in the worst," he gasped, stepping backward, "in the worst way! I took her husband! Oh, God, God," and he collapsed to his knees, then prostrated himself completely, unable even to breathe.

Rachmiel tried to move closer, but Tabris leaped up and shoved him backward, clothed solidly in battle armor and an instant after that holding a sword which blazed brightly. They stood that way for a moment, two angels on a cliff top against the speckled dome of the sky: the peacemaker, a son of God, and another who mourned but would not be comforted. Rachmiel looked at Tabris from where he crouched and wondered at the raw power of the angel, how much was frenzy and how much God's gift. Shimmering all about him, the energy pulsed like a green quasar, radiating more than anger and betrayal—there was self-hatred too, as though by attacking Rachmiel, Tabris could annihilate himself, or else—and Rachmiel knew this with sudden cold certainty—prompt God to condemn him once and for all time. Knowing this was precisely why when Tabris did attack, Rachmiel stayed immobile and took the blow.

Tabris would have dismembered him and tossed him into the Pacific if God had not made Rachmiel completely incorporeal, like light, so that Tabris' sword passed through his body and lodged three inches deep in the stone.

Rachmiel shuddered, wrapped in fear but determined not to allow Tabris to try to force God's hand.

Tabris heaved up his sword, an effort that involved his whole body and made him gasp, and then he used his whole body again as he sliced through Rachmiel in the other direction, as though swinging through a dust cloud.

Rachmiel winced under the burst of Tabris' anger. The sword was useless against him now, but God never could shield him from emotional weaponry. It was against his nature not to feel what another creature felt, and Tabris realized this the instant Rachmiel did. He grinned maliciously.

"Why hesitate?" Rachmiel asked, his voice trembling a little.

Tabris blasted him then. His anger was not as fully blown as Rachmiel had expected, but it hurt him anyway, blacking his vision for the moment so that whenever it ended, and Rachmiel had no idea how much time had passed before it did, he found himself lying on the ground. He pushed himself up halfway, ignoring the fear in which his whole soul was enveloped, to look around. Tabris sat against a rock a short distance away, watching him darkly.

They stared at each other, kindness and truth, Compassion and Free Will, neither moving, Rachmiel seemingly frozen in place halfway up from the ground. Neither one could speak for a long time. Tabris had reverted to emotional emptiness again, and Rachmiel's heart had grown so terrified that he had no will power left even to be brave and ask Tabris if he were all right. A small, small part of Rachmiel wanted very badly to leave, to fly to Elizabeth and guard the room until Tabris promised he would never return. That part of Rachmiel clamored on the surface of his heart, shrieking that he didn't care any longer what happened to Tabris, how Tabris felt, or if Tabris was sorry. He had been hurt in his one vulnerable area.

Tabris had to detect that noisy panic, but the part of Rachmiel's soul that dictated his next actions was the same one that comforted Elizabeth after she threw a temper tantrum. He struggled to sit up, moving cautiously, and then looked away from Tabris.

"Listen," Tabris said, "I'll go get Voriah and then leave you forever."

Rachmiel made no answer, but clearly he did not agree to the proposal.

"I'll take myself off your hands. You have a daughter at home who needs you."

"So do you. She's fine. Don't leave."

Tabris looked up and his eyes gleamed, but Rachmiel did not see it.

Rachmiel shook his head, trying to think of something to say.

"Rock, I'll just go."

"That doesn't solve the problem, and you can't leave Elizabeth. You're still on probation. I'd leave her myself before I put you in danger of damnation." He looked up fiercely. "No nonsense out of you, all right? No begging that I kill you or send you away."

"I won't do that," Tabris said, his eyes somewhat sharper.

They continued looking at each other, and then Rachmiel stood up, regretting it the instant he tried when his vision swirled like multicolored sand in a dust devil.

Tabris was there. "I really hurt you, didn't I?"

"Kind of you to notice," Rachmiel said lowly, leaning into the hands and wings that suddenly supported him and held him in their warmth. He closed his eyes against the harsh glare of the daylight, suddenly realizing—daylight? And who knew which day's light it was?

"Same day," Tabris said. "I knocked you out for about six hours."

Rachmiel considered standing on his own, and Tabris released him just long enough to decide to postpone his independence a little longer. He felt Tabris close the hollow of his wings over him, against his back, and forced himself not to panic, to recover his strength quickly and willfully.

A moment after he did that Tabris apologized.

The nonverbalization caught Rachmiel unexpectedly, giving him a rush of elated surprise and relief, and he responded with his own unsaid apology for probing at the deep inner wounds of an angel who had lost the love of his son.

Tabris held him tightly.

Rachmiel closed his eyes. "You asked if any angel could love you," he said. "At the time I didn't. Now I do. There's a brilliance to your soul that has to be loved, it's that impressive. You've still got a pure heart beneath all that control and denial."

"But I hurt you!" Tabris said, his arms closer around Rachmiel than was necessary for support only. "I knocked you unconscious!"

"But you opened your heart to me even after you thought I hated you. Maybe you thought you deserved the punishment, but I don't think so. You apologized and you meant it, and for a moment I saw God's glory in your heart, and I knew you had to be loved, by God and by me."

Tabris was actively resisting the urge to push him away, but only because he knew Rachmiel would collapse on his own. The concern seeped from Tabris' heart, his one nonverbalization following the next as though they were looped together like chain links, and he was unsure why he had suddenly released his self-control. He had spent the past six months in spiritual rigidity, avoiding the pain that would come when he let another angel see what he really felt, and yet now, so soon after he had come closer to hating Rachmiel than he had any other creature outside himself, now he had opened his heart to him.

"If you're so determined to love me," he said with forced harshness, "you should know what you're up against."

Rachmiel shuddered at the fear that had managed to creep into Tabris' voice. Tabris felt the residual fear on Rachmiel and recognized the urge to pull away and hide, too achingly familiar to him. He grabbed Rachmiel tighter, and then, without giving himself time to change his mind or become terrified to the point of paralysis, he released all the restraints on his heart and engulfed Rachmiel with his soul.

He felt Rachmiel's nonverbal astonishment, the genuine love that proved his earlier words no lie. For a moment Tabris had the oddest visual images: sunflowers, children, Ferris wheels, fish, and opals. Then he relaxed more, trying not to call to mind that he was a murderer, failing from the sheer strain of simultaneously remembering yet not remembering.

Rachmiel stilled him, as if his heart's fingers had spread and pressed down on his soul, calmed him. The touch said that nothing could rob Tabris of this one true friend, this co-guardian who loved him the way God did, appreciating all the intricate structures of his soul and realizing the architecture of God. From the inside and outside at once, Rachmiel could see Tabris the way Tabris himself could not, and Tabris felt wonderment as he congratulated God on yet another masterpiece. Tabris felt embarrassed but not ashamed. He wanted suddenly to hide, to deny that God had made him specially instead of mass producing angels and naming one of them Tabris, an alphabetical serial number. Rachmiel shushed him, seeing all of Tabris' potential and being impressed with his findings.

Then the two-toned angel rebelled, showed Rachmiel the guilt, the anger, and the loathing he could feel, the lack of trust in God that could make a guardian a killer. He showed him all the resentment he held toward the angels who did not understand, the rage against the ones who pretended they did—until a while ago, the fury against Rachmiel himself. On the pages of his memory were written all the times he had wished himself damned, the briefest instants when he had wanted to fling himself away from Love entirely so that he could hate the things that now he found so frustrating and then could justifiably hate himself.

Rachmiel grieved but not because Tabris had done something evil. Rather, because Tabris had suffered so much at his own hands.

My hands failed first, Tabris thought.

Silencing him, Rachmiel showed Tabris around the interior of his soul to prove that what could be so frustrated without hating, failing only in small ways for short moments, was indeed a glorious creature and loved by God anyway.

"Not as much as before," Tabris said, speaking because that was too painful to nonverbalize.

Rachmiel pulled up his memory of the parable of the ninety-nine sheep who did not stray while the shepherd went in search of the one who had, reminding him that the shepherd loved that sheep more than before once he had retrieved him.

Positions had reversed. Tabris was shaking from the strain on his soul and Rachmiel had grown stronger doing what his nature required of him: identifying with a creature in anguish. Instead of holding him up, Tabris was leaning on Rachmiel, who stood taller under the other's weight.

Tabris showed Rachmiel what he felt was proof that God no longer held him in the same love: there had been no immediate punishment following the crime. He remembered for Rachmiel all the other angels who had been punished for far slighter offenses, making them truer to their own natures: the crowning example was the Archangel Gabriel, cut away from Heaven for a year as the result of a tiny infraction in 600 B.C. He nonverbalized, *God loved them enough to reform them, why not me? Why just probation?*

Rachmiel's eyes suddenly swirled, and Tabris swallowed, realizing with acute distress that God had possessed Rachmiel and was just now wedged inside his heart, inhabiting his awareness. Even though he had known that God saw his heart through the guards he maintained against other angels, the added vulnerability of his position made him uncomfortable. Rachmiel smiled, the orange and red of his eyes spinning in a way that reminded Tabris of twin hurricanes on a satellite photo. Through Rachmiel, God nonverbalized into Tabris with the instant understanding that humans call inspiration.

God revealed that a harsher punishment would have caused Tabris to despair at the beginning of his recovery.

His punishment had been severe as it was: Sebastian had been taken from him.

His capacity for the Vision had been slashed, albeit by Tabris' own choice.

He had to live with the memory and the knowledge of his crime.

These punishments alone had nearly crushed him. In fact, all that had kept him solvent after the trial was the hope that God still loved him. Any words of reprimand would have been not only redundant but also crippling.

Tabris nodded, still fighting the urge to snap his heart shut like a clamshell, but then the swirl left Rachmiel's eyes and the other angel stood away from him, renewed in strength although still linked to his heart.

"You're shaking."

Tabris nonverbalized that Rachmiel was observant. Beneath the sarcasm lay a very deep knowledge that he was at the end of his efforts.

Rachmiel stopped reading into Tabris' heart and smiled a gentle smile.

"Yes—I'll be all right," said Tabris.

"Thank you. You don't look ecstatic."

"I'm very tired. Let's go."

Rachmiel did not mention how Tabris' eyes had brightened for a moment, nor that Tabris was no longer an emotional black hole and had become more like a man-made lake with a concrete dam—emotionally present to Rachmiel even though carefully controlled.

They flashed to Elizabeth.

23

LISTENING INTENTLY TO HER TEACHER, ELIZA-
beth did not detect the return of Rachmiel and Tabris.
The substitute guardian greeted both, then said, "You
took a lot longer than eight hours—Voriah summoned
me when Alan woke up."

"Thank you," Rachmiel said. "Is she all right?"

"Fine—she had trouble waking this morning. At
about three-thirty she woke with a start. Did something
happen?"

"Something. I suppose she just turned off the light
and went to bed?"

"No, her mother had tucked her in at about ten.
She's been fine all morning."

Rachmiel nodded and the other angel left.

Tabris had overlooked the other angel's time dys-
lexia (he had never been a guardian), and noticed only
that others always reported to Rachmiel and avoided
even looking at him.

"Force of habit," said Rachmiel.

A growing sense of angelic wonder filled the classroom: the other guardians had noticed how much more
open Tabris was today than he was yesterday. Perceiving
their surprise, he locked his soul and sealed his expression. Rachmiel moved toward Elizabeth, holding her for
a moment and saying he was sorry for not being around
earlier in the day. Tabris stood perfectly at attention, his
uniform in order and his sword ready at his side while
Rachmiel slipped onto the desk where Elizabeth sat,
swinging his legs a little.

"Did you miss me, kid?" he asked. "A little, in the deep recesses of your heart, did you understand I was away?"

Tabris still stood at attention. No matter how much Rachmiel claimed equality, no matter how often he deferred to Tabris' decision, Elizabeth still was his. Tabris never could love her as he did. Rachmiel looked up and realized in an instant that he still thought of himself and Elizabeth as the angel-human team and never included Tabris in that interior image. Deep within his protector facade, Tabris had realized this. Perhaps he even understood.

Rachmiel nonverbalized, *Sebastian will return to you.*

Tabris turned away, pacing as though patrolling a perimeter. With great effort of will, Rachmiel stopped his train of thought, deferring it at least until they could speak privately.

Tabris had emitted a nonverbalized negation of Rachmiel's whole sentiment: denying that Sebastian would one day love him, that he even wanted that love, or that there could be a happy ending for the angel named Free Will. The trembling hope had lain naked to Rachmiel's sight for the barest second before being swallowed in enforced cynicism, self-doubt, guilt. For a moment Tabris' eyes had brightened, wanting to match the certainty before retracting the mistake, hoping then that having actively expressed a desire would not be the cause of that desire's never being fulfilled.

Like a suit of armor serving as a decoration, Tabris stood by the door, immobile but very impressive, impervious, and seemingly soulless. Tabris had dropped out of emotional existence, no longer showing even a faint spectrum of suppressed emotions—he had sucked all his energies into himself as though no longer feeling anything, and he managed to maintain that pose for the next ten hours.

While Casifer idly played a clarinet, Sebastian sat reading Heaven's equivalent of the *Summa Theologica,* written by none other than the guardian angel of Thomas Aquinas. He had trouble concentrating. Finally he closed the book and laid his head down on the leather cover.

"Is something wrong?" Casifer had continued playing so the question must have been nonverbal, concern emitted in the rough and formed into a familiar human expression only in Sebastian's mind.

"Maybe."

Casifer put down the instrument. "Cass," Sebastian said, "where is he right now? My guardian," he answered the nonverbal query. "Where is he?"

"I suppose he's guarding Elizabeth, wherever she is."

"That's annoying. I mean, shouldn't he be here?"

"Not if you're angry."

Sebastian sat smoldering for a little while.

Casifer sighed. "Of course he feels guilty. He has to feel somewhat guilty or else he'd have been damned."

"Then why isn't he here? Why do you have to do his job?"

Casifer sat closer to the boy. "He had no choice in the matter. I was assigned to you immediately after you died, and he was placed with Elizabeth after his judgment."

"So that he could kill her, too?"

"That's not fair, Sebastian. Tabris always did a good job for you. He provided everything you needed all your life."

"Except for the one thing that mattered." Sebastian looked at his small hands. "He didn't love me enough to let me develop into whatever God was making me. He cared for his own free will but not for mine."

Sebastian looked into Casifer's face, his eyes rapidly darkening, growing smaller.

"You'll have to forgive him before you enter Heaven."

"I don't think," Sebastian said, "—God help me—" through clenched teeth, "that I want to."

"He's a creature of God," Casifer said. "He's your guardian, but he's also your brother. Before God he's just as small and frightened as you are. He's hurt and angry, too. Try to see him that way."

"He had to do better. That's why *he* was put in charge of *me*."

Casifer put his arms around the boy and squeezed him tightly, rocking him slowly until he stopped resisting and relaxed in the angel's arms.

After a long time of just sitting and rocking, Sebastian spoke in a cracked voice, a child's voice. "Why didn't he come himself? Why didn't he send Rachmiel?"

And Casifer found he had no response for this angry and abandoned child—more abandoned than angry. He continued holding him for a while.

Tabris dropped the uncaring mask for Rachmiel with the understood condition that whatever he said or did was private. No one would be told, no one else would be invited. For the first time, Rachmiel comprehended how much strain Tabris endured keeping himself so strapped. No wonder he had needed long periods of solitary time. Sprawled in the easy chair by the window while Elizabeth finished her science homework, Tabris closed his eyes as if he would sleep and sighed.

"He'll come back tonight," Rachmiel said. "I'm sure he will."

"I'm not. You're acting as though he were you. He's more like me, far more liable to distance himself and mull over it than to approach me. No, Sebastian won't return again. Not soon, at any rate. He'll probably visit me right before he gets into Heaven because it's a requirement that he cancel all outstanding debts or something. There'll be some silly act of forgiveness, and I do mean act as in putting on a show. Then he'll be acquitted of the prerequisite and he'll enter Paradise."

"No lie ever entered Heaven."

"No, lies leave Heaven."

Tabris looked sullenly at his hands. "God won't ask the impossible, though." Rachmiel swallowed, tasting bitterness on his tongue that had to be a reflection of Tabris because it certainly was not emanating from Elizabeth. Tabris looked at him and smiled. "Maybe I took out both of us. Maybe God can ask the impossible. He has high standards, and maybe by killing Sebastian I've assured that he'll remain in Limbo because he can't ever forgive me."

"Now stop it!" Rachmiel exclaimed with enough force to startle Elizabeth, who returned to work almost without realizing it. "You're being ridiculous!"

"You know what I like about you, Rock? I like how I can stay calm, and you begin to fly completely off the handle as I get more and more withdrawn. You think I'm perfectly serious all the time."

"Aren't you?"

"What scares me most is that I don't know. I play with ideas verbally, and I don't know how many of them I believe. I don't think I'm lying, but the irony of what I'm saying is in my blood."

They stayed quiet for a while. Rachmiel looked over Elizabeth's shoulder and pointed out that she had written concave instead of convex on problem three, said it again, and then turned back to face Tabris, who was frowning as he thought. "You know, if he does forgive me I won't know what to do."

"That's not difficult," Rachmiel said. "You hug him."

Tabris shifted his eyes, the color of honey mixed with blood, and regarded Rachmiel with disdain of—or hunger for—his innocence. "No, I mean longer term, as in, what do I do about Elizabeth? She's my job, but so is he, and I can't do both. So maybe it's best that he won't do it meaningfully in this lifetime."

"Tabris, no offense, but God works quickly." Rachmiel stood. "You're right, though. You'll have to choose one or the other."

What remained unspoken was the understanding of why a guardian angel never was assigned two human charges in all eternity, even if the first had been damned. If Sebastian were near Tabris and Elizabeth while she was awake, then the Tabris-Sebastian bond would spiral into the Tabris-Elizabeth bond—more so because Sebastian and Elizabeth had been made for one another. In essence, Elizabeth would begin to sense Sebastian's thoughts and feelings, would hear voices, and would lose her mind. This problem could be solved neatly by keeping Sebastian and Elizabeth separated, but that meant Tabris had to choose between them.

"I've been making choices all my life," Tabris said. "I'm not sure why this one is so difficult, but I dread it. In the natural order of things, I shouldn't be here. But I am, and I have a responsibility toward her. I think she needs me."

"I won't dispute that," Rachmiel said. "You work extremely well with her. But I could manage alone again if I had to."

Tabris smiled a curvy smile, an icy smile that had seen the Lord about to reject him and then had looked past that into the Divine determination to extract good from evil, freedom from fate. Rachmiel felt the spiritual temperature drop enough to make him shiver.

"You, ah, had an idea?"

"With two of us around she's strong, stronger than with one. But even that original strength was sufficient. You read Milton—'Sufficient to stand but free to fall.' Well, with the two of us, her temptations will be greater, but so will her accomplishments. If I leave, the good she produces will still be in proportion to her temptations, but that will necessarily be less."

Rachmiel said, "I don't think God would affect her that drastically because of any choices you make," and then regretted it.

"Right. Wasn't Sebastian's growth stunted because I cut him off?"

Rachmiel fidgeted, emitting bright clouds of worry.

"So I have to stay," Tabris said. "For Elizabeth's good. But if Sebastian ever decided I was worth the effort to forgive, he'd probably want me to stay with him again full time. I couldn't abandon him once more, Rock. I'd—I'd have to be crazy. But then I think about Elizabeth, because she's my responsibility now. I gave up Sebastian. Now he belongs to that other angel, and that's the only guardian he knows."

"That's not true. You're important even though you're with someone else's family. He has Casifer, that's true, but Casifer is clearly a substitute. The one he really wants is you. Casifer knows that too, but he stays because he's a lot like me and that's what Sebastian needs right now."

Tabris startled with questions.

"We're giving emotional support, unconditional tenderness, gentility of spirit. You're like Sebastian, though, and you'll need to be there before the end to give him proper spiritual formation."

"He can't enter Heaven without me?" Tabris asked, bolting upright. "That's crazy! That means that if I'd been damned he would have been condemned to eternal Limbo! Rock, you've got to be wrong!"

Clearly Tabris had not been as serious as he had sounded before when he had suggested the same thing so casually.

"It's more than just forgiveness, though," Rachmiel said. "He needs you, the guidance and example only you can provide. You're the best role model he could have."

"No," Tabris said angrily, "my *potential* is the best role model he could have. What I am isn't . . . it's what he shouldn't be, shouldn't ever do. Rachmiel, I failed my one child more than I ever knew! I can't possibly know all the damage I've caused. Or rectify it." He dropped into the chair, actually fell backward, and said, "If I don't deserve Hell, no creature ever did."

Rachmiel flashed to his side, holding his hands tightly. "Don't say that. There's mercy too, the mercy that saved you and gave you this time to prove yourself trustworthy. Please don't do this to yourself."

Tabris snatched back his hands. "Stop fawning!"

"But you're sulking!"

"Please! This isn't self-serving behavior. This is confusion. Don't you know me by now?"

"No," Rachmiel said quietly, "I don't."

Tabris felt the fiery comeback dissolve in his mouth, and he locked gazes with Rachmiel.

"I'm sorry."

"It's okay. Just—don't keep bandying about damnation as though God's in Heaven rubbing His hands together in anticipation, just waiting for you to mess up. He's not like that."

Tabris lay back in the chair so that he could look at the ceiling. "I still don't know what to do about Sebastian and Elizabeth, at any rate."

Rachmiel smiled gently. "Let's pray over it."

Tabris realized suddenly that Americans throw money at their problems and angels throw prayers. "How about you pray and tell me the results?" he said hesitantly.

"You have to be open."

"I am open. I'm just not getting too open. I don't want God to flood me, not yet. Can you . . . scout out the situation for me?"

Rachmiel's mouth twitched, but Tabris could feel him grasping for God's heart already.

God's voice sounded in his mind, *Why must you hide from me?*

Tabris flattened as though he had been swatted, prostrate and shaking. "I—I'm right here."

God's disapproving response nearly flattened Rachmiel as well. "Please," said the orange-winged guardian, "can't you enlighten us? I'm not asking for a solution."

Tabris realized that the answer would come only if he were the one to ask, and he wondered if he really wanted to know all that badly. Then he thought about Sebastian, about having to choose between responsibility and longing, about the way Sebastian would make his eyes round the way he always had done when asking for an important favor from his real father. He had to know

now in order to be able to refuse to stay with the boy when the time came, if that time ever did.

"Why do you want to know?" Jesus asked, standing solidly in the place which only moments before had been empty.

Tabris closed his eyes and he began shaking, but not out of fear this time. The Lord had seen into his heart and knew exactly why he had wanted God to speak—that he already suspected very strongly what the answer had to be.

"I mustn't scapegoat you," Tabris said. "That's against my nature. I'm sorry."

Jesus moved closer, bent down, touched his shoulders and his two-toned wings. The touch terrified Tabris for an instant, but then filled him with calm.

"It has to be Elizabeth," Tabris said. "She's my responsibility. There'll be time for leisure in a hundred years or so. But God, he's only going to grow up once."

"He's grown a lot in the past six months," Jesus said.

Tabris choked on one small cry that had managed to work its way as far as his heart before he stopped it, although its roots extended as deeply as his soul.

Jesus tried to coax him to sit upright but Tabris resisted, so He bent and put His head beside the angel's. Then, after a moment of unspoken words, He departed.

Tabris rolled onto his side, curled like an unborn child.

Rachmiel touched his arm, and when Tabris sat upright the sunbeams that fell onto his eyes were swallowed by the dark discs in the center.

Rachmiel's eyes said, *So it's decided.*

"Apparently so," Tabris said. He shook his head, then looked at Elizabeth. Suddenly he was standing behind her, looking over her shoulder at her science homework and sighing. "Sweetie, if I'm giving up Sebastian for you, the least you can do is learn the difference between concave and convex."

Rachmiel smiled tenderly, and it did not escape his notice that Elizabeth paused and began thinking about it for a moment before deciding her wrong answer was right. "That probably *is* the least she can do."

Tabris nodded, almost pained. "I suppose. I need a good workout, Rock—will you spar with me?"

"Mentally."

"No—come on, put on a sword and let's use metal. I'm tired of using my intellect. I want something more base, something far more automatic than theology. I'm tired of working hard to understand God, my soul, myself. Let's slaughter each other."

"Mentally."

"I'm not interested in dialogue!" he gasped, clenching his fists.

"I am."

"I'm going to find Miriael," he said, his eyes glinting. "Have fun with Elizabeth."

As he flashed out of the room, between being with Rachmiel and being with Miriael (if there can be a "between" when the travel is instantaneous) he changed his mind, so that when Rachmiel followed him to Miriael, Tabris was elsewhere.

24

TABRIS LANDED IN HEAVEN.

Destination, or whatever the demon was calling himself now, was standing a few feet away from him, smiling snidely in the white-blue light that streamed in through the glass windowpane. The building in which they stood—airily empty of furniture and panelled with oak varnished to a slippery shine—was Tabris' carefully selected spot out of all Heaven's infinite acreage, built on the top of a snowy mountain. This small, square one-room cabin with large windows overlooked an ice-choked stream and a vertical drop that would make a human being's heart pound in fright at the frozen sight of it.

"Spar with me," said the demon.

"Why?" Tabris said, his eyes as narrow as needles' eyes.

"To be rid of me forever. To work off energy. To prove something to yourself." He paused. "The reasons are infinite. To arouse your hunger for life. Take your pick. It's all the same to me."

"My damnation."

"Oh please, not even God is that unreasonable. Maybe if you had surrendered over New York Harbor then you'd be in serious trouble, but this is just recreational fun, isn't it?"

"Not if you've taken an interest, Destination."

"What a corny name," said the demon, turning to look out the window at the snow which reflected the sun's glare. "I'll change it, what do you think?"

"It's really no concern of mine."

"I will—Hell's a free country. What to change it to, though?"

"Could you think elsewhere, Nameless One?"

"I'll bounce ideas off you. Recklessness? No, too long. Primrose Path? That's sweet but too feminine."

"How about Condemned-by-God?"

"That's taken. Let's see." He smiled wickedly, showing if not all his teeth then certainly most of them, human-like teeth for his being a demon. He had been an angel first. "I know, Tabris—America! What better name for a creature as unfettered as I am? Reckless, irresponsible, always taking the easy way out, addicted to recreation and my own personal ease at the cost of everyone else . . . it's perfect. I should have thought of it long before now!"

"Are you pleased?" Tabris asked.

"Unbelievably so." He turned about, looking at himself as though he were a model in a new dress. "It fits my soul. Come to think of it," and he looked up, "it fits yours too, you short-sighted assassin, sacrificing your son for a second or two of freedom from awesome and ridiculous responsibility."

Tabris lunged at America, catching the demon off guard. He had expected to have to taunt him for a half hour or more before getting even a slightly pulse-raising reaction, and he was hard put to defend himself at first, even after he summoned his sword and began blocking the blows.

This was no sparring. Both knew it, that Tabris' intention was far more deadly than ever it had been before. Even with Miriael, supposedly to the death-blow, there had been a sense of restraint on his motions which kept Tabris from dealing a fatal blow. As a result, Miriael had won most of the time, and Tabris had begun to wonder if he were still the warrior he once was. If anything, this match proved that he had not lost his skills by putting them into hibernation.

Again and again they clashed, Tabris hardly slacking his pace, expending all his rage at this his pretended friend. For a while the demon held his ground, wounding Tabris to match every wound he felt until both angels had been covered with each other's blood and each breathed loudly because of the pain. Frenzied, Tabris seemed hardly to notice whenever he scored or America did. He moved like a mighty engine, relentless and timeless. The demon began faltering, the fear shining in his eyes, and Tabris pinned him inside the cabin with his very will—far more effective than a Guard because it was so specific, so pointed that the demon writhed and tried blasting out of the room a number of different ways and failed every time.

Tabris slashed until the demon slipped in a pool of his own blood and dropped to the floor.

Keeping him pinned with the force of his will, Tabris stood over the demon. Fire blazed in his eyes and sweat mixed with ichor on the shiny feathers of his two-toned wings.

"You lose," he whispered.

The demon watched with wide eyes. "I can't have lost—not after so much time with you. You'll still come to me. We're still friends."

"No," Tabris said, his breath still heaving his whole chest with the effort every few seconds. "We're not. Maybe before, but not now. No longer. You've lost me."

The demon turned his head to see his reflection in the bloody puddle that was freezing on the panelled floor. "Tabris, please—"

"I know now what you're doing. I won't fall, though, I see that. Not willingly. You aren't going to force me to choose against Him anymore. I'm stronger, I've got His love and you don't, and that could turn back a thousand of you."

Tabris glowed, smiled as he sensed the Spirit's power in his heart. "I see now—you were enticing me to trust you, to play with you because there was no one else. You tried to isolate me."

"You did that yourself," said the demon. "You left me precious little to do on my own."

"Shut up. I know you, I remember what you were—Zeffar. The angel of irrevocable choices."

"We belong together," Zeffar said.

"We belong as far apart as we can be unless your choice is God."

Zeffar spat in his own blood.

"Then it's done, and you've chosen death, but you were as free as I was."

The demon sneered. "And your choice as irrevocable? These name games are garbage. I put off my name for a reason, because I refuse to be just what God made me. I'm not just an allegory of some part of Him. I want to be more."

"And as long as that's what you want, a caricature is all you'll ever be."

The demon snapped up his head. "You're the one to talk about caricatures! You puppet! You're a puppet—God knew! He knew it all along! He knew you were going to kill Sebastian on his bicycle when he was twelve years old—and not only did He go on to create the both of you, but He matched you up as his guardian anyway! And he kept Casifer from being a guardian just so that he could pick up the pieces after you shattered Sebastian's soul! How could He do that? Why didn't He do more to warn you? And now this kid is stunted for all eternity because He arranged this farce of Free Will!"

Tabris glared, shaking, but his will held.

Zeffar had tears in his amber eyes, and maybe they weren't entirely a pretense. Maybe, but Tabris had passed beyond pity's reach as far as Zeffar had surpassed Mercy's. This last attack might have left him disturbed, but he had heard the intent behind the words more than the words themselves. Zeffar had waited too long to fire his biggest gun, and Tabris had passed out of range.

"Is this it?" Zeffar whispered. "Forever? Have I really lost you to Him after all?"

The dark eyes narrowed.

"Give . . . Give me a call sometime," Zeffar said, the vibrant color of his spirit fading, his teeth worrying at his lower lip.

Tabris released his will, and the demon fled.

Looking at the blood slowly vanishing from the floor, Tabris fingered a wound on his arm distractedly and thought, *God, that was close, too close for me.* He knew that if he had sparred, had played the way Zeffar had wanted, if he had tried to reason his way through Zeffar's Möbius theology, he would have continued to doubt until eventually Zeffar had been the only one he trusted—and then he would have fallen.

"God, that was too close," he said again, this time aloud for the benefit of the oaken log walls of his cabin. "Thank you." He smiled as an inspired *You're welcome* tickled in his chest, and he walked to the window to stare at the snow cap of the mountain.

"If he ever lets me," Tabris said, "I'll bring Sebastian here."

God filled his heart with comfort, sad Himself that two creatures designed for one another should be hurting each other so deeply. "I don't blame him," Tabris said. The fingers of God tapped out a question on his heart. "Myself, of course," said Tabris. "That should be obvious."

"You don't tell me any longer," said God.

"I know," Tabris said. "I can't let you in. You understand, don't you?"

Suddenly Tabris noticed the humble log cabin, tiny, frigid, stained with blood and smelling of both sweat and wounds. The message was clear: God would come into any place, no matter the size or the dirt, if one of His children needed Him. Could—no, would. He would fly to the rescue like a mother running into a flaming house to save her children, no matter the pain, the danger, the filth. The child mattered, and now that child was Tabris.

"I'm not a house," he said.

God said, "A soul is much finer than any building."

Tabris tilted back his head, looking at the ceiling he had not seen in thirteen years, or perhaps fourteen—time had only mattered when it mattered to Sebastian, and since then it had become an obsession. Moments that once had flooded from somewhere into somewhere else had become a mystery when they were inhabited by a changing creature he loved. Moments meant so much to creatures that perished after a finite number of them—they were saved in the boxes of the mind, hoarded, cherished, hated, and feared. Tabris had begun looking with Sebastian's eyes toward future moments which they might spend together, the milestones as important as the oatmeal breakfasts and the ordinary afternoons and the times when Sebastian untied his shoes before going to bed at night. Time had been his addiction after that. How long had eternity been before Sebastian? Creationists had argued with evolutionists about whether creation occurred in six days or six billion years, and Tabris had been confused—he had forgotten the time it had taken, and remembered only that God's hand had manufactured the little pieces that made space and fit them one into the next to create a seamless garment for the creatures He called humans and sons of God.

In human minutes and seconds, how long would it be until the next time he saw Sebastian? There had been a delightful pain in his presence, paradoxical because the boy could wound him more deeply than any creature could. Only God could strike deeper. Because he loved the boy, purely because of that, Sebastian could hurt him, all but destroy him, and Tabris would return again and again in the hopes of forgiveness and reunion.

"You and I both," God said.

Tabris gasped. "Am I that bad?"

"Come home," God said.

"I can't," Tabris said, realizing that in his own way he was playing Sebastian to God. "How can I let you into my heart when I've broken the one law you gave me?"

Tabris thought of humanity. "But that's different," he said, meaning the cross.

The image of Sebastian rose into his mind. God posed Tabris a question: even if Sebastian had not forgiven him, would he like to see him again?

"Yes."

"Then do the same for me."

"But I'm not angry at you!" Tabris said, his voice jumping in pitch. "I never blamed you!"

God surrounded Tabris with peace until the two-toned angel chose to absorb some of it. God had not meant that Tabris was angry with Him.

Tabris looked at his hands, then moved away from the window and sat in the corner of the empty cabin, drawing his knees to his chest, placing his hands flat on the cold wooden boards.

"Can I see Sebastian again?" he asked.

Tabris realized that God would not deny permission but Sebastian might. Tabris also knew that he himself might deny permission to God in the same way.

"If you want," he said softly, "just for now, I'll let you in a little."

God cuddled him, telling him not to be afraid, to take his time, not to rush into any decision from feelings of guilt or weariness. If he wanted God to fill the void in his heart, He always would be there.

"You're identifying yourself with Sebastian and then me with you," said the Spirit. "Don't project your pain onto me. I miss you, but not to tears. I want you home, but when you're ready."

"Is that why the father ran out to meet the prodigal son on the road, but didn't follow him to the distant land?"

"You make your own choices," said God. "If you choose me, I'll help you with every step, but if you run away I won't follow."

"Free will," said Tabris.

"Irrevocable choices," said God.

Tabris shifted so that his back rested in the corner where the two walls met and interlocked. "How long will I have to wait for Sebastian?"

"Until he wants to see you again. He's been praying for both himself and you."

"Thank him for me. Someday I might be able to return the favor."

"What's stopping you?" said the Spirit, so tangible in that small cabin that if Tabris closed his eyes he could imagine Him sitting cross-legged a few feet away.

"I feel like I should do some interior cleaning first. Of course," and Tabris grinned in self-mockery, "if I don't invite you in, I'll never do that interior cleaning."

The Spirit smiled at him, loving what He had made.

"How about this—if Sebastian forgives me then I'll pray."

"You're holding your soul hostage," said God. "I could just as easily say that I would prevent Sebastian from forgiving you until you prayed to me."

"You could," Tabris said. "And I'd pray immediately."

"I know you would," said God. "That's why I don't ask. When you open your heart to me, I want it to be for me and not Sebastian, even though that would be a perfectly acceptable motive. I'll take you any way I can, but you're still a guardian and your charge has to be your first cause now, before yourself, even before me. I designed guardians to be that way."

"But your will and their benefit would never be opposed to one another," Tabris said. "I thought my stunt proved that."

"The charge comes first," said God, and Tabris nodded with tears trapped in his heart but radiating from his spirit.

"I've sinned against Sebastian and against you."

"But I still love you, my son."

Tabris closed his eyes weakly. "Make him return to me—please. I know you can't compromise his free will, but could you tell him that I want to be on good ground again."

"I will," said God.

"I can't stand the deep-set anger in his eyes. It's almost as bad as when Rachmiel—"

He bolted to his feet. "Rachmiel! He has no idea where I am!"

God let him know that Rachmiel was worried but not afraid. Tabris bowed as though leaving His presence and returned to Rachmiel, who looked up immediately on his arrival.

"Tabris!" he said with a bright look in his eyes. "I'm glad you're back. Where were you?"

"Heaven." He relaxed his stand a little.

Rachmiel nodded. "You never got to Miriael."

"I changed my mind." He looked at his hands. "That's not to say I didn't get in any sparring. Zeffar returned."

"The demon?"

"I drove him off, for good this time. Not without some blood loss, but the job's done." A shadow crossed his face and he shifted nervously, wrapping his hands together and looking at his arms. "I'm all healed now. You'd never tell."

Rachmiel moved closer, opening his wings. "I can tell—he did hurt you. You're radiating nervousness and loss."

Tabris closed his eyes as though he had just been hurt again.

Rachmiel's eyes rounded.

Tabris smiled hesitantly, a little more on the right side than the left. "I'm not wounded that much, I'm just not shielding my whole soul."

Rachmiel gaped.

Tabris looked up, caught halfway between laughing and sulking. "That shouldn't surprise you. You're the one I trust."

Rachmiel nodded quickly, but he really was stunned.

"I know I haven't been as open as I might have," Tabris said, "but I realized today when I sent away Zeffar, you guys are the ones I should trust. I've had my priorities all mixed up, all wrapped in toward myself. I'm sorry, Rock. I'll try to be better."

Rachmiel hugged him tightly and was almost unwilling to let go, as though Tabris would be gone forever if he let this moment pass away into the rest of the moments God was stacking in that unreachable place called the past. Deep within his heart, Rachmiel clasped his spiritual hands together hopefully, and God clasped His hands around them.

A thought struck Rachmiel. "Maybe Sebastian will come once Elizabeth's asleep."

Rachmiel gasped suddenly as though he had been punched, feeling the knifelike pain in Tabris' heart. "No," he said, his eyes dark and liquid. "Not tonight. Maybe not ever."

"No," he whispered. "What did God tell you?"

"He didn't say that definitely," Tabris said, "but the child is like me, too much like what I am now. If after six months I'm only beginning to recover and still can't forgive myself, how can he? At least I used to love myself. He never knew me before the other night. Besides, he's got another guardian now."

Rachmiel's face reflected all Tabris' sad despair of ever regaining his son's love. Sebastian did not come that night, or the next few nights either. Tabris was very surprised when Sebastian showed up on the fifth night.

25

"HELLO," THE BOY SAID NERVOUSLY, THE LIGHT of God gleaming in his eyes. "How are you both?"

Rachmiel had half an instant of panic before flashing the three of them out of Elizabeth's bedroom—she was awake, and there might have been danger if Sebastian had stayed. Once they were away by a good distance Rachmiel answered, "Very good," almost vibrating with excitement. "Yourself?"

"I'm nearer to Heaven than before, and that's always amazing," Sebastian said, flashing a strong smile. "Actually, I was wondering if I might borrow Tabris for a few hours."

Rachmiel could sense Tabris' heart pounding so hard it hurt, and wondered if Sebastian had grown sensitive enough yet to detect it. "I'd love to," Tabris said in a soft voice. "Where's . . . ?"

"Casifer stayed behind."

Tabris nodded slowly, as though just now daring to believe the child was here with him. "And Rachmiel?"

"If you'd like," Sebastian said, "but I hadn't really planned it."

The boy was just as nervous as Tabris, which made Rachmiel's soul almost scream in anticipation. "I'll stay with Elizabeth," Rachmiel said, mentally reaching for stability from the ten year old who lay on her stomach doing homework. "Go, have a good time. Send postcards."

"Angels have a postal system?" Sebastian asked.

"He's picked up my sense of humor," Tabris said. "Don't mind him."

Rachmiel nonverbally pushed them away from the area, then froze in place for a second and began laughing with relief. He returned to Elizabeth, who while doing a math problem suddenly rolled onto her back and smiled at the ceiling—a smile that intercepted Rachmiel's eyes and made him feel warm with God's love.

Sebastian and Tabris landed in an open field in an unbelievably flat part of the world. Tall stalks of crops would wave in the breeze through future months, and already seedlings were pushing their heads out from beneath the soil, but now the flatness was emphasized by a bareness like a bald man's head.

"I love this world," Sebastian said. "I didn't much care for it when I was here, but now I do, now that I can see it in greater detail, with all its diversity of life. It's such a shame my breed ruined it, but every now and again I have a glimpse of it as God intended, and my heart stops."

"What do you like best?" asked Tabris.

"I like the oceans," he said, "I suppose because they're so unchained, so formidable, but they're still under very regular control by the moon and by all the laws of nature. That's what I've learned about most while I've been in Limbo. The ocean is really fascinating, isn't it?"

Tabris agreed nonverbally. Sebastian looked up again, his eyes shining almost gold with reflected starlight, a color that filled Tabris with hope he would not dare to feel fully. "How many stars are there?"

"I could give you a number," Tabris said, "but that removes all the drama and wonderment."

"I suppose." The boy looked around at the plain. "You could tell me so much trivia, I'd bet, like how many hairs there are on my head, or how many angels can dance on the head of a pin. I suppose that's all nonsense, though, since there's only one thing worth learning about, and that's God."

Tabris beamed. Sebastian returned the gaze even though he could not return the intense pride and devotion that were churning in the guardian's heart.

"I guess you're wondering why I wanted to see you."

Tabris' face changed completely, but Sebastian had looked down and did not see the rounder eyes, the tighter mouth, the trembling of his hands.

The boy began walking closer to Tabris, then lifted one hand and slipped it into the angel's.

"I'm not that subtle, I guess," the boy said, "and you're supposed to be able to read my soul especially well, but you see, I've been praying lately, and I've been working hard at it. You'd be proud if you knew all the advances I've made, and I can see God more clearly now. I feel I know Him better."

"That's good. It's a big step toward entering Heaven."

Sebastian smiled, lost momentarily in thought, perhaps inwardly debating whether he should change the conversation entirely to the abstract matter of the steps one made before entering Heaven, or if he should continue as planned.

"I guess," Sebastian said after a moment, still holding his guardian's hand as they walked together, "that I've learned a lot about God lately, seeing Him in action, looking back through my experiences and seeing what He's done for me. And . . . well, God's always forgiven me. I've done some pretty bad stuff, you know, but He always took me back when I asked. And I want to be like Him."

Tabris' hand tightened its grip on Sebastian's, and the boy swallowed, suddenly almost too nervous to continue except that he almost had done it. "So, I was wondering the other day, how can I be called a son of God if I'm not acting like Him? And I prayed about it. I—I'm really mad at you sometimes. I don't understand why you did it, but I'm trying. I want to forgive you the way God forgave me. I haven't done it yet, but I've been trying."

Tabris startled, and Sebastian continued, "I thought it might help if we could pray together."

Tabris' face had turned bone white.

"What's wrong?" Sebastian said.

"I . . . This is blackmail!" he shouted at God. "I thought you wanted me on my own terms, when I was ready! You said I could wait it out!"

Sebastian's eyes had grown as large as tea saucers, but he calmed when he felt God coalescing before them. "I'm not forcing you," He said. "This is Sebastian's idea."

"You know, the family that prays together stays together," Sebastian added helpfully.

"You can't!" Then Tabris turned to the boy and crouched down to his eye level. "Listen, Sebastian, I—I'm having difficulties here. I haven't prayed, I mean *really* prayed, not human prayer, since November. All along there's been coercion, Rachmiel and Voriah and your mentor, but I'm not ready yet. You can't force that."

"How will you know—when will you be ready?"

"Someday. It takes time."

Sebastian almost pulled his hand away, but Tabris returned his full attention to God. "And you're approving this? It's blackmail!"

"Sebastian will forgive you in time whether you help him or not," God said. "You're free to refuse. I still love you, and I will even if you don't ever open your heart to me."

Sebastian touched Tabris, almost crying. "It's okay. It was just an idea. It's just that I'm tired of being angry. I wanted to be on good ground with you again. I understand if you don't want me, if you'd rather I worked through it on my own."

Tabris grabbed the child, snatched him from the brink of letting go and held him close. "No, this isn't between us, it's between God and myself. It always has been."

"Don't you trust me?" asked God.

"Apparently I don't," said Tabris.

"I do," Sebastian said, his arms wrapped in a hug around Tabris' waist, his fingers pressed up through the thick matting of two-toned feathers. "I'll trust for both of us."

The offer of the loan was not what gave Tabris pause. What made him hesitate was the fact that the child had hugged him and really, genuinely wanted them to pray together. The angry love erupted from Sebastian's heart and battered his own the way a six-year-old daughter can scream and pound her fists on her father's shoulders. He knew that the boy was worth the pain. He realized suddenly all that he would discard by brushing him aside now. He might still earn the boy's trust sometime in the future, but this one moment would have been lost forever.

Tabris, guardian angel, knew that the first priority had to be the child. He felt the old spirit reemerging which would have risked damnation for the sake of his charge.

"I'll do it," Tabris said, hardly realizing all that he was consenting to, ignorant by choice. The prospect of flooding all his dark corners with light would have made him shake if he had dwelled on it.

Sebastian looked up, met the hot protectiveness in Tabris' eyes, and made no deferrals or reassurances.

They sat on the ground. Sebastian explained that for some reason he prayed best seated even though the angels he knew prayed best standing. Then he made himself quiet and Tabris followed suit.

Sebastian smiled and breathed deeply, preparing himself to meet the Lord, and Tabris felt his own spirit tremble—afraid and hesitant before the moment arrived.

Sebastian opened his heart and God flooded in, meeting the boy on his own ground, moving into the youthful soul and filling him to capacity.

Tabris ground his teeth together, thought of Sebastian, and reached forward with his heart to meet God on holy ground.

God and Tabris encountered like strangers at first, Tabris finding Him and then circling with rabid wariness, like a man protecting his house from a thief. Then, reluctantly because he knew what would happen, he swung open the gates and let God inside.

He visualized an old woman returning to the house in which she grew up, walking from room to room accompanied by shadows of the past, remembering the bed where she was born, recalling the old positions of the furniture, disliking the changes made by the new occupant but still loving the house as her own. There did not come a torrent of grace as Tabris had expected, something overwhelming that would leave his mind raped and exposed utterly. What God did for him was to slowly reabsorb him, to ease him back step by step and make certain there was no shock.

Gradually his vision of God in everything heightened until once again he saw the tiny motes of life that made up the air, the ground, the small puddles in between the rows of crops. Tabris had been hungry for this, and he watched again as God made Himself apparent in all the world, but now that he saw it he felt strangely terrified. There was nowhere to run even if he had been able to.

Sebastian squeezed his hand, and Tabris could not squeeze back, like a tourist in New York highway traffic too afraid to take his hand off the wheel even to change the radio station.

God steeped him slowly. Tabris relaxed forcibly, letting all his guards stay open, allowing God entrance to all his soul, even the parts engulfed in shadow that made him feel so deeply ashamed. When God reached those, he gripped Sebastian's hand with sudden and violent fear, and he twisted onto his knees.

God stopped abruptly at the peripheries of the one area Tabris had wanted to forget, the place in his soul where he had killed Sebastian once and had continued killing him every moment afterward, that one place where he had abandoned God deliberately and continued to do so and would do so forever.

Sebastian was asking to link his heart to Tabris', and Tabris said yes, since Sebastian was the reason for this whole painful venture. The boy touched his soul tentatively, and Tabris allowed him to curl their two souls momentarily, the way he had with Rachmiel.

All that Tabris found in Sebastian he loved, loved it so much that for a moment he forgot to be self-conscious and released himself utterly to this braid—Sebastian, Tabris and God, woven together into the fabric of eternity.

He remembered this soul—the one he would have damned himself to save.

Sebastian looked up at him, his eyes large and mixing anger with need, and Tabris remembered with a near shock that he had a spiritual form—he had forgotten for a short time that he existed as a creature apart from God, and now he felt reluctant to leave those spiritual waters.

But the boy had seen all those twisted areas in his heart, the ones God had framed and would not enter.

Tabris met his eyes, and Sebastian looked down, away, as though wanting desperately to ask the questions he had always feared answering—things, Tabris realized, that he had never asked Casifer.

"Why did you do it?" Sebastian asked.

"Because I didn't trust enough in God?" Tabris said, shaking his head. "That shouldn't matter—it's done. I wouldn't do it again, if I could make the choice now."

"But *why?*"

Sebastian's eyes were round. Now he was completely the frightened child, shifting his spiritual balance like a kitten who has just been stepped on and is wary of human feet.

Tabris backed away, scrambling to grab the armor he had worn for so long during that desert of time between November and April, and discovered to his horror that God had His hands blocking his one protection. Sebastian breathed in short gasps, fighting off crying. "But that shouldn't be important," Tabris said. "It happened. It's over. Now we just have to make do with the way things are. We try to fix things up. That's all. Knowing why can't make it any easier."

"Yes it can," Sebastian said. "How can I forgive you if I don't know why you did it?"

"How could you forgive me if you did know?" Tabris said. "If I told you, you'd never understand, it would just mess up your spirituality for ages. You'd be working in Limbo to undo the warps to your character that would be there if I told you, if you knew. I'm not a good role model for you—that's why we were separated! To tell you now would defeat the whole purpose of patching Casifer into this mess!"

Sebastian looked utterly defeated, even though he had not slumped forward, had not looked down, had not started to cry. Somewhere in him, however, there had come a change, a renewed doubt, and Tabris sensed it.

They sat for a moment, looking at each other, until Tabris stared at his hands in his lap.

"Because I loved you."

Sebastian frowned and brightened simultaneously, an odd combination.

"Because I loved you," Tabris said. "But I loved you too much—I couldn't bear to see you sin. Not again. I couldn't see you lose the love God had for you. I wouldn't watch you risk damnation again, ever. It would have killed me to lose you."

God flowed through Tabris' heart as easily as his blood, making the words more ready for his mouth, making the emotions simpler to sort through and explain.

"But," and he looked down, "I lost you anyway, didn't I? All I wanted was to keep you safe, but they took you away from me. I've been replaced and assigned to Elizabeth as though you never were a part of my life. But you were."

Sebastian was leaning forward. "You loved me?"

Still looking away, Tabris nodded.

"And do you love me now?"

Tabris might have choked, might have grabbed the child and gushed with words that would make Sebastian feel loved and cherished, if he were Rachmiel. For the moment he could only nod.

It was enough for Sebastian.

The link between their hearts—God—still coursed through their souls, a forced bond that once had been natural and pure. The strain on the tie hurt Tabris a little, but he bore it. There had been a realization—Sebastian hadn't wanted to know why it happened. He said he did, and maybe he wondered about the cause, but there had been a larger question, something much more important that he had needed answered. Somehow, his answer had gotten it just right. He tightened his emotional hold on God and thanked Him.

Tabris closed his eyes and said softly, "I still love you, Sebastian. I can't help it. I would choose to love you again, even knowing you can't forgive me. In the first days the love was put there by God, but later on it was mine. You're an amazing creation. I'd have been damned for you. I got overprotective. That's all. I know you couldn't ever understand, but that's why. I didn't think before I acted. I was too fast to stop myself. There was this desperation to get you into a safe place. But by doing that I lost you."

Sebastian moved closer to him, his spirit still razor-sharp, but Tabris was unsure if the pain he felt were Sebastian's or his own. The tension had begun mounting in his two-toned heart, though, and he almost vibrated with the need to ask, imitating Rachmiel in his nonverbal announcement of the question before he even said the words, as though his heart were the horn on a speeding train.

"Can you forgive me?"

Sebastian looked into Tabris' soul, explored it with his own, and Tabris winced as the boy came on the shadows, the iron bars and concrete floor of that one God-forsaken moment in his past. The realization struck him instantly: no amount of explanation would be enough in this state. Sebastian could no more love him than the other angels while his soul stayed stained. Tabris knew that he had one more step to take before the boy could love him honestly. Before he could be forgiven by his son, he had to be forgiven by his Father.

With God surrounding the one instant which sin and time had engraved on his soul, but not entering it, Tabris bowed his head and asked to be forgiven. He asked God to descend the spiral staircase and enter that tiny chamber in his soul, the dungeon of his heart, to purge it with light and burn out the plague that had filled his spirit with sin and dust.

God forgave him that easily, taking away the corruption from the act, righting the balance as only He could have, and Tabris realized with sudden relief that he was clean again in the one way that mattered. God had cut out the dead parts of him and replaced them with living spirit, renewed his energy, returned his purpose, refreshed his love.

Witnessing this, Sebastian gasped as he saw the Divine light suddenly beam through Tabris the way it did through Casifer and Rachmiel—with sun-like constancy rather than the periodic flashes of a light house—as all the darkness and twistedness were gone from Tabris, replaced by clarity and internal refraction. Sebastian smiled, then, slowly, and looked into Tabris' eyes.

"Can I forgive you now?" asked the boy, his eyes bright gold, his hair so hazel it might have been blond.

"Can I forgive myself?" Tabris asked.

Sebastian watched him a moment, and then nodded slowly.

When Tabris realized he was crying, it was too late to snatch the tears from his cheeks. Sebastian reached up to hug him, and Tabris closed his two-toned wings about them both, like a bivalve hiding a very precious pearl.

Hugged by his guardian's arms, wings, and heart, Sebastian laughed out loud. Tabris bowed his head to touch the boy's forehead and he let the relief relax him. God joined them both, present and welcome in their hearts, and Tabris thanked Him repeatedly for the strength to do what he had done and for the privilege of success. Sebastian was doing the same. When Tabris looked into Sebastian's eyes, he found a reflection of his own eyes, and they were shining like sunlight.

They sat, later, by the pond behind the Hayes' house. Tabris had been telling Sebastian a story, and after he finished Jesus arrived.

For the first time in six months, Tabris did not prostrate himself in fear. He smiled broadly, asymmetrically.

Raguel had arrived beside Him, but until he spoke Tabris did not realize he was present at all.

"Congratulations," said Raguel.

"Congratulations?"

"Your probation is ended," said Jesus. "You're not going to face damnation any longer."

Sebastian gasped, nonverbalizing but making his point in words also. "That's great!"

Tabris seemed stunned. "But what about Elizabeth? How do you know I won't do the same to her?"

The Lord smiled. "Now you won't. You've changed your own soul enough that you would never fail that way again. And now you have Sebastian to help you also."

"So I get to be a guardian to my guardian?" asked the boy.

"You still have some growing up to do, little man," said Tabris, giving Sebastian a mock push, and the boy pretended to grab him in a wrestling hold and fight for some imagined title.

When they looked up from playing, Raguel had departed, but God had not—and never would.

26

RACHMIEL BRIGHTENED THE INSTANT TABRIS RE-
turned.

"He forgave you!" he exclaimed, flinging his arms
around Tabris' neck, feeling the strong response of his
soul in return. "That's so amazing!"

Tabris smiled, a compulsive grin that seemed to
overtake his whole face. "How did you know?"

"You look so different—your eyes are as bright as
honey! Even your hair is lighter. You just look happier,
and you've relaxed the controls on your spirit. You're
nonverbalizing. I knew he'd do it! Tell me how it happened."

"We prayed together," Tabris said. "I asked God to
forgive me, and I let Him into my heart. I forgave myself
too."

Rachmiel's mouth opened, and his eyes pulsed happily.

"And," Tabris said, "I'm off probation."

Rachmiel gasped and hugged him again while
Tabris laughed with surprise and the peculiar notion that
he would be crushed. "This is wonderful! So you're out of
danger for good?"

The other household angels arrived and knew instantly—Rachmiel's agitation and the changes in Tabris'
soul worked together like a news broadcast. Congratulations and hugs were shared by all. Voriah called Casifer
and Sebastian, and they joined in the midnight fun. For a
short time the angels had a little spiritual party, each
exulting and emitting a festive atmosphere that swept
through the group like a strong wind, without the benefit
of streamers or balloons or the things humans use to
make rooms seem festive when God is not the primary

decoration. Tabris was brilliant with relief, and he stayed for a long time with Sebastian by his side as though he could hardly believe God's gift.

In the middle of the laughter and talking, Sebastian said to Tabris, "You're staying here, right?"

"Yes," Tabris said, feeling his heart vibrating suddenly—he had forgotten about this, the second abandonment. Sebastian's eyes rounded.

"Are you all right?" the boy asked.

"I'm abandoning you again, aren't I?"

"No, I don't think so," Sebastian said. "You've got a job to do here. I'd rather you were with me, but it can't be helped. You're only a word away. You can come for me whenever I call you, and I can visit you. And we'll be together afterward."

"In eighty years," Tabris said, his eyes still uncertain, a little darker than before.

Sebastian smiled, so brave a child that Tabris nearly felt his heart burst with pride and love.

"Tabris," the boy said, "I love you, and time doesn't mean anything to love. We have God holding us together—that's everything!"

Tabris brightened like a sunrise, his eyes brilliant gold and warm with the reflected light of God.

"I'll be waiting," Sebastian said, and grinned with Tabris' asymmetric smile.

After the angels had dispersed and Casifer escorted Sebastian back to Limbo, Rachmiel and Tabris sat against the foot of Elizabeth's bed, bright-eyed but a little spent.

Rachmiel had been emitting almost constant joy all night, and Tabris sat up to look at Elizabeth who was, as he had suspected, smiling in her sleep. He settled back onto the floor, pulling up his knees and leaning forward with a bright grin.

"What?" asked Rachmiel's sudden squint.

"You look like you've thrown a party and now dread cleaning up the mess," Tabris said, putting the words into a picture even as he spoke, so that Rachmiel had the benefit of seeing himself as an exhausted man with his shirt collar unbuttoned, his tie unknotted, sprawled on a chair amidst used paper plates and fallen streamers. He laughed aloud. "You need a vacation."

"Thank you, no," said Rachmiel, winking, nonverbalizing that his heart had settled in this nest for the time being, and this household made him feel secure—the souls more than the walls.

A thin shaft of morning sunlight managed to elude the cloud cover and pierce the dark interior of the room.

Tabris raised his eyebrows at Rachmiel, as though to say, "Time for you to do your stuff."

Rachmiel shook his head. Tabris squinted.

"Well, I figured, since you're going to be here for the next eighty years, maybe you should try."

Tabris suddenly had a glimpse of the future, a long trail lined with joy and heartbreak, and drudgery, frustration, and relief. He could see a red-haired woman leaving home, having her own family, running for public office, changing the world in the hundred different and small ways that every life must change it—ways which count too drastically to measure. He saw himself as a part of her future.

Tabris sprang onto the bedside and put his head next to Elizabeth's.

"Sweetie, wake up," he said. "Morning's here, Sleepyhead."

She opened her eyes and Tabris felt the warm glow of God's love expand in his heart until it filled him and overflowed into the young girl by his side. Laughing, he focused some of that love back to the Father and told Him again how good it felt to be home.

About the Author

Jane Hamilton is a recent graduate of Cornell University with degrees in English and religious studies. She has been interested in angels since her childhood and has studied them seriously for the past five years. She is currently pursuing a master's degree in English at the State University of New York at Brockport. *The Guardian* is her first novel.